# GHOST
# PAINS

## JANE
## SEVERANCE

SHEBA
FEMINIST
PRESS

First published in 1992 in the UK by Sheba Feminist Press, 10a Bradbury Street, London N16 8JN.

Cover illustration by Pip Phelan
Cover design by Spark Ceres
Typeset by Photosetting and Secretarial Services, Yeovil, England
Printed and bound by Cox & Wyman Ltd, Reading, England


ISBN 0 907179 45 2

British Cataloguing in Publication Data
A record for this book is available from the British Library

*This book is dedicated with special thanks to Carol Traumann, without whose encouragement I never would have completed this manuscript.*

# ONE

The nurse behind the desk of the emergency room had worked a double shift. That was because half of the staff at the hospital were out with this flu going around. At 3 a.m. she was stupid from lack of sleep, and when the pick-up truck drove up outside the double glass doors, at first she did nothing but stare. After all, the girl behind the wheel got out by herself and, though she was somewhat clumsy, she wasn't bleeding obviously, or bent with pain. Strangely, the nurse wondered for a moment if she hadn't seen the girl before, if she hadn't been in earlier that evening. But that was unlikely. She was just so tired that she was imagining things.

It wasn't until the girl began to unlock the tailgate, with hands that were stiff from the cold, that it occurred to the woman that maybe she really did have an emergency and that she might need some help. She pushed the buzzer that woke the doctor from her twenty minute nap and threw her heavy coat on over her clothes.

A cold blast of wind blew a handful of snow into the nurse's face as she stepped through the doors, jolting her wide awake. Another teenage girl had climbed out of the back of the truck and snow had already dusted her head and shoulders. She and the driver, between them, were trying to haul something off the tailgate, trying to be gentle.

As the woman came up behind them, carrying a stretcher she had grabbed from behind the counter, the taller girl turned and for the first time she saw her face. Again the nurse had a sense of *déjà vu*, of having seen her before in almost this exact instance. But even stranger than the feeling, was the look that the girl had in her eyes. It was almost as if she were not standing there beside them, hunched against the wind. Her eyes said that, instead, she was somewhere very far away.

# TWO

'I've been to London, I've been to Dover....'
    Lyn Frasier sang to herself, as she arranged the six cards in her

hand. She pulled two and placed them face down on the stump they were using as a table.

'You dealt me a lousy hand,' she sang to her older sister, Darcy, 'but it's not going to keep me from beating you good.'

'Big talk. You're already ten points behind.'

Darcy did not look up to answer, but twisted her mouth down, considering her own hand. She ran her fingers through her short brown hair, an automatic reflective gesture, and then pulled them down.

'Yuck!' She rubbed her fingertips together fastidiously.

'What do you expect?' Lyn was still singing. 'You haven't washed it in a week. You're lucky that you didn't find something alive.'

Her own blonde hair was tightly french braided away from her face, and she didn't intend to touch it until she was under a shower. She squirmed with delight at the thought of hot water pounding down on her. She was already heady with anticipation, couldn't stop singing. It was just one more thing to look forward to.

Darcy cut the deck and Lyn turned over the top card. It was the Jack of Diamonds.

'Ha!' She crowed. 'Two points, and wait till you see what it does for my hand! I'm going to skunk you.'

'We'll see.' Darcy started to lay down a card, then reconsidered and pulled it back. She stared intently at Lyn's hand, as if somehow she could see through the backs of the cards. Finally, she put down a Queen.

'Fifteen for two,' said Lyn triumphantly, slapping down a five. She moved her brass peg up two holes on the board. It was a narrow rectangle of zebra wood, something Louise had made years ago. Louise was her mother's partner, the other carpenter in the family. The wavy line of the wood showed subtly on its polished surface and, distracted, she picked it up.

'Hey! You're dumping the pegs out!'

Darcy scrambled to catch them before they were lost in the grass.

'Oh. Sorry.' But Lyn wasn't, really. Suddenly she didn't want to play cards anymore. She swept them into a pile carelessly, then picked up the board again with both hands.

'How do you suppose a puzzle that was also a cribbage board would go over? Like maybe if the holes went around the edge pieces?'

'What about if it was a stand up toy or sculpture?' Darcy suggested. 'It could be a little train with holes along the top.'

'Good idea. I'll write that down.' Lyn started to paw through her blue daypack for a pencil, then stopped, grinning sheepishly, as she caught Darcy's smile.

'Well,' she said, 'it is a good idea to write ideas down so I don't forget.' But she knew that she was wasting her time trying to defend herself. She was famous at home for her lists and everyone teased her.

'Well,' Darcy replied, grinning back, 'if you make everything that you've got written down already, you're not going to have room to display it. Wasn't the deal that you only get one side of the booth?'

'Only the shelves on one side. Aunt Annie's still got the wall space.'

It wasn't a complaint. She was happy that, after two years of nagging, her aunt had agreed to let her display any of her woodwork in the booth where she sold her textile art each week.

'Let's see your list: "Puzzles, stacking ducks, balance toys, coffins for canaries and hamsters."'

'Let me see that!'

Lyn snatched the small, spiral notebook out of her hands. 'Oh, I see Nikona's been at it again. Nothing is safe.'

'Hey, I thought it was the best item on the list. You would have made your fortune right there.' Darcy finished restacking the cards into a perfect pile, then stood and stretched. 'Is there anything left to eat?'

'Yeah, that same package of oatmeal that we talked about before.' Lyn jerked her thumb over her shoulder, pointing down the hill. Their second-hand backpacks sat together where the trailhead met the road. 'Are you going to cook it, or eat it raw, or just bring it up every ten minutes?'

'Hmm.' Without answering, Darcy paced the five steps that she had defined as her territory when they had reached the rendezvous point that morning. They were early, and there was a whole mountain behind them to explore, but they had done enough of that during the previous seven days.

Lyn looked at her watch. It was too soon to start listening for the truck, but she was listening anyway.

'Who do you think is going to come get us?' They had already discussed it a number of times, but Darcy was always willing to talk things over and over. Both Lyn and their cousin, Nikona, thought that this was excellent quality, but it drove Aunt Annie crazy.

'Make up your minds!' she would shout at them from her workroom, 'Don't talk it to death!'

'Louise for sure. She's going to be so jealous. I thought she was going to cry when she sprained her knee and couldn't come.'

'I know. It was such shitty luck that it happened right before we were going. I know Mom wouldn't have let us make the trip alone if Louise hadn't talked her into it.'

When she heard Louise's name a clear picture came into Lyn's mind: There was Louise in the workshop behind the barn, totally absorbed in something on one of the high benches. Her grey hair was, as always when she worked, stuffed up out of the way beneath a baseball cap, and she was singing to herself. The room was cosy from the heat of the wood stove, and over to the side Lyn could see the little workbench Louise had built for her when she was four. Above it were hanging a little hammer and a little saw, and beneath it were pushed a child-size toolbox and a box of woodscraps. Of course, there also was a picture of Louise at the kitchen table hunched over her first cup of coffee, her face sour, as it would remain for the first hour that she was up.

She came back to the present with a start. Had she missed anything? Darcy was sitting quiet, a faraway look on her face. Immediately, Lyn knew what was wrong, and inwardly she winced. What was it, that little chill that ran between her and her sister sometimes when their mother was mentioned? Was there a pattern? Was it every fiftieth or two hundredth time? Or did it just pop up, as unexpected for Darcy as it was for Lyn? Sometimes, when Darcy reached back past Lyn's remembering Lyn wished that she could poke into her sister's mind to hit the switch that would erase the first six years of her memory; that with one touch she could give her the gift of knowing Mom only the way she did.

'Maybe Nikona will come,' she ventured, trying to keep the conversation going. Sometimes she wished she had the guts to ask Darcy, to come right out and say, 'Hey, what are you thinking? What makes you freeze?' but she didn't. The truth of the matter was, in fact, that she didn't want to hear about it at all, just as she didn't like to look at Darcy's face when her hair was smoothed back from her scarred temple.

'Yeah, Nikona.' Darcy answered as if the pause had never occurred. 'If she can get away from...' she paused dramatically, then both shouted together, 'Computer camp!'

'I thought if I heard one more word about computer camp I was going to scream,' Lyn confided. She tried to wipe her dusty hands off on her clothes, but there was not a single clean spot on either her shorts or her t-shirt, so she settled for brushing them together.

'You and everybody else in the world. I was ready to send a bomb to the scholarship committee.'

'You know,' said Lyn, in the tone of confession, 'I was really pissed when she decided to do that instead of coming with us. We planned all winter, and she didn't think twice, didn't even ask us how we'd feel about it.'

'Yeah, but...' A slight tick appeared in Darcy's right cheek, so small a stranger wouldn't have noticed it. But Lyn knew it, because it showed up every time there was strife, or even the possibility of strife within their family. She recognized it with some annoyance. Honestly, couldn't Darcy just mellow out for a few minutes and let her bitch? It wasn't as if she were going to rip Nikona's head off when she saw her.

'... she really looks forward to being around other kids like her.'

'Her "peers", as I think they refer to them in the gifted and talented program.' Darcy rolled her eyes back in her head. She was joking, but Lyn thought that she probably felt the same way she herself did when it came to the topic of Nikona's 'peers': as if all the time they'd spent together, the work, the fights, the confidences at night after they were in bed, were worth nothing because they weren't taking college. But she said nothing. Darcy would think that she was attacking Nikona in her absence, and she'd feel duty-bound to defend her.

'So, what'll you do the rest of the summer?' she asked suddenly, as if posing a brand new question, rather than rehashing another well-worn topic. At least it was unlikely to produce chills or twitching.

'Oh, hoe sugar beets.' Obligingly Darcy answered in the same way. 'And hoe sugar beets. And maybe hoe sugar beets some more, if they need the help. I hope so. I need the money. I don't even have enough to pay my athletic dues after this trip.'

'Ah, the joys of hoeing sugar beets.' Lyn preened in a satisfied manner. 'Something I hope never to have to do for money again as long as I live. You'd better hope you have time between working in our own garden and quilting.'

'You'd better hope that yourself, 'cause there's no way you're getting out of chores just because you'll be making stuff for the market.'

'Well, it was worth a try. Do you suppose Aunt Annie has accepted any new quilts yet? I hope not.'

Darcy laughed, but not unkindly. 'You know she has. I bet she has a whole pile, and every one of them has a note that says "Rush for wedding" pinned on to it.' She held up her forefingers ruefully, both covered with tiny needle pricks, almost healed, and pulled a face that made Lyn think of Aunt Annie when she'd say, 'Quilting's our bread and butter. I can't count on selling a wall hanging, but somebody always needs a top quilted.' Of course, she was just as likely to turn around and say the same thing about bee-catching or the produce stand, or any of the other half dozen businesses by which they kept the farm going.

'You ever wish we just got an allowance?' Darcy asked.

'Wow, what a concept.' Spending money, like other kids. Not putting a percentage of the money they picked up on odd jobs back in the kitty. She considered for a moment.

'Yeah. Sometimes. Like, I just feel like I work more than my friends, that I have to share jobs that their moms do for them. Living with old hippies, like they say about us at school - everything's got to be communal. I hate it sometimes! But we get to say more about what goes on. That's a good trade. Kathy's dad, he just decides everything for all of them, it doesn't matter what the rest of the family thinks. We've always been in on weekly meetings.'

'Yeah, that's the good part about living with old hippies. And sometimes they even listen now, too. You were smart to bring that stuff from your woodworking class to a meeting instead of nagging Aunt Annie. Then everybody saw how good it was, they were willing to front you and be on your side.'

'Yeah.' For a moment Lyn saw a horrible picture. Nikona and Darcy were rolling in money they had made hoeing sugar beets, but she hadn't sold one thing at the Saturday market, couldn't even pay back the front money, couldn't go to an occasional movie or buy Christmas presents. Not to mention the humiliation of it all. No, surely that wouldn't happen.

'...and basketball camp.' Lyn blinked, having lost the original thread of conversation. Oh, yes, they had been talking about what Darcy would do during the rest of the summer. She looked at her sister, sitting hunched forward on her heels. Her voice had taken on the tone that other kids reserved for fantasizing about the ultimate sexual experience. Though she said nothing more, her eyes sparkled so brightly that Lyn knew that she was pre-living the two weeks in her head; that she had already gone through every shot and screen and feint.

To her dismay she felt the familiar stabs of resentment and jealousy. Dammit, she didn't want to feel that way. Hadn't she argued on Darcy's side when she showed them the camp brochure Mrs Jennings had given her, pointing out how great it would be for her to be offered a basketball scholarship in her senior year? Passing on the things she had heard the coach say about Darcy's talent, even though she knew the camp fee would probably mean cutbacks that would affect her. The feeling just sneaked up on her, the same way that the resentment about Nikona did. It was hard to be content all the time with being just Lyn-B-Student-Back-Up-Voice-In-The-Choir, tag along behind Queen-of-the-Basketball-Court and Miss Hi-I-Learned-to-Read-When-I-was-Three. But she didn't want to feel badly towards either one of them!

Slowly, deliberately, she relaxed her hands, clenched in fists, and called another picture. Herself, running down the dirt driveway, so young that her hair was still pulled back in pigtails. Yelling frantically, not even sure what she was missing, only that the big girls were trying to leave her. Nikona and Darcy, walking side by side, heads together, then swinging apart, almost like a dance, each one reaching a hand back for her. She didn't know if it was one memory or a collage of many, she just knew that they were willing to include her more often than not, that the three of them were tighter than most other sibling acts she knew. It had been that way ever since she and Darcy had come to live on the farm at ages six and three; it was the same now, twelve years later. Then, because just a touch of the ugly feeling remained, she added one private consolation: 'Anyway,' she thought, 'Mom loves me the best.'

Then, ashamed, but comforted, she was able to say to Darcy in a bantering tone, 'I hope you have a great time and come home an All American Pro. And Nikona and I are going to wear all of your underwear while you're gone and put them back without washing them.'

'Oh, yeah,' Darcy replied, putting the cards in the velveteen bag that contained the board, 'I forgot to tell you that we already did that to you last week.'

They were comfortably quiet then. Who would have thought that they would have gotten along so well alone on the trip which they had originally planned for four? Lyn thought, easing herself into the shade. Soon, this afternoon, her mother would be there, and she had so many things to tell her. About the incredible coldness of the mountain lakes, and the way that she had felt compelled to swim in each just the same. The fields of snow they had skiied on with their feet and the fields of wildflowers through which they had hiked.

She looked across at Darcy, who was engrossed in her own thoughts, and wondered if this would be one of the times that she would be withdrawn from their mother. Oh, dutiful, certainly, and doing nothing overt that would cause pain, but every muscle of her body, every line of her stance screaming her discomfort and need to get away. Or was it only so obvious to Lyn, familiar with the tick, the other little nuances? She had never heard anyone at home mention it. For a group of women who so encouraged sharing feelings there were a lot of things they didn't talk about. But it did seem there were times when she had observed her mother dropping her arms quickly from a hug, turning away from Darcy with a look of sorrow in her eyes.

But she didn't want to think about it now. She wanted to think about what she was going to tell everyone about the trip, or to make plans for the money she was going to make, not solve the unvoiced problem between her sister and her mother.

A harsh sound brought her from her musing. It was far away still, but she thought that she knew what it was, and leapt to her feet. Sure enough, three switchbacks down was a cloud of dust moving up the road, and the sound had now distinctly become the voice of the old grey truck, missing a muffler. They were early. She let out a little squeal of excitement, then recalled herself, looking sideways at Darcy. But she couldn't play it cool for more than a moment.

Then she was over the side and down the hill, scrambling to the place where the trail met the road. She was vaguely aware of Darcy coming slower, pausing to gather up the cards and their waterbottles and her daypack, but she wasn't thinking about her sister's feelings anymore, how she might or might not act. Her thoughts were running ahead of her, meeting her mother.

# THREE

The alarm that had jerked Lyn from her sleep was cut off almost immediately, in the middle of its first ring. It was too dark for her to see the clock, but she knew without looking it was exactly five-thirty, not one minute before, not one minute after. Darcy ran her life on set schedules, and, in the tiny bedroom, Lyn was also a slave to this one. Without moving she watched Darcy by the pale light of the street lamp that shone in the back window, moving stealthily so as not to wake her. Lyn wondered why she had never told Darcy that in spite of the way that she dressed in the bathroom, eased the water off and on, opened and closed the apartment door as quietly as a thief, that she woke when her alarm went off every single morning and was never able to go back to sleep until five minutes before it rang, reset for her an hour later.

Was she being nice? Darcy's primary goal these days was to get along with as low a profile as possible; she would certainly feel guilty if she thought she were disturbing Lyn. Or was she being mean, letting Darcy tip-toe around in the dark, running into things, when she could easily tell her that it was fine to turn on the light? She didn't know. A lot of motives which would have once seemed clear were no longer so. She found herself examining them with puzzlement sometimes, like the rocks and bones she used to pick up in the fields and drag home in her pockets.

She crawled out of her sleeping bag as soon as the front door of the apartment was quietly pulled closed, and, without thinking about it, gave the bag a kick that landed it in the corner, on top of a pile of dirty clothes. There was no particular feeling attached to the kick, it was just what she spent a lot of her time doing these days; kicking things that couldn't kick back.

It was cold in the room. That was one reason she didn't complain about being woken early. She never really got warm during the night. But, though she knew it would be much warmer in the bathroom, she lingered for a minute by the window. Darcy had insulated all the others in the two main rooms with rags and plastic trash bags scrounged from the dumpsters. It kept out the third-storey wind, but it also turned the apartment into a cave. This window by the fire escape was the only one not covered. Lyn had ripped the plastic down four or five times before Darcy had given up on it. They hadn't talked about it. Her mother, Connie, thought she wanted it off so that she could sit and smoke outside, and Lyn encouraged the myth with stray cigarette butts when she wanted to hurt her. Now she stood by the window until she saw Darcy's small figure pass beneath the street light and out of sight, running.

She started the water in the tub first thing, before even looking in the mirror. It took a long time to fill enough even for a make-do bath, and she needed to wash her hair. The vent in the bathroom was the only one that gave off measurable heat, and she basked over it. The warm air brought back some coloured fragments of an early morning dream. Unobtainable pictures of the farm. Aunt Annie, and Jean out on the lawn in the spring, early, after Jean had dropped her first load of kids off at the grade school. Mr Green, her special cat.

She didn't mind the alarm when it pulled her from her dreams; memories that attacked her unfairly when she was defenceless. Automatically she closed a door against them. That was her life now; days divided neatly into tiny compartments cut off from one another. The first box of the day, the waking box, was now closed, the dream with it. There was no going back to it. It was the only way that she had found to keep any control at all. For a moment, deep beneath the surface, like a subterranean river, she felt the anger pounding. Not yet, too soon in the day. She pushed it back without even being aware, knowing only that she was now into her getting-ready-for-school box.

As she washed her hair she tried to think of nothing before or after the task at hand, tried hard not to think that this morning's dream had been a little different to her usual night yearning, tried to ignore the snatches of music and the feel of celebration it had left in her head. On the street, in the other apartments, people were waking and starting their days. The garbage truck was in the back alley, the pipes were banging as someone tried for hot water downstairs, Connie was snoring on the couch. Lyn noted the sounds in her head without commenting. They were all simply sounds of the new day.

There was a card tucked behind her make-up. A present from Darcy, who liked surprises, and who also had a regular route through the trash bins of the shops two blocks over, that often produced treasures, things that could be fixed up and used. The chair in the kitchen had come from them, and so had the curtain in the bathroom. This was the front of a greeting card, a painting of three cats sitting on a quilt, cats so black massed together that only by their eyes could one tell their number.

Lyn smiled again thinking of her fat, black cat on the farm, and was surprised to feel how awkward the smile felt on her face. A long time since... bang! She slammed the door of the box, catching the thought inside in it. Now she would simply move to the next. She thought of sticking the card up in the mirror, but instead took it to her bedroom and propped it up on the table, never once voicing the reason: that it was hers, and she didn't want Connie, who also loved cats, to get any pleasure from it.

She hesitated a moment before she heaved the window in their bedroom up, checking the weather, the state of the fire escape. Her blue down jacket protected her blouse, but she wanted to make sure that she wasn't going to sit in a puddle, or something worse. Her clothes were part of the armour that protected her at school. No one needed to know about the way she and Darcy had sweated over the blouse, trying to fit the pattern around the stain on the remnant material, finally hiding it beneath a tiered tie. Nor did they need to know that the grey wool pants, fashionably peg-legged, had started their life as part of a fat man's suit they had gotten at a bag sale.

As she always did, Lyn placed her sleeping bag carefully on the sill. She sat down and folded it back over her lap. For a moment she seemed to catch a smell of woodsmoke, clinging from one of the camp-fires that she and Darcy had lit on the mountain. But that was impossible. Any smell had been washed out, was as long gone as their packs, which Connie had traded away for a couple of drinks one night in the bar. Darcy, at least, had caught on in time to sell the tent herself.

Once again she felt the far away rumble of anger, this time closer so that she knew it was there, thought even, for one moment, of letting it out. Just a little. Just enough to feel its power and life. But, no, she knew better than that. If she gave in this early in the day she would, at the very least, have a headache later. Darcy didn't think she even tried and Lyn wished, for a moment, that she could show her the effort that she put into control. But wishes were as useless as dreams.

For one sharp moment she saw a picture of a very small blonde girl being ridden horsey on a knee, heard the voice of Jean, who had more consistently liked the three of them as small children than as adolescents, chanting, 'If wishes were horses then beggars could ride.' Then the picture was gone, and without acknowledgement Lyn leaned out the window, and rattled the coffee can that sat on the fire escape.

They were there in a flash, probably waiting at the bottom of the stairs. The bigger kitten, the grey one, was talking before he even got there, complaining about the night and the morning and the lateness of breakfast.

'Yes, yes, it's a terrible life, isn't it? You have to sleep out in the cold, and last night you chased away at least a dozen burglars and mountain lions and who knows what all so I could be safe. Yes, you are very brave.'

Lyn put a double handful of the generic cat food onto the plate. They had to come right beside her, right up on the sill to eat, but it didn't bother them anymore. She could, after weeks of slow and patient work, touch them and pick them up now.

'How was your night? Did you stay home and warm like good kitties?' Home was beneath the dumpster directly below. After she had traced them there, weeks before, Lyn had torn out the tattered cardboard box that they had been living in, along with a skeleton of a brother or sister, and replaced it with an old tyre. The inside and bottom were stuffed with clean rags, leaving a space just big enough for two kitties to cuddle in. She knew from watching Sadie rig up a similar set-up for chicks, how well the rubber retained their body heat. Sadie was really the only one of the five women who liked chickens. The rest of them appreciated the egg money, but only Sadie treated them like pets, could tell them all apart. Lyn had regularly helped Sadie feed them in the morning, and Sadie would tell her about their latest tricks....

No, she wasn't going to think about that. She spoke to the kittens to distract herself.

'You're getting to be a big girl,' she said to the calico, who had finished eating and was washing her face with her paws. She held out a finger to her, straight and steady, and in a moment the kitten came over to sniff it.

'Yes, you are beautiful,' Lyn told her. The little cat walked back and forth twice beneath her hand. 'If you came inside you could sleep on the bed,' she said in her most cat-tempting voice. 'You could sleep on the heater.'

Lyn slid off the window sill and into the room as she spoke. But the kittens would not be lured, even though they sat outside the glass with woebegone expressions after she gave up and closed the window.

'Dummies,' she told them through the glass. 'I'm going to get you in here eventually. So why spend all winter outside in an old tyre?' For the moment she didn't think of all the times she had fantasized that their shelter was larger, so that it could be her refuge too.

In the living room Connie's snores had given way to mumbles, probably caused, Lyn knew without looking, by the cold. She had trouble arranging her makeshift bed when she came in drunk, and the blankets usually ended up in a pile by the couch. As she walked into the living room Lyn did not look over to see if she was right, to judge by whether Connie was sleeping in her clothes, what state she had been in when she arrived home. Connie's banging entrances no longer woke Lyn during the night. She only woke if Darcy got up to put Connie to bed, and then she often stayed awake for several hours afterwards.

But right now she was only concerned with Connie's old jeans jacket, thrown, soaking wet, over the corner of the one arm chair. Luck was with her, Connie's wallet was in the inside pocket, instead of in her jeans, or left on the table in the bar for a friend to return later. Lyn didn't bother to be stealthy; she knew from experience that Connie wouldn't wake easily at this point. Other mornings, when her control had not been so tight, she had tried to wake her deliberately, dropping books she didn't need, rattling pans she was not using. It had not been an effective punishment. She had developed others that worked better. The cigarettes on the window-sill, for example, were a good one, or the casual display of a hicky on her neck. Either of those were good for a fight. There were several others she had in mind. But not this morning.

There were no bills in the wallet, but Lyn emptied out all the change. There was a photograph of Nikona in the first plastic compartment of the wallet, a snapshot that showed her working in the garden with her blonde hair, the same colour as Lyn and Connie's, tied back, looking at a tomato as if it were the most amazing, the most unique thing she had ever seen. As she did every morning, Lyn considered removing the photo. What was Connie trying to prove by carrying it? Lyn had removed her sophomore photograph long before. She didn't want Connie showing it to other women in the bar, making up a life to go with it, telling stories that made her seem as if she cared. Darcy's photo, a basketball shot, she passed over. Darcy had to take care of her feelings herself.

Lyn put a dime and a penny back into the coin department, so Connie wouldn't know if she had spent the money herself, or if Lyn had rolled her. She thought that Connie half suspected that she stole from her, and she didn't care. In fact, as a punishment, it was not bad.

But she didn't want to have Connie start taking her wallet to bed with her. She could not stomach taking it off her inert body.

The thought made her glance over at the couch without thinking. She froze. She had caught Connie at her best in the dim light from the bathroom. Her blonde hair, the same style, the same length that Lyn's had been before they moved, fanned out on the pillow around her. Her hands were folded like a child's, beneath her cheek, and her face had lost its usual worried look. Lyn was too far away to smell the bar smoke.

Against her will a picture flashed into Lyn's head, a memory from two years before, when the women's softball team had been so depleted by vacationers that not only Darcy and Nikona, but also Lyn had been pressed into temporary service. She saw her mother standing on the pitcher's mound at the high school. It was dusk, and they were the only two people in sight, along with Dutchy, Sadie's ugly dog who would field balls. Her mother pitched Lyn a soft underhand throw that even a baby should be able to hit. Only Lyn couldn't. She wasn't any good, not like the big girls. She was just the stupid right fielder who gave them the legal number of players, who struck out every time she came up to bat. But her mother smiled at her as if they were spending the most pleasant of evenings, as if there was nothing in the entire world she would rather be doing than helping hone Lyn's batting skills.

The picture lasted only for a moment, but every detail burned itself into Lyn's mind, down to the rip in the hem of her mother's shorts, the way her earrings caught the light of the setting sun.

She came back to herself. She was still staring at Connie with her mouth open, clutching the change in one hand. She was talking to herself under her breath, keening, rather, the same words over and over.

'Oh, my mother, my mother, oh my.... Why...?' She stopped talking immediately, but it was the only thing that she could stop. Already she could feel the anger, gushing out, though she had not said a word, filling the room like a presence. Beyond control. Her boxes tumbled as if they were a house of cards. Goddamn it. She kicked the leg of the couch, and the pain brought her back under control for a moment. That was the trouble with feeling anything, anything at all. It didn't last, didn't make her feel good. It just carved a hole in the dam she had built up around the anger, and as soon as the feeling was gone the anger poured out.

She couldn't seem to stop staring at Connie, and the longer she stared, the more furious she became. Why, why did she do this to herself, did she do it to Lyn? Why did they have to live here, away from Nikona and Aunt Annie, from Sadie, Jean and Louise? She didn't believe any of the stories that Connie had told about the fight. They didn't dovetail, didn't fit in with the people she knew. No, they were here so that Connie could get to the bars every night. Why didn't she just stop? If not for herself, at least for her daughters? Couldn't she see what she was doing to them? Or did she just not care?

Hastily, Lyn tried to shift away from that question, but it pushed back, full force. Did she just not care?

The answer could only be yes, no matter how much she wished it different. It couldn't be anything else, because if Connie cared she would do something about the drinking. No, she just didn't care, and Lyn hated her for it, hated her, hated her....

A key scraped in the front door. For a moment Lyn thought of dashing into the bedroom, feigning sleep until she calmed down. But it was too late. Darcy was already half in, a hesitant smile on her face that irritated Lyn immediately.

'Hi.'

'Is there anything to eat in this house?' Lyn knew her voice was ugly, accusing. She wasn't mad at Darcy, but she couldn't hold back, either. It was like when she played soccer, there was just a certain point at which she could not be called off the ball by another player, a point at which she was committed. If Darcy wandered into the way of her anger it was not her fault.

Darcy's face fell, and Lyn felt the sneer in her growing. How could she be hurt anew every single time? Didn't Darcy see that it just made her more scornful, that she could have been stopped by one sharp word? But, no, she stood there looking wounded, turning over the question, trying to find a way that it was not a weapon.

'Did you look in the fridge?' Darcy asked finally.

She did not question why food should be her job. She was talking more and more slowly these days, Lyn had noticed, trying to examine all of Lyn's words for barbs, Connie's for signs of tears or eruption. It was an awful, self-feeding cycle: Darcy talking slowly to avoid irritating Lyn; Lyn being irritated because she talked slowly. Neither one of them knew how to stop it.

'Of course I did.' She hadn't, but she knew what it would look like: a depleted version of the refrigerator back home - vegetables, grains, maybe some tofu. In other words, nothing she could pick up and gobble before she caught the bus. She wanted the junk food she had never eaten until six months ago, sugar and caffeine. Well, one of the boys would buy her something on her break. Darcy stuck her head into the refrigerator herself.

'Eggs?' she asked, 'Falafel?'

'No.'

Lyn didn't want either, but she felt slightly appeased. Maybe now she could talk to Darcy without attacking her. Maybe she could even ask her if there was something special about today, as her dream had suggested.

No, she couldn't.

'If you can't find the mate to that earring, you might as well not wear it.'

It was out before Lyn even had time to analyze what it was that was really bothering her about the way Darcy looked; before she had time to make a list that included the too-short sweat pants, the safety pin that replaced the tie in her hood, and her sweaty hair, which would stay slicked back until she hit the showers at school.

So what was bugging her? Darcy always looked as if she dressed in the dark, she always had. It had never bothered Lyn before. But now, as she watched her, again turning over the words before replying, Lyn felt a rage totally out of proportion.

She had often thought, 'We don't even look like we're sisters.' But now she thought, 'We don't even look like we're from the same planet!' It was cruel, she knew it, but that didn't stop her from thinking it, didn't stop her from thinking, 'I'm glad we don't go to the same school.' Worse, it was only by biting her tongue that she kept from saying those things right out loud.

She tried to calm herself by imagining Nikona, who thought herself quite the sharp dresser, wearing Darcy's left behind jeans, rolled up three times, looking just as silly as Darcy did in Nikona's sweats. But the only picture she could get was Nikona standing in the hall of their old school, following Darcy with her eyes and saying, in a voice that equally combined warmth and annoyance: 'There goes old Darcy I-Don't-Give-a-Shit Frasier.'

'I haven't actually lost that earring, I just decided to give punk a chance.' Obviously Darcy had decided to ignore Lyn's tone. Okay, Lyn could go with that now that she had blown the top off the steam.

'I hate to break it to you, but one earring is not going to make you punk, particularly that earring. You're going to have to have at least five holes in that ear.'

'Yeah, put in with a hole punch. So I can wear bones and curtain rings and sandwich ties.'

A sudden flash: the three of them punked out before a Halloween party the year before, dancing in the kitchen for the five women as they screeched a New Wave version of 'Down in the Valley' that Nikona had worked up on her mandolin. Jean, who tended to be a fusser, in the background saying, 'Are those my tights? Did you get those out of my closet? Is that going to come out?'

But Darcy was still talking.

'I thought I'd have a token ear at first. To work people up to it. So that nobody would be too freaked out when I showed up on the court in leopard stretch pants and a purple tank top with the straps pinned together.'

Basketball. Why did she have to bring it into everything, the brass ring, the escape Lyn didn't have? With difficulty Lyn twisted back another bitter reply. Another quick picture: Sadie dancing with her in the front room while she was still small enough to be carried on a hip. On the stereo, Holly Near sang 'You are not my enemy.' Remember that. Darcy wasn't her enemy. She was just handy.

So instead she asked, 'Then you're saving a haircut for a finale?'

'You got it.' Darcy put the bowl down and made as if to run her hand over the spiked front of Lyn's hair. She still hadn't gotten used to it. But Lyn shrank back, and with a hurt look Darcy turned back to the stove.

'You couldn't carry it off, anyway.' Lyn disregarded Darcy's wince, unsure whether she had feared being hugged or hit. It was foolish to expect either one from Darcy. 'You'd look like a little kid whose sister had given her a hair cut with the dog scissors.'

Darcy raised an eyebrow.

'Don't remind me. I took the blame for that one.'

You took the blame for them all, Lyn thought, but what she said was, 'I don't know how they could have thought you did it yourself.'

'Oh, nobody was thinking. Not Mom, not Aunt Annie or Louise or Jean or anybody. They really wanted us to fit in without hassles, same clothes as the other kids, same pencils and notebooks, and then there we were with crew-cuts on the first day of school. They were afraid that everyone in the town would think they were perverts, that they wanted us to be boys or something.'

'They should have just shaved them the rest of the way and let people think it. That would have been an improvement over those damn kerchiefs.'

'Yeah, I thought mine was going to grow to my head before I got to take it off.'

'You wore yours? Nikki and I took ours off the minute we got to school!'

They stared at each other for a moment and then burst into laughter.

'I'll tell you what, though,' Darcy said, 'it was so utilitarian. You could wash it with a bar of soap. If I got my hair cut like that, I'd save a mint on shampoo.'

She pointed with her spoon to the front of Lyn's head then ducked back into the fridge for a bowl, and scraped it into the hot frying pan. Without much hope Lyn jockeyed to look over her shoulder. Was it something she might want to eat?

'What do you care? You steal all your shampoo out of the lost and found in the girls' locker room.'

'It is not stealing if it's been there for a week. I think there may even be a federal law to that effect. It got me some good tennis shoes.' She stuck out a foot.

'You are deluded. Those shoes were meant for the trash to begin with. What are you cooking?'

It was funny. Sometimes she resented Darcy's efforts to take care of her. They made her feel young and incapable. Yet other times she fully expected to be shopped for, fed, and knew Darcy would do it without protest or expecting thanks. For just a flash she thought that, strangely, it was kind of like the way that their mother related to Aunt Annie.

'Oh. Just falafel.'

Lyn loved the way that Sadie, who had an almost magic touch with food, used to cook up the patties made of ground chickpeas with garlic and spices at home. But Darcy's, though they were edible, were bland and boring. Kind of like, as a matter of fact, Darcy's whole routine. Still, she picked at the edge of the patty when Darcy slid it onto her plate.

Darcy had long ago given up defending her food. In a big family you were either overly protective about what you were eating, like Nikona, who wouldn't even trade bites in a restaurant, or you were totally mellow, the way Darcy was. It was as bland as Lyn had anticipated.

'Not to be rude, but this is pretty disgusto.'

'So don't eat it.' But Darcy didn't pull the plate back out of reach.

'It's not so gross that it couldn't be saved. What you need is about a gallon of...'

Lyn stopped. She hadn't seen where the conversation was going. This was getting onto dangerous ground. The haircuts were far in the past. It felt as if they had been talking about two different people. But the hot sauce was last year. If they talked about that time, maybe Darcy would want to talk about what was happening now. Lyn didn't want to do that.

But Darcy was already off and running.

'The great hot sauce ritual. Bushels of peppers and onions.'

Lyn couldn't resist, 'Which I had to chop.'

'All by yourself, right?'

'Well, you gave a hand once in a while.'

'Once in a while? Are you sure it wasn't like I was the chief tomato chopper, in fact, the Queen of Tomatoes?'

'Okay, you helped. Everybody helped except M...' She snapped her mouth shut in the middle of the word and looked away. There was a silence, and she knew they were both seeing their mother, tilting her chair back against the counter, playing her banjo for entertainment so she wouldn't be asked to help.

What was it between them that they couldn't talk anymore? She had tried to tell Robin at school:

'It's like... well, partly it's Nikona not being here. Like we've always been a team and now it's like... well, trying to drive a car with the steering wheel gone or something.' She had struggled, trying to find the right words. 'Whenever I was mad at Darcy I'd find Nikona and she'd say, "Yeah, that makes me mad, too. But you know what really pisses me off..." and we'd go through every damn thing that she did. But we'd always end up laughing and talking about the good things about her.

'And Nikona never clammed up. It was always "Hi, this is how I feel." She thought people really were interested when they said "How are you?" I mean, you had to tell your own stuff in self defence, or you'd end up listening to hers all day long.'

She'd screwed up her mouth in concentration and Robin, sitting on the floor of the bathroom, had screwed up hers in unconscious imitation.

'And, well, I know it's stupid but... well, at first it was like we were in shock. Like we couldn't believe it was happening, it was too weird to talk about. Then, after that was over, it was as if we felt that talking made it too real, that it would go away, be some kind of bad dream, if we just didn't say anything.'

For a moment she had tensed, fearing she had left herself wide open to receive a plug for Robin's Alateen group. But Robin had just nodded like she really heard.

But it was not just those things that kept her silent, Lyn realized now, as she watched Darcy scrape the dishes from yesterday. There was more. It had something to do with the way Darcy cooked for her, collected her laundry automatically. She saw in her mind a picture of her very first day of school. She could hardly see herself. Darcy, holding her hand, dominated the picture. Darcy was much more shy than Lyn, but that day she had overcome it so she could protect Lyn, shout back at any of the children who tried to tease her about living with a bunch of hippie-dykes. Darcy had always taken care of her, been her protector.

Except that she hadn't. Not when it came down to the line. Not when Connie had picked them up. She hadn't stopped Connie from bringing them here, hadn't shouted down the lies that Connie had said about the other women. Darcy had lapsed into shocked silence, just as Lyn had. It was her job to take care of Lyn, and she hadn't done it. When Lyn was being honest with herself, she knew this was really why she kept her feelings to herself. Why share them with Darcy? She hadn't come through when Lyn had needed her the very most.

The sink was full and Darcy had her hands in the water, scrubbing the dishes with her fingers. She was humming to herself, and the look on her face seemed peaceful. Did she really feel that way? Lyn wondered. How could she? Unless she had discovered some better way to not feel, not remember. Lyn knew it was possible. She was the kid who didn't remember anything, not one single thing before she was five years old and her mother had been two years sober. But it was crazy to think that Darcy had just blanked out eighteen years the way Lyn had when she was three.

Only if she hadn't, how did she keep on going, calm and quiet? Because with Lyn, in spite of the boxes in which she tried to capture her emotions, there was always something. Like the dream or the hot sauce, or the woman she had seen in the park yesterday who so resembled her mother in the slow, dogged way that she ran. Always some damned thing to remind her where she wasn't and who she wasn't with. If Darcy didn't feel the things she did, how could she tell her the fear she had lately; that she no longer controlled the wave of anger inside her, but merely rode on its crest like a surfer.

She wanted to tell her. It was too lonely, frightening to carry inside. She couldn't tell her boyfriend Rick, it was beyond the surface things they usually talked about, and she had already dumped enough on Robin without reciprocating. It had to be Darcy.

Lyn opened her mouth to speak. Then, as Darcy turned from the sink, Lyn looked over her shoulder and saw the homemade calendar on the wall. For the first time that day, she noticed the date.

The words of confidence died in her throat. No wonder she had dreamed of parties and dancing, had almost been smelling chicken curry and carrot cake: today was the day they should have been celebrating their mother's twelfth year of sobriety.

# FOUR

For a moment, Darcy stood startled, absently wiping her fingers on her sweatshirt as she leaned against the counter. What had sent Lyn suddenly slamming out of the door without a good-bye? Probably something she had said or not said. Her fault again. She sighed deeply and ran her fingers through her hair.

For a moment she considered just standing there, just standing and thinking nothing until it was time for her to leave for school. Then, with another small sigh she pushed herself away from the counter. If her mother did not get up she would lose her job.

She pulled the can of coffee out from the back corner of the last cupboard, where it nestled, along with the paper filters, behind the washing-up liquid where Lyn would never run across it. There was really no reason to hide it. Except that seeing it would piss Lyn off. (Just like everything else did these days, said a flicker of anger from deep inside her, coming and going so fast that she didn't even know it had been there.) If Lyn was pissed off over the coffee ('Why can we buy *that* for *her* if we're so short on money?') she would create a fight and, please, anything but that. It was all Darcy could do to cope with their lives at all, without watching the angry scenes Lyn created daily with their mother.

*They are in a small place, a place in which she will not fit much longer. This is the safest of their hiding places. Even though it is dark, only a thin box of light outlining the doors, and it smells like old garbage (and even feels like old garbage under one bare foot), it is a good place to be. Hidden away from the screaming voices that travel from the kitchen to the living room to the bedroom and back again, the clinking of ice and glass that she can hear clearly no matter where her parents are. Lyn is curled up against her chest, clutching her shirt with clawlike hands. Tears roll silently from underneath Lyn's closed lids and fall on them both. She will not give them away with a sound. She is almost three, but the only word that she speaks is 'Sissy'.*

*Darcy's hands are clamped over her sister's ear. She cannot identify the feeling inside her, the flicker of resentment because she cannot put her hands over her own ears, bury herself in the chest of a protector. She feels both love and resentment towards Lyn, and guilt because of the resentment. Lyn is her baby. It is her job to take care of her. It is no one's job to take care of Darcy.*

The water was almost ready. As she waited Darcy wondered again what had sent her sister flying from the apartment. She tried to recapture that moment of closeness when they had laughed over the hot sauce, but already it was fading into the daily greyness as if it had never been. She could hardly believe that for a moment she had thought about reminding Lyn of the date. What had she been thinking? That together they would reminisce about the yearly parties?

...lavish parties, thought Lyn, as she leaned against the street sign at the bus stop, much more exciting than anything that happened on a mere birthday. Like the time that everyone came in second-hand finery — prom gowns and tuxedos and tall hats. She remembered being carried by Jean, who had her hair pinned up, braided with silk flowers, and reaching up to touch the shiny paper stars that hung from the ceiling.

In the apartment, Darcy drew a deep breath, remembering the year, her mother's eighth of sobriety, when it had snowed unexpectedly hard. After the storm the full moon had lured the partygoers out. She saw the moonlight shining off Sadie's glasses, useless from the melted snow, heard the voice of Sadie, who, absorbed in her manuscripts, usually had little time for the girls, saying, 'Let's wipe them out, Darcy!' as she thrust a packed snowball into her mittened hand. The memory tore at her stomach so that she doubled over in pain, but she still could not help remembering.

When the spasm passed, she stood and, without knowing why, went into the bedroom. From the one uncovered window she could see Lyn at the bus stop and for a moment she just stood and watched her back.

Lyn was thinking of the fifth party and her mind was filled with pictures: her mother standing in the downstairs bedroom shut away from the crowd, her hair down, her banjo hanging around her neck by a blue and yellow strap handwoven by Aunt Annie. She was wiping her hands on her pants, nervous because it was the first time she was going to play in front of a group. The noise, the wonderful smells filtered through the memory, and in the background Lyn saw herself on the bed, staring over her mother's shoulder at their two faces reflected side by side in the mirror on the dresser.

Lyn brushed back a strand of hair, refusing to acknowledge the wetness that she felt against the back of her hand. Damn it, she wasn't crying, she wasn't remembering. Because it didn't do a damn bit of good. But even as the denial shot through her it was followed by a collage of pictures she couldn't turn off.

Her mother, up on the roof with an apron full of nails, down on the porch swing in the evening with a book in her lap. As she struggled desperately to get a hold on the unwanted feelings that the pictures produced, Lyn suddenly knew that all these things had happened when she was age six or seven. She knew by the feeling that went with them, welling up inside her like an alien voice.

'My mom can do anything!' she heard herself bragging, shrill voiced, at school. A whole new series of pictures flashed through like a slide show gone out of control, so fast she had trouble recognizing them all: Her mother in the garden, at a sewing machine, planting a tree, playing at a dance. What was the common theme? Oh, yes. In every picture there was Lyn, too, a miniature version of the woman, putting her little hands on top of her mother's big calloused ones, imitating whatever she was doing.

Had that been when she started to realize the uniqueness of the bond between them? It seemed as if she had always known that she was her mother's favourite. Of course, Connie denied it when Lyn asked, saying that she loved all three of them equally well. But Darcy and Nikona never called Lyn a liar when she threw it at them in childish fights. She had needed that specialness, needed to know that she was number one to someone, that it didn't matter that she wasn't a prize winner, wasn't the smartest or the best player.

And it was only fair that her mother loved her best. She loved her mother best. All the time. She never held back like Darcy did, choked by old memories, feelings. Sometimes Lyn had felt sorry for Darcy. Connie loved her best, just the way Aunt Annie loved Nikona best, as if she also were an only child. Sometimes, though, she had thought that it served Darcy right for not being able to forget.

Now the tears were frozen on her eyelashes, and the bus was not due for another twenty minutes. Where was the mother in the pictures now? Gone, and she had not taken Lyn with her. Gone, and worse than dead because she had left Connie behind; a shell that caught Lyn off guard, so that sometimes she hoped. Gone, and everything she had said before must have been a lie. Must have been a lie because if she really loved Lyn, she wouldn't leave her, would she? No, she wouldn't. All of it, all her memories, were negated, voided, by the last six months. She had nothing to hold for comfort.

The window was cold against Darcy's face, but she couldn't seem to pull away from it. Lyn looked little from the distance. Darcy put her hand up on the cold glass beside her cheek, as if somehow she could hold onto it, use it as a handhold to keep from falling back into the memory she felt battering at her, at the back of her throat rather than her mind, as if it were some kind of vile sickness. The first party.

*They are getting ready for a party on the farm. This in itself is not unusual. They are women who enjoy parties and rituals. Jean in particular likes to invent celebrations that can be repeated over and over, rituals of seasons and harvest and growing.*

*But this party is different from the ones that six-year-old Darcy has seen on the farm in the last year, and she is nervous. The woman they say is her real mother (a statement she outwardly accepts calmly, but knows in her heart of hearts is just not true) has been living on the farm with them for some months now. The four women talked to her and Lyn about it at great lengths before she came, reassuring them that she wasn't drinking any more. They were so trusting that Darcy didn't have the heart to tell them her mother just said that whenever she wanted her own way, or was trying to make up for something. It was just talk, just like the way that some of the kids at school would hit you on purpose and then say sorry.*

*But even though she thinks that it is a lie, it does seem to Darcy, from the cautious distance she keeps, that perhaps there are some changes in her mother. Enough changes in fact, that a stranger might not be able to pick her out from the other women if they didn't know about the monster inside her. The trouble is, Darcy does know.*

*But when she is alone she wonders, talking to herself, if perhaps the monster has not been curbed, securely chained this time. She knows that it is not dead, for sometimes when she looks up from under a table or behind a door she catches a look in her mother's eyes that tells what she is thinking as clearly as words. As clearly as if she said aloud, 'I want a drink.'*

*But she hasn't had one while Darcy has been around. Not while Darcy has been at school, either, because she questions Lyn every day afterwards. She understands vaguely what the women have told her, that it is the drinks that change her mother, make her do bad things, and she supposes that thinking, wanting, is all right, as long as her mother doesn't actually have one.*

*She also understands that things have not been easy for her mother here and somehow this fact makes the not drinking more significant. First there was the death of Linda. She was an old woman, who had been dying even before Darcy and Lyn came. They hardly even got to see her at all and easily put aside the funeral. But Nikona wept and went to her mother over and over, asking when she would come back. Nikona called Linda 'Grandma', even though she wasn't Aunt Annie's mother, the same way that Darcy calls Nikona's mother 'Aunt', even though their mothers are not sisters.*

*Linda's death was hard on all the women in the house because they loved her, but it was hard on Darcy's mother in a different way. In one way it was good for her, because it meant that there was room for her to come and live now. But Linda had an important place in the balance of the family, a place now empty, that her mother cannot possibly hope to fill. Sometimes Darcy sees her struggling to try. No one has said that she should, but Darcy is familiar with unspoken pressures and can almost sympathize. No one has said that she should read at third grade level, as Nikona does, either, but it doesn't stop her from feeling stupid sounding out four letter words.*

*Then there's her work. Connie's job is to help Louise, who is a carpenter. She's good at that. She has a natural aptitude, says Aunt Annie, the way Darcy has for sports, or Nikona for music. But the other part of helping Louise is working in the apiary, and Connie is afraid of the bees. She never mentions it, but when Darcy sits far back in the weeds watching the two of them in their veils, she can see her fear rising off her like a cloud of steam. Not mentioning the fear has something to do with being grateful; kind of the way if Aunt Annie finally gave in to your nagging and took you with her to the Saturday market, you never, never whined, for fear you'd never get to go again. That also seems to be the same reason Connie is letting Louise try to teach her to play Linda's old banjo even though she hates it. Darcy once heard Aunt Annie say to Connie 'For Christ's sake, you don't have to be so damn grateful all the time!' and was honestly surprised. She thought it was only reasonable that Connie would feel that way.*

*There are more things about the hard times her mother has been having, some that have to do with the place she had been before she came to live with them. Darcy knows vaguely that she went somewhere after that night Aunt Annie had come swooping down in response to her phone call and taken them away in her old car. She can still make herself shiver at the thought of that night, of the memory of Aunt Annie holding her tight against her chest as she stood on the lawn and screamed at her mother. A shiver that came not from her usual fear of fighting, but from awe at Aunt Annie's sheer power. It was so great that it had taken her mind off the blood trickling down her face and soaking Aunt Annie's flannel night gown. She had chosen to ignore it when Aunt Annie sobbed over and over, in a voice that Connie, collapsed on the stairs, could not hear, 'Connie, I love you. Connie, I love you.'*

*After that, her mother had gone somewhere that helped her, and it was hard. But Darcy doesn't really know where and she doesn't care, either. Aunt Annie has tried to talk to her about it, but she has wilfully put on a blank face and not listened. She had gone to the hospital for eight stitches, and she doesn't suppose her mother cared.*

*Her uneasiness on this night has to do with the fact that this is the first time her mother has been there during a party. Darcy has seen her mother during parties before, when her parents were together, watching from the dubious safety of the bedroom. Her mother gets very excited and Darcy isn't sure if, in that excitement, the monster can be kept chained. It is not just her doubt, she knows that her mother isn't sure either, and that sometimes she thinks it would be easy and harmless to take just one little sip out of one of her little bottles, just to make it seem more like a party. Nikona had found the bottles in Connie's shirt drawer and showed them to Darcy, both of them very aware that looking through other people's things was not acceptable.*

*Without mentioning her find, Darcy has heard Nikona questioning Aunt Annie over and over in her shrill voice: 'Well, what if she does start doing bad things again? What if she does?' Nikona's blatant dislike is another thing that makes it hard for Connie. Darcy is leery of her, Lyn simply acts as if she is not there, but Nikona is vehement about her feelings. The day that*

*Connie had arrived she had jumped off the porch and kicked her in the shins and the relationship has not improved much since. She still has the habit of sitting across from Connie with narrowed eyes murmuring, 'Hurt my sissy.' Nikona is loyal to those she loves and won't be changed by any amount of reasoning. Perhaps this is one reason why, neither then nor later, does anyone talk openly about Connie's problem. Always it seems to be something that they are pulled aside for, one or two at a time, and lectured on uncomfortably, as if at times Aunt Annie herself doesn't believe what she is saying.*

*Darcy doesn't know why she doesn't tell about the golden bottles. Maybe, like Nikona, she hopes her mother will be sent away. Or maybe she thinks the bottles are like Nikona's old blanket in the hall closet. She never uses it or even touches it, but she likes to look at it once in a while, to know it is there.*

*Or maybe somehow Darcy understands that her mother's monster will never stay chained unless she is able to do the job herself. At any rate, that is what she is thinking of as she sits in the front porch swing, watching the first early guests arrive. (Really they are friends of Aunt Annie's that she has been determinedly trying to graft onto Connie, because not one of Connie's old drinking buddies was invited.) Thinking of the tempting shine of the bottles and wondering if even now her mother is upstairs drinking while Sadie puts the last touch of frosting on the cake and Aunt Annie runs down the lawn to greet her friends dressed in a long flowing skirt.*

Darcy blinked. Somehow, without being aware of it she had retreated back to the kitchen during the memory. The water in the pot was boiling, little spurts of steam lifting the edge of the plastic plate she was using for a lid. She turned it down, not quite ready to deal with coffee yet. She had got used to stealing a few moments at this time of day, when Lyn was waiting for her bus, her mother still asleep. There was a pile of textbooks sitting on the kitchen table, and she pulled a thin red spiral notebook from beneath them. Automatically it fell open to the middle, past the pages of chemistry notes. She smoothed the page with her hand, wrote the date and 'Dear Nikona'.

The first time she had tried to write a letter she had only put one line after the salutation.

'Dear Nikona', it had read, 'My mom has really freaked out.'

There she was stuck, no matter how long she pored over the otherwise blank page when she was supposed to be listening to the lecture in class. The questions she had could not be formed in a way that would fit nicely on the paper. Then, one day after breakfast, she had picked up the notebook and the words had flown.

'Dear Nikona,

'My mom has really freaked out. You must know that she's drinking again and it's just as bad as it ever was before. Remember when they'd send us outside to play so that your mom could bawl mine out? I wish she were here to do it now.'

Here she had hesitated, trying to formulate a thought that wouldn't quite come together. Why the hell, she had wanted to say, was that the way that the other four adults — Jean, Sadie, Louise and Annie — had continued to keep her mother in line? Had they ever tried anything besides shaming and guilt? It was mixed with love but if there had been something else, some kind of control that her mother had welded herself, would she have fallen so completely apart once away from their influence? But it had sounded too much like criticism and at this point criticizing made her far too vulnerable.

She had continued.

'I don't know what to do. I want to come back but Mom says that all of you told her to leave, and to take us with her. I don't believe that. I can't. But remember Christy Davis from Junior High? Remember how her parents got divorced one year while she was at camp and her dad moved away? They never even talked to her about it, she didn't know it was coming. She hasn't seen him since and they were really close. And Danny Iglesia's mom left him and his sister. But I don't think you'd vote that way, even if everybody else did. Sometimes Mom says that she was tired of getting bossed around, that she left on her own. When we first got here she and Lyn had a huge fight and Lyn told her that she was going home. Mom told her that if she did she'd make trouble for everybody. She said she'd call the police and have your mother arrested for kidnapping, she said she'd have the Internal Revenue Service audit everybody's businesses, and that she'd find your dad and tell him you weren't being taken care of, so that he'd try a custody suit again. And a lot of other stuff. I don't know what to believe.'

She had been writing too fast to put everything in, to explain about the nights she had spent wondering which threats were real, or even feasible. Like, could Nikona's dad even take legal action now that she was almost out of high school? Of course, it wasn't really the possibility that mattered, it was the intense anger that had flowed out of her mother towards the women with whom she had previously been so close.

'Most of the time she's just kind of whiney, but sometimes when she's mad, she gets real mean. Then I think she would do that stuff and only be sorry later. So we can't come back, even if I could leave her alone. You know it was always her and Lyn, but now it's me that takes care of her, that she tries to talk to. That's because all Lyn will do is fight.

'The only good thing is basketball. The coach here is better and we're in a bigger league and get to play lots better teams. Ms Ernst thinks that I can get a scholarship even though I didn't get to go to camp, and she's helping me apply to some colleges with good engineering departments. The only thing we need to do now is send them a video tape, and we're waiting 'til the end of the season to film it. It feels so good when I'm at a game, but sometimes I forget that I'm not with my old team, and I try to toss back to Lacie, because I know right where she'll be. Only it's somebody else. If I get a scholarship I can go away, which is what I really want. I think about having my own room and eating meals that someone else fixed. (Except you should see the stuff they serve at the high school - I wouldn't eat it even if I could afford it, because I know it would just give Sadie a fit. Lots of preservatives. Are you still a vegetarian? I'm still eating chicken, but we almost never can afford to have it.) Only I know that if I go that will leave Lyn and Mom together and I don't know what they'll do. I can tell Lyn is angry when she thinks about me going away, but she doesn't talk about it. She just walks around with her arms crossed over her chest saying ugly stuff. (Imagine that time she was pissed off because they wouldn't let her go out with that eighteen-year-old guy with the motorcycle and multiply it by ten or twenty.) I feel like they're both pulling on me to stay. But I want to go. I want to get away from it.

'Did you really tell her that we couldn't come back?'

She had known even as she was writing it that she would not send it. It made her too vulnerable. It didn't matter if they had not really been cast out, if, as she suspected, Annie and Louise and the others were worried about them, maybe looking for them. What good would the contact be? It would only bring their family trouble they could ill afford after working so hard to establish themselves in the small community. She could still remember hostile years, when people in the streets muttered about the 'dykes up the road', when there had been children at school who were not allowed to play with the three of them. They had settled in since then. People accepted or ignored them as they had become caught up in the web of small town life. Neighbours traded work and overflow from their gardens, bought honey and had their roofs shingled and recognized themselves as bit players in Sadie's books.

But the balance could be easily upset by any of the things Connie had threatened, and Darcy could not bear to be the one to bring that down.

Still, she didn't throw the letter away, or even tear it out of the note book. Instead she continued to write almost every day to the younger girl she called her cousin.

Today she began with,

'Do you remember when I used to say I wanted to be an invisible woman? That was from a story my first kindergarten teacher read us, about a boy who could make himself disappear. Everybody thought that was really great - they started talking about all the tricks they could play, how they could steal candy and not go to bed and stuff like that. But what I really thought was the best would be not being noticed. I didn't want to do anything different than what I usually did, I just wanted not to be noticed. I wanted to be able to fade away when my parents fought, and I didn't want her to be able to find me when she was crying. It made me so mad when she cried. She yelled at me when I cried, made fun of me and called me a baby. So I thought if I really tried hard enough I could make it come true; if I really concentrated or said the right words I could be invisible. Sometimes I think about that now. And you know I still think that it's possible. At least, a lot of the time nobody notices me unless I say something. Or, maybe I just don't notice them.'

The water had been boiling for some time now, and she put down the pen so that she could pour it through the filter. She had barely set the pot down again when she heard a voice behind her say, 'Hey.'

She was so startled that for a moment she almost windmilled backwards onto the floor. She did hit one hand against a cupboard door with a loud smack. She had not expected to hear her mother's voice, flat and harsh from smoke. For just a moment she recalled a snatch of song, a duet Connie and Louise had played at a coffee house long ago. She could hardly believe that the sweet dulcet harmony had come from the same person. Then it was gone, and the woman standing in front of her, blocking her way out of the kitchen, croaked, 'Hey', again.

Darcy didn't really need to look at her to know what she needed to do. She knew she needed to: 1) run a bath (and coax her mother into it); 2) get coffee (and hopefully breakfast) down her; and 3) fold the blankets up so she wouldn't be tempted to crawl back into them (though maybe it wouldn't be necessary to detour her, since she had risen alone).

Automatically she thought in a list, breaking the task down into steps. Who had taught her that? Jean, years ago when she and Nikona had been trying to whine their way out of cleaning the hen house.

'Every job can be done,' she had told them both as she handed out the hated shovel and rakes which they held with limp, unwilling hands. 'It doesn't matter how hard or nasty it is. You've just got to break it down into steps, do 'em one at a time.' She had reached into her shirt pocket for a cigarette and seemed surprised not to find one there, though she had given up smoking five years before. She'd settled for pulling a blue bandana up around her nose and had continued to lecture, her voice muffled, as the two girls rolled their eyes at one another. 'First we make sure that we do this more often. Like once a month at least, so it's not such a big job and you're not such pills about helping and I'm not so tempted to rap you both on the head. Next we get our tools together.' She had indicated the shovels and wheelbarrow expansively, as if they were a John Deere equipment yard. 'Then...'

'We shovel shit,' Nikona had inserted quickly. She was only eleven and they were not supposed to swear, but Jean had not been able to keep her face from twitching under her bandana, which of course Nikki had taken advantage of.

'We shovel shit, we shovel shit,' she had sung, marching Darcy into the coop ahead of her.

Darcy's mouth twitched with a trace of a smile at the memory. How would her mother like to know she compared that to getting her ready for work, that in fact she would clean out a coop everyday if only she never had to do this again?

At any rate the advice was still sound. It was how she got through every day, every morning of rising with her mother. By looking only at the small portion of the task in front of her. Not what she would have to do tomorrow or this afternoon, but just the small steps of the morning. Automatically she groped for the coffee, getting ready to hand it off on her way into the bathroom.

Then she stopped, wary. She had become an expert at reading her mother's moods. Now that she was closer she could sense that something was wrong. She tensed herself, wondering if it would be one of Connie's tirades, her anger at everyone and everything flying out to stick on her. Then Darcy noticed the trembling lips, the teary eyes. Oh, god, no. That meant that this morning she had gotten up with a purpose. This morning she was going to apologize.

This was the worst. For one quick moment Darcy wondered if it wouldn't be possible for her to sidestep quickly and be out the apartment door before her mother even knew what was happening. She no longer cared about her own lunch or her mother's clean clothes. She didn't even care if her mother went to work. All she cared about was avoiding being bawled on and listening to gasped apologies. It seemed like too much on top of everything else, to ask of her this early in the morning.

She could see though, that casual escape would not be possible. Her mother blocked the narrow kitchen determinedly. Darcy couldn't push by roughly like Lyn would. Still, bluffing it out was at least worth a try.

'Good morning!' she cried in a hearty voice, looking away from the tears that were now starting to puddle. 'Just in time for coffee!' She gestured towards the filter and the institutional plastic mug at the same time flattening herself against the wall, hoping to lure Connie past.

But mere coffee was not a good enough distraction today. Now her mother's face was screwed up into what Lyn called (and not always behind her back either) her boo-hoo face. Desperately Darcy said in a loud voice, practically a scream, 'I'll just go start your bath so it will be all ready after your coffee.' She wasn't thinking clearly, so badly did she want to be out of the kitchen. Anywhere else.

Then she made the fatal mistake of trying to brush by and she was trapped. Her mother grabbed her in a tight bear hug, a hug that seemed impossible for such a skinny little woman and began to cry against her chest. Remotely Darcy noticed that the sobbing and gasping was raising quite a cloud of steam around both of them in the cold air. Trapped again and no way of getting out unless she broke the hold and tossed her mother onto the floor. Quickly she swept the thought out of her mind and resigned herself to standing stiff as a store dummy, both arms at her sides. She hadn't even been able to get into her preferred break position, one arm between them, ready to push off the minute the grip loosened. There was an intense moment of sobbing. Then her mother gasped out in her kick-me voice, 'Oh, honey, I'm so sorry. And you're such a good girl!'

Oh, shit. Of all the forgiveness speeches, and she had them memorized, this was the worst. There was no reply Darcy could make to this opening statement that would not simply prolong the scene. Certainly none of the things she longed to say.

Like, 'No, I'm not. I think all the same things that Lyn does, I just don't have the guts to say them.' Or, 'No, I only put up with this because I know that in a year I'll be gone, and Lyn will be stuck here with you.' Certainly not the thing she longed to say the most, and thought might even stop the whole spiel, 'Yes, I am and you sure don't deserve it right now, do you?' It made her feel guilty even to think that one. She tried to wriggle into a more comfortable position, to dislodge her mother's chin from her chest. She wasn't thinking anymore about starting her mother towards work. She thought only about loosening one arm and dragging them both back towards the coffee. She knew her mother's hysterics only too well, knew that some lucky times all it took to break a tirade was to shove a hot drink under her nose. 'I ought to carry a thermos with me,' she had told Lyn once, trying to joke away the embarrassment she felt when her sister witnessed these scenes. But Lyn had only stared humourlessly.

She freed her right arm, the one nearest the counter, and groped behind her for the coffee, tuning out her mother's first few sentences. She didn't have to hear them to know what was being said. Her mother's voice rose hysterically, breaking her protective haze.

'You've always been so good,' she was snuffling, 'ever since you were a little girl. You were more Lyn's mother than I was and you were just a baby too. Oh, honey, I'm so sorry I've done this to you!'

She shouldn't have to listen to this. Because apologies didn't mean anything. Not one damn thing.

*She is little, sitting on the front steps of the apartment building, Lyn firmly clutching a handful of the second-hand dress, decorated with teddy bears that Aunt Annie brought over on her last visit.*

*Aunt Annie has just been there with Nikona. Only later does she know that Aunt Annie is her mother's friend, her only friend left from high school and only much, much later does she realize and muse in amazement that, at the time she was wielding so much influence in her child's life, Annie was barely out of her teens herself. For now she is only Darcy's saviour and Darcy envies her daughter Nikona, who gets to go home with her, with a passion she has never felt before or since. Darcy knows that Aunt Annie's visit is the reason her mother is now talking to them. She was able to hear only the tones of the grown-ups' long talk while the three of them played in the hall. (Mostly Nikona played, because Lyn does not play and it's hard for Darcy to move with her clutched to her side. Nikona, however, is nothing if not creative, and eventually built a make believe town right at Darcy's feet so that she could participate without moving.) The tone, however, had told her enough. There was Aunt Annie's high voice made stern, going on and on, interrupted only by an occasional weak, wavering sentence from Darcy's mother. Darcy has long ago decided her mother is a much bigger baby than Lyn is, and she knew it was only a matter of time before she started to cry. Sure enough, after a little while she heard sobbing and waited for Aunt Annie to stop lecturing and begin comforting as she usually did. But this time was different from all the rest, for Aunt Annie continued in a firm tone.*

*Darcy suspects that this unusual exchange is somehow the reason that her mother is apologizing this particular time. She is not quite sure because she is not listening, has not been since her mother came and sat beside them and burst into her standard opening lines about being sorry and changing. Listening to her mother's promises are just too painful. Darcy knows that they are just lies that her mother tells to make herself feel better. But sometimes she can't help but believe them a little, and that makes it hurt all over again.*

*Instead of listening she is watching Lyn eat the core of an apple that Aunt Annie gave her. She has a vague idea that the actual core is not eaten and knows she should probably stop her, but she is too tired. All her energy must go towards shutting out her mother's voice. Generally Aunt Annie cooks for them both when she comes to visit and stays to watch them eat and sometimes takes a bath. This apple, though, was a last-minute thought, produced from Nikona's lunch box after Aunt Annie peered into Lyn's face to say goodbye.*

*Darcy didn't get an apple, but she is holding something else Aunt Annie gave her tightly clenched in one hand. In fact, maybe that was another reason that Lyn got an apple (and it looked so sweet and juicy) so Aunt Annie could pry her away from Darcy long enough to give her the envelope. It contains five quarters and Aunt Annie's phone number is printed on the back. The quarters are for the phone booth in front of the store on the corner which luckily has a little seat in it so Darcy can climb up to reach the dial. They practiced that and dialing the last time Aunt Annie was over. The money is for phone calls and nothing else. Aunt Annie only said this once. She knows Darcy won't spend it on candy or leave it where her mother will find it. Nikona is the smart girl, Lyn is the baby, but Darcy is the good girl. Darcy is to call Aunt Annie if anything bad happens. (But how bad? If they have eaten only popcorn for two days? If Lyn is sick and has to lay in her own vomit because Darcy is unable to lift her? If -— oh, please, god, no — their father returns and the fights begin again?)*

*Beside them her mother goes on and on. Darcy wonders how long it will take for her to make herself feel better with her lies, and if eventually she will be so convinced by them that she will take them to the store like a good mother. Then maybe Darcy, too, can have an apple.*

'Stop it!' Darcy wasn't aware she had said the words she was thinking aloud, or that she had worked her arms up to give her mother a push until she saw her stagger backwards and saw her mouth crumple. Oh, no, now what had she done? Guiltily she grabbed the cup of coffee and stuck it in her mother's face. Though it might have done the trick two minutes before it was no longer enough. Now her mother was sobbing in earnest, her hands over her face because Darcy had pushed her away. Awkwardly Darcy patted the air around her shoulders, making what she hoped were comforting noises. She hadn't meant to make her mother cry. She only wanted not to hear the lies she was telling. It wasn't that she didn't think her mother was truly sorry; She knew she was. But she also knew that she didn't have the strength, the faith or whatever it took to change what she was doing. She might believe every word she said as she said it, but Darcy couldn't. She knew her mother would be out drinking again tonight, or the next night or the next. And she didn't want to hope.

Her mother had accepted the coffee but she was still sobbing behind one hand. Darcy heard Lyn's name mumbled, and she thought, 'It's not fair!' Sadie's voice, deep and serious, darted through her mind saying,'Of course it's not fair. Where did you get the idea that things worked out fairly? It's not fair that you can walk and run when other people are in wheelchairs, or that I can see when other women are blind. It's not fair that Nikona's ahead in school and other kids can't even read. Hey, get ready to deal with it, fair or not.'

Right. She tried to square her shoulders and not to think about how in this job of being her mother's mother, which was so thankless to begin with, she wasn't even first choice. Her mother would much rather be comforted by Lyn. Maybe that was Darcy's own fault. She never had been able to warm up, could never quite let go of the deep, deep fear of betrayal. But it wasn't just her - it had seemed so futile to try and establish a friendship with her mother, knowing that they could never be close the way she and Lyn were.

She jerked her head, reminding herself that she had to deal with what was happening now. What was real for both of them was that Lyn was not there any longer. She was now just as cold as she had once been warm. Darcy would have to take care of this mess herself, no matter how unpleasant and draining it was, no matter how angry it made her. As she thought this she heard Sadie's voice again, one more sentence she had blocked the first time.

'And it's not fair that some women have to deal with alcoholism.'

Immediately she felt a fresh wave of guilt, this time because she was angry at someone who was sick. She knew it was a disease. So how could she think about pushing her mother down when she started to cry or about snatching the bottle out of her hand in the evening and shattering it against the wall? She turned away, aware that she was not a good daughter, wondering if that was one of the reasons her mother had started to drink again after such a long dry period. Yet, even pressed with guilt she could not hold her when she was like this. It turned her stomach. But to make up for it she spoke in a voice that she forced to be bright and cheery.

'I'll just go start a bath, and you can have another cup of coffee while you wait.' She sidled out of the kitchen, trying not to see the little hand gesture her mother made, as if to clutch the hem of her shirt when she passed.

Then while she was still able, she left. She no longer cared whether her mother went to work, or that she was leaving her homework in the kitchen. It didn't matter what appeasements the guilt demanded.

Without a goodbye she ran down the stairs at top speed, pausing to put her sweatshirt on only when she was safely out of the building and down a whole block.

# FIVE

Connie took her cigarettes and coffee into the bathroom. She didn't turn on the bath water, but sat on the closed toilet, letting the warm air from the vent play up around her. The thought of breakfast nauseated her. Besides, it was too much bother, like the bath. A lot of things were too much bother these days. But that was because she worked hard. Naturally she didn't feel like doing anything but going out after a long day of dry-walling in an unheated building. There was nothing strange about that. There had been years when she hadn't gone out at all, not even once. She deserved it now. It helped her relax and face the next day.

She wouldn't have to work so hard if she weren't supporting two grown kids. But did her daughters ever think of that? Certainly not Lyn, who never said more than two words that weren't cold or cutting. It was hard to believe that six months before they had been playing softball together and that Lyn had hugged her tight after every double play. She had known that the kids would have to make some kind of adjustment to the move, but she hadn't figured on Lyn acting this way. Well, give it time. No one could say it was Connie's fault. Lyn had acted crazy when she was a kid, too. Every time Darcy had left home without her she had screamed and ripped things down and eventually wrapped herself into a weeping, rocking ball. Now, maybe Connie hadn't been the world's best mother, but she hadn't had the world's easiest kids either. Sure Annie could put her down for keeping Darcy out of school. Nikona was bright and pretty and easy to take care of. But what was Connie supposed to do when Lyn acted like that? Because even though she'd never, never hit her kids the way her old man had pounded on her and her brothers, everyone had a limit, and she knew that Lyn's constant screaming would drive her past hers. So wasn't it the lesser of two evils to keep Darcy home?

She put out her cigarette on the counter and lit another. Well, she thought, kids were supposed to go through weird phases. It was just her bad luck that both of hers were going through one at the same time. Almost as hard to deal with as Lyn's smart talking was Darcy sighing and acting as if the weight of the world was on her shoulders. Acting like she was trying to help, when all the while disdain was plainly written on her face, just as it had been for years. All those years that Connie had tried her damnedest. Every time that it seemed as if she had really gotten through and everyone had forgiven and forgotten she would catch that look in Darcy's eyes and know that the nightmare past was still with her. Annie said that it was herself she had to be at peace with not anybody else, but how was she supposed to accomplish that when her eldest daughter still winced when she hugged her?

Maybe she could understand Darcy better if she were less quiet and inwardly drawn. She herself had been a hellion at eighteen. First in love with Annie with no way to understand it, and then marrying Don in a rush of anger when Annie got married, figuring in some confused way that if she couldn't be with Annie at least she'd be like her. It had gotten her out of the house, too, and away from the fear of striking back at her father, whom she loved dearly when he was sober.

But for the most part she thought she could understand or outwait the kids, no matter how much it hurt temporarily. It was the women that she couldn't forgive. In a sudden rush without warning she was back at the farm house the morning after the party.

# SIX

*As she pulled the battered red Datsun up in the gravel driveway she had seen signs of women working. The grey truck was gone. Louise had gone out on a job without her. She felt guilt for a moment, but didn't want to hold it, so she consoled herself with the thought of all the days she had worked with a cough or a cold, when she could have legitimately stayed home. It was too good a morning and had been too good an evening to feel guilty.*

*As she'd opened the door Sadie came off the porch carrying a laundry basket full of wet sheets. Connie had called a greeting and then moved forward to help her, aware as she did of how bright and full the day seemed, how the birds were singing more clearly than usual, and how the scent from the flowers that grew by the porch hung spicy in the air.*

*Then Sadie had spoken to her. Three words, and they were like a bolt of lightning that changed everything violently forever.*

*'You've been drinking,' she'd said. Connie remembering not her face, but*

*the way that her small hands had tightened up on the wicker handles of the basket and the tone of her voice. Saying, 'You've been drinking' in the same tone that she used to discuss neighbours that beat their animals or neglected their children. Raw horror pouring out of Sadie who was usually reserved and never spoke before thinking twice. Those were the things she remembered, that and the way, among the smells of the flowers hanging heavy in the air, Sadie's smell had suddenly changed, and Connie realized she was afraid of her.*

*She had reached out one hand, wanting to touch her, to explain to her that it was okay. Yes, she had been drinking, but it was okay. She had realized that the night before. She wanted to tell Sadie about the party she had been to, how she had stayed in the car at first, afraid because it was the first time in twelve years she had been somewhere liquor was being served without at least one other family member there for back-up. How knowing her two kids had gone camping and she didn't have to be responsible for anyone but herself had both thrilled and frightened her. Oh, she could have gotten away before and the girls would have been loved and cared for. But that wasn't the point. Sadie wouldn't understand the fierce jealousy that sometimes gnawed her when she saw the girls with one of the other women, or the consuming need she had to try and make up for years of bad mothering. It wasn't something she had wanted to go into that morning. She had only wanted to tell Sadie about the fear turning to excitement when she she had finally gotten herself to the door and had seen that the party was wild and grand and filled with new women, women who hadn't heard her stories a hundred times over on winter nights, who didn't have her neatly and forever pegged as 'Oh-yeah-that's-Connie-she-has-two-kids-nearly-grown.' She wanted to tell Sadie how she had been able to shed that self at the door for the first time in years, and how, almost as if in reward, someone had paid attention to her in that special, smouldering way that also had not happened in years.*

*Sadie was an indrawn person. She always seemed content with the same cycles over and over; dealing with the family, loving Jean, her longtime partner, and dealing with whatever passions were left over on the pages of her manuscripts. Connie wondered if she could even understand just what it had meant to her when she had realized she was flirting. There had been almost nothing, not since the painful time years before when she and Annie decided that everyone would function best if they were just friends. Annie found solace in her good friends who were sometimes lovers and in short, intense affairs that left her emotionally drained but eager to work. But Connie wasn't like Annie. Nor was she like Louise who, after Linda's death, seemed*

*to become almost asexual, finding her comfort instead in her spiritual ties
with the earth, and in her family. Connie was a young woman still and it
seemed that night as if she had only just realized this fact after years of
ignoring it.*

*But before she had been able to tell her any of those things, before she
could recall Sadie's horror-stricken voice by assuring her that no harm had
come from her drinking the night before, the screen door was wrenched open
and Annie came flying down the steps. She had obviously overheard them
in her studio. She still wore her work apron and as she bounded towards
them seam rippers and thimbles were jolted out of the pockets onto the grass.
Already before even seeing Connie her face was drawn up in a mask of tragedy,
tears streaming down both cheeks.*

*'Connie,' she'd said, 'No... what...' and then simply, as she drew nearer,
'Oh, god, oh, god.' She'd run her hands through her long dark hair in a
gesture of despair that was familiar from long ago. A handful of pins from
the pin cushion she wore on her wrist became dislodged and caught in her
curls. 'No Connie, no, My Heart, not again.'*

*Those were the last words that Connie termed caring. Suddenly it had
seemed everyone knew what had happened without the story being told and
without listening to even one single word of explanation they had decided
to set themselves into a unified front against her. Without even listening
to how she had suddenly known the problem was past and the need for strict
control was no longer there. She didn't need anybody to take care of her,
shield her, keep her in a box anymore. She had been angry, suddenly, when
she thought of all the times that someone in the house had decided to
accompany her at the last minute. It all seemed artificial, as if no one had
ever legitimately wanted to go to a party or dance for any reason except to
oversee her. Well, she didn't need to be taken care of anymore, damn it! She
didn't need to be taken care of or told what to do or to live her life according
to the stipulations other people had set. She was a grown woman, she would
choose what she would do. For the first time she would choose whether or
not to drink.*

# SEVEN

She shook the memory from her head, savagely stabbed out the half
smoked cigarette on the counter. Damn the kids! she thought suddenly.
Goddamn them both! If they hadn't gone away she never would have

touched another drop.

Another memory, this one artificially bright, garishly clear. She and Annie returning from a concert that had been far too crowded, both soaked with beer that had spilled when a flimsy table was accidently overturned. Darcy in her pyjamas, coming down the stairs to greet them, rubbing the sleep from her eyes. Standing for a moment a few feet off, deciding who to go to first. Wanting Annie, but knowing that choice would hurt Connie. Finally turning to her mother, who squatted down in triumph and opened her arms.

Then she'd screamed. As Connie gathered her up and pressed her to her shoulder she'd begun to scream the moment she was close enough to smell the beer on her clothing. She didn't struggle, she didn't strike out, she merely covered her face with her hands and screamed. She didn't calm until almost fifteen minutes of rocking in Annie's arms, after her mother had left the room in tears. Dammit, thought Connie, she never would have taken a drink if she'd been able to hold the knowledge of one of her daughters waiting for her at home.

She made an impatient movement of head and hand, throwing the regret away. What did it matter? She reminded herself that drinking was not the problem. The problem was...she had forgotten what the problem was as she removed her wallet and started to dig through it. She was sure that she remembered someone giving her a joint the night before. Sure enough, there it was stuck back between her out-of-state driver's license and old library card.

As she sat in the bathroom never once did she recall the significance of the date.

# EIGHT

It seemed as if the first bell had only just rung, but already it was time for the welding students to take their mid-morning break. Lyn pulled off the leather cap that protected her hair from sparks and laid it down on the bench beside her torch. She untied the heavy apron that matched. Most of the boys were already out the door and on their way to the snack bar still in their coveralls, but automatically she began to take hers off. She gave most of her breaks to her classmates and she needed to look good, to maintain her image with them. Especially if it turned out that she had to break up with Rick.

But before she had pulled the zipper all the way down she changed her mind. Today she would visit Robin. No one from her class would notice. Not for the first time she was glad that Rick's break did not overlap with hers.

'Lyn?'

Startled, she turned, thinking for a moment that Rick had somehow gotten out of class early, maybe wanting to apologize for the way he had been acting. But it was only Randy from carpentry, stopping on his way down the hall.

'I thought maybe you hadn't seen the clock,' he said, blushing a little, as if to acknowledge the transparency of his excuse. 'I made some cookies last night. You could tell me if they're edible. I might even spring for a carton of milk to make up for using you as a tester.'

Her stomach growled as he held out the plastic bag. But she had made up her mind that what she really wanted to do was talk to Robin. The boys from the three classes would all be standing up by the snack bar horsing around with each other, and she suddenly felt that the effort to be her school self — cheerful and fun and maybe not outstandingly bright — would be just too much.

Still, she smiled at Randy before shaking her head. He was nice and he'd had a crush on her for at least a month. She had considered him for a possible next boyfriend in case Rick didn't give up the sex angle. But he just didn't fit the bill. Rick was popular and had friends in all the shop programmes. She was fairly safe from hassle as long as she was with him which, of course, was just what she had planned even before the first time she smiled at him. But Randy was more of a loner. He hung out with one or two good friends rather than a group and sometimes was even teased himself. The cookies, both making them and then admitting it, were the perfect example of the type of thing the other boys would give him a hard time about. No, Randy would definitely not do.

Still, he was sweet, and she could afford to be nice. 'Thanks anyway,' she told him, 'but I've got some things I really have to take care of during break.' She nodded vaguely in the direction of the girls' bathroom, assuming that he wouldn't ask for any specifics.

'Oh, well. Maybe next time.' He made a great effort not to appear disappointed, but couldn't keep his face from falling just a little.

To console him, and because she felt bad about rejecting him for the very qualities which would have attracted her the year before, she said, 'Maybe I'll still have time to join you,' even though she had no such intention.

Immediately he brightened again. 'Great!' With a swift movement he tossed her the bag of cookies, then turned to leave. She didn't watch him. Something else had caught her eye, something that had been dislodged from a fold in his flannel shirt when he swung his arm up. She stuffed the cookies haphazardly into the front of her coveralls, then bent to retrieve it. It was a chip of wood, a wedge of cedar. As she smelled it and handled it, she felt the same seduction that hit her whenever she looked in the door of the woodworking shop. For a moment she turned it over in her hand, imagining it shaped and sanded along its lines to be made into an ornament like the one that Aunt Annie hung in the window of her workroom, small, but perfect.

Then she saw a quick picture of her mother, her head bent over the jigsaw with such concentration that she was biting her lower lip. Beside her on the bench lay a small pile of cedar boards, already cut to size. Behind her, through the open door, Lyn could see two branches of the crab-apple tree in blossom.

Angrily she dropped the chip onto the floor and then gave it a kick that sent it scudding across the room. She jerked the door open and hurried down the hall before she could be trapped by anyone else.

Robin was standing in front of one of the three mirrors, brushing her long, dark hair. Usually she wore it pinned up beneath a purple bandanna to keep it out of the muck, so it was only the third or fourth time that Lyn had seen it down. It was fluffy and curly, like a dark dandelion gone to seed.

'Look,' Robin said, starting the conversation as if they had spoken minutes ago, rather than days, ' do you know the maximum penalty I could get for killing a teenage boy? Not an appealing one. Likely to be missed by no one but his mother and then only out of duty. Keep in mind that I'm under age.'

'Sounds like probation at the most to me,' Lyn replied. Her mind was still on the picture of her mother, the smell of the wood shop, and determinedly she boxed it away. Think of something else, like the way that Robin's speech patterns reminded her of Nikona, who rarely used any kind of social amenities such as greetings or farewells. 'Maybe you'd get a sympathetic judge.'

– 43 –

'Hey, I'll call you in as a character witness. You can tell them I was driven to it.' Abruptly she stopped, and Lyn could see her blushing a deep red in the mirror. She felt a matching redness creep up her throat. Robin knew even in jest that no matter how much Lyn commiserated with her privately there was no way that she would stand up for her in public.

Well, damn it, Lyn thought, it's not my job to take care of her. It's not my fault that I've figured out how to survive with these guys and she hasn't. She felt a sudden anger that she could not assign.

'So,' Robin said in a new voice, changing the subject, 'what did you and the football player do this weekend?' Like Lyn, she was reluctant to probe the boundaries of their friendship. Not surprising, when what it boiled down to was that Lyn would admit to knowing her only when they were alone. That would rankle anyone, would spotlight exactly how desperate for kindness the united front of hostility in the mechanic's shop made her.

'The football player and I fought about sex this weekend.' Lyn matched Robin's cheerful tone. She could guess at the kind of things the boys might have been doing this morning to make Robin feel murderous, but she didn't want to. As long as she didn't hear about it and wasn't there to see it she could pretend it wasn't happening.

'Sounds like that's about all you and the football player do these days,' Robin observed, as she drew her hair back to make a ponytail. 'You ought to try finding some other things that you like as well. I hear that a lot of people are into going to the movies.'

'Oh, let me braid your hair,' Lyn said, surprising herself. She and Nikona had experimented with each other's hair since they were little, but she hadn't realized how much she had missed that touch until she took Robin's in her hands. For a moment, as she began a french braid at the crown, she wished that her own hair were still long on top. But, then, who would brush it and braid it for her?

She said, suddenly serious, 'If you want the truth, I'm afraid that the football player and I are going to break up over this one.' Robin was posturing in the mirror, and again Lyn was reminded of Nikona as she tried out different faces and stances with her new hair style, going from stern to sad to elated. As she watched her Lyn thought of the day she had registered at the Career Education Centre when she had first met Robin.

It had been in this same bathroom. Robin had been pounding on the tampon machine with one hand when Lyn had entered. Not as if she expected that this would make it work, but more like a person driven to the end of her tether.

'Do you have a knife?' she had asked Lyn without preamble. 'I'm going to cut my throat.'

'No,' Lyn had replied, feeling shy. It was her first contact in the school, which was much bigger than the high school she had attended back home with Darcy and Nikona. 'But I do have a tampon.' She dug it out of the pocket of her day pack and tossed it.

'A blunt weapon at best,' Robin had said, looking at it thoughtfully before slamming into a stall. She had continued to speak from behind the door. 'Right now I would say that the cutting the throat idea still gets top billing. But if I can't do that, not bleeding through my coveralls in front of that class full of jerks runs a close second.'

Lyn had been silent. She was thinking of the shape of the girl's blunt hands. She had noticed them as she caught the tampon, and somewhere in her tour of the building, she had seen them before. She remembered her quick glance into the mechanic's shop. Her eye had been caught by a blue Volkswagon. The left hand of the student working beneath it popped into view several times. Finally, just as Lyn prepared to leave, it come to rest flat on the cement. That was when without warning, one of the boys in coveralls had walked by and as if by accident, had dropped a socket wrench on the floor an inch away from it. The clatter had made Lyn start, but as if it were an old trick played often before, the hand had not moved other than a slight twitch of the last three fingers.

'Hey,' she said, as Robin came out of the stall, her coveralls still peeled down around her waist so that she could button the black cotton shorts she wore beneath them, 'you're the hand in mechanics. I mean, the one that almost got the wrench dropped on her hand.'

'Hey,' Robin said, echoing her tone as she tucked in her blue striped tank top, 'you're the only person I've ever met who's noticed that kind of thing going on. Everybody else just thinks I'm a paranoid bitch who's losing her mind. I was beginning to believe it myself.'

'You mean that happens all the time?' Lyn was shocked out of her shyness.

'Let me tell you.' Robin had turned to face Lyn, leaning against the sink. 'You want to know how come I was trying so hard to get a tampon out of this piece of shit machine? I mean, most girls would carry an extra, right?'

'Always,' Lyn had agreed. 'My aunt says that every woman in the

US has tampon anxiety.'

'She's right. But I can't carry a pack because my locker had the door taken off the first day of school, and when I was stupid enough to leave a book in it while I was working someone slashed the inside up. Fifteen dollars for a new algebra text. I can imagine the fun they'd have with a box of tampons.'

'Well, doesn't the teacher do anything about it?' Lyn asked incredulously, shuddering at the picture that was being painted in her mind.

'You've heard of the term 'Male Chauvinist Pig'? It was invented specifically for this man. He thinks I should be back in the kitchen in a pink dress, pregnant, making biscuits. Preferably with someone smacking me now and then so I remember my station in life. I think that if he had his way girls wouldn't be able to read, let alone lay their hands on one of his precious automobiles. He not only sees nothing that happens, he stirs a lot of it up. And I'm sure he feels like he's perfectly justified and striking a blow for the return to America's moral standards. I think the guys would probably mellow out eventually if they were on their own.'

Lyn hadn't been able to keep from laughing at the grimaces and grins the girl put on her mobile face, square, like her hands, to illustrate her story. But it made her anxious. She had made up her mind that this was the school in which she wished to enroll. But she didn't think she could face that kind of pressure every day.

'Have you tried having your folks talk to the principal?' she asked, even while rejecting that option for herself.

Robin's face had fallen and the tone in which she answered was subdued. 'My mother is... well, by the time she gets home she's not really in touch with reality. She doesn't deal with this kind of thing well at all. She did come in once, but it just made things worse.'

Lyn couldn't have said, either then or later, what it was that made her blurt out, 'Does she drink?' Maybe it was the embarrassed way that Robin talked around the problem, just as she imagined she herself would if cornered.

Robin had shown her a new look, eyebrows pulled together, mouth in a little frown. Lyn felt herself blush scarlet and began to grope for an apology. But before anything but a stutter came out Robin said, 'Yeah, she does. But how'd you figure that one out?'

'My mom drinks, too.' Lyn felt a rush of relief as she said the words she had not been able to say to Darcy. 'It just sounded a lot like her.

I mean, I realized that she wouldn't be able to help me either.'

Robin's face had lit up. 'You're new! I should have known, nobody ever uses this bathroom but me. You're coming into the mechanic programme, right? All that stuff I said before was a lie. It's great, nice guys, nice teacher. You'll love it!'

Lyn had looked away from the hope, hidden behind the joking, shining in her eyes. 'No. I hate cars. But maybe something like welding?'

She surprised herself with her answer. Up until that moment she would have said that her choice would have been woodworking. She hesitated, starting to change it. Then came the memory of small hands resting on big hands on a plane and then the same big hands shaking and reaching for a drink.

'Welding,' she said again, almost angrily. Then she asked, 'Are you the only girl in the shop programmes?'

'Me and three carpenters. We are the pride and joy of the guidance counsellor. In the spring he trots us around to talk at all the junior highs so that we can be role models for the ninth grade girls. Unfortunately I'm not much of a public speaker. I didn't convince anyone.' She had spoken lightly but Lyn had been able to see that the hope of an ally had been very real.

'Why do you stay if it's that bad?' she had asked curiously, even then planning how she could avoid the same ostracism.

'I've already completed almost a year and a half out of three. I don't want to throw it away. I want to do something with mechanics. Maybe planes, maybe race cars. Maybe something totally different, but definitely with motors. I know this sounds like I'm really bragging,' she made a face, 'but I'm really good with them.' Then she'd laughed. 'Besides, I can't stand to think about that bunch of creeps in there winning. Somebody has to stick it out long enough to be the first girl.'

'Hmm.' Already Lyn was casting memory's eye back over the other girls she had seen that day, the ones that had looked cool and popular as they talked to the boys. She was sure they were never hassled the same way that this girl was.

'The fox,' she had said, not realizing that she had spoken aloud until Robin said, 'What?'

'Oh, there was a boy down the road from us a couple of miles. He had a tame fox for a pet. I mean, really tame, like it would do tricks like a dog, and the house cats would get in and sleep with it.'

'And?' Robin's look had been puzzled, not following the point of the story.

'It ran away one night.' Lyn had not added that she was the only one not surprised by this, that she had looked often into its eyes and seen that it was only waiting out a masquerade, that it always remembered that it was still a fox.

And I can do that, too, she had thought. I can do that, too.

'What?' Daydreaming, Lyn had lost the drift of the conversation.

Robin repeated herself patiently. 'I know you've talked about this sex thing with Rick before. But am I being stupid, or did you ever tell me why you don't want to do it with him? Do you just not like him enough?'

Funny, but that was what Rick had said to her that weekend, that she didn't care enough about him. Only he didn't say it like it was anything they should talk about but as an accusation to try and manoeuvre her.

'Kinda, sorta. I mean, that's definitely part of it.'

Robin did not ask why she had been going out for three months with a boy for whom her affections seemed lukewarm. Although they had never discussed it Lyn was sure she had figured out the master plan, knew why she dated who she did.

'But other stuff, too. Even if we could get around hassling about birth control and safe sex and where to do it, it just seems so heavy. So, big deal. I don't think I'm ready to handle any more big deals right now.'

'Yeah, I know what you mean.' Robin turned from side to side, looking at the finished braid in the mirror. 'Boy, am I cute, or what?' Then, not waiting for an answer, 'I went to bed with this guy last summer, and it was just what you're saying. It was like by doing 'It' our whole relationship was supposed to change. We couldn't just go out and go swimming or look for fossils anymore. We had to always be thinking of ways to be alone. I felt like I had to act like I was in love with him after it happened, when really all I wanted to do was still be buddies.'

Lyn was too stunned by the story to pay much attention to the moral at first. 'You mean that you... you and some guy...' She had heard the other girls talking about sex before, but who would have thought that square little Robin, who was always joking, would have an affair?

'You don't need to act so surprised. I told you I was cute.' Robin looked at Lyn flirtatiously, mocking herself again, but also a little offended at Lyn's total astonishment.

'No, no, it's not that.' Lyn tried to backpedal. 'It's just that you never said before, and all the boys call you...' She stopped in dismay. Rattled over the confession, she had now really put her foot in her mouth. Now Robin would not only know that the boys called her names behind her back, but she would know that Lyn knew and did not defend her.

'A dyke?' Robin did not appear surprised. 'Yes, that's one of their favourites, isn't it?'

'But why don't you...'

'Tell them that touching little story? No thanks. And I'm not going to have a quickie with one of them just to prove that I can do it, either. Besides, it's not as if they're using it literally. It's more like it's just the worst name that they can think of. I mean, that tells you something right there.'

A picture of Jean, tall, gaunt, walking down the city street once when they had all gone in for the Saturday market and a rare night out. Next to Aunt Annie, Jean was Darcy's favourite of the aunts, maybe because, like Darcy herself, she sometimes seemed slow in the way that she turned other peoples' words over and processed them. Someone behind them had hissed 'Dyke!' Lyn remembered wincing, thinking that Jean would never think of a quick come-back. But Jean had surprised her, turning slowly with one eyebrow lifted, and simply saying, 'Yes?' Unashamed, taking the ammunition out of the word that had been meant as a weapon. For a moment she wanted to blurt the story out to Robin the same way she had blurted out her mother's drinking on the first day. No. Maybe it would just lie quiet until she brought it up, as that confession had. But what had just been fact at home was a possible source of derision here. Not from Robin, but possibly Rick's friends, or even Rick himself if it leaked. No, it was better to keep playing her cards close to her chest.

'You are so cool,' is what she finally said. 'You just don't seem to let that stuff bother you.'

'Ah, that's the Zen of Alateen,' Robin replied, again joking and serious at the same time. Then, dropping the joke altogether, she added, 'One of the things that I talk to the other kids about all the time is how not to be mad at my mom. I guess it just spills over into other things. The old accepting what you can't change.' She looked at her watch. 'Time to go back into the fray. Wish me luck!' She slipped out into the hall before Lyn could answer.

Which was just as well, Lyn thought as she waited a moment before following, because she had no idea what her answer would have been. Robin mentioned Alateen now and then, matter of factly, not pushing. But there was something about it, something she could not put her finger on, that made Lyn's skin crawl.

It was only half an hour later, after she had once again become engrossed in welding, that she relaxed enough to know the reason. Even then it did not come to her in sharp words or a clear statement, but more like osmosis, so that one minute she did not know and the next, without pondering, she did.

It was simple. The reason that she had trouble with the way Robin found peace was that she herself did not want to let go of her anger towards her mother.

# NINE

*'Down by the willow garden*
*Where me and my love did meet*
*By chance we fell to courting...'*

The tune, one Connie knew from Louise, ran over and over through her mind as she worked, almost as if Louise herself was working in the next room. Louise knew hundreds of songs and she sang them to herself end to end as she worked. Connie remembered this one, and the staircase they were building the first time she had heard it. But she couldn't remember the rest of the story. It seemed as if something bad had happened to the girl in the story. She could recall Louise telling her about it, and other songs related, over lunch one day. That is, she could recall the look on Louise's face as she talked and ate, could name the tree in whose shade they had sat. But she couldn't remember the words spoken.

Louise had a fine, strong voice. She played the guitar and sang in the kitchen while evening dishes were being done and was the lead voice whenever the band could pick up a dance. But the times Connie liked best were when she was singing to herself on the job.

She missed that. She missed Louise. She was fifteen years older than Connie with a face weathered beyond even that. So many talks they'd had over the years while they were working together. There was a sort of healing calmness in being around Louise. Connie remembered it even from the first time they had worked together, when she was too inexperienced to do much more than fetch tools. It was different than what there was between her and Annie. Annie loved her, but she also knew her past. Sometimes she felt held back from growing by Annie's expectations of her. But Louise didn't know her as Connie Screwup, Connie-Needs-To-Be-Taken-Care-Of. She had only seen the best. It was all she expected. Sometimes it seemed that if only it had been Louise she had been able to talk to first when she got home, if she could just have explained to her what had happened, that things would have gone differently. She'd probably be working with Louise now, listening to her sing.

'But you're not, Ace, you're dry-walling for Joe.' She spoke aloud to herself. And Joe himself had popped his head out of the kitchen as she came back from lunch and said, 'See me before you go, huh, Kiddo?' His voice was pleasant enough but it was definitely a command rather than a suggestion, and Connie's stomach had twisted in anticipation around the three beers she'd had for lunch. She'd drunk them from the can while standing in front of the phone booth outside the grocery store, rubbing a quarter between her fingers and wondering if anyone on the farm would accept a collect call. In the end she had turned away.

But once upstairs and back to work she sneered and repeated the order to herself over and over under her breath. 'See me before you leave, huh, Kiddo? See me before you leave.' Oh, how it rankled her to work for Joe after being Louise's partner for so long. He was fussily precise and an authority on everything. He insisted on telling her how to do things she had been doing well before he got out of high school. Working for a kid who was only twenty-five! Sometimes she wanted to tell him to cool his act, coming on like it was nice of him to hire the old lady. He was getting quality stuff here! She did have to admit that he no longer poked his head in the door every five minutes to check on her, as he still did with George, the punker downstairs. Now he contented himself with a grand tour in the evening. He never found anything wrong, but still it made her want to throw a hammer at him.

The request was doubly irritating. She had hoped that he would leave so that she could slide out just a little early that day and hit the plasma centre. It had been three days since she had 'donated', as they referred to it, and she was eligible to go in and sell another pint for ten dollars. Maybe that was what Joe wanted to talk about. Maybe somehow he had found out that she had been leaving early when he wasn't there. Well, he could afford to be fussy. He had no children, he had no idea how easy it was to run short on cash when you were supporting two. It was important that she have at least a little cash for herself after working all day. As soon as you had kids everybody labelled you 'mother' and put you in a category in which going out and having fun was not permitted. Maybe she'd quit her job. Except that finding another would be such a drag. It seemed as if everyone who had interviewed her had looked at her strangely. But that was because she was a woman working in a non-traditional field. It wasn't because she was drinking.

'Connie.'

She started. Caught in her inner tirade she hadn't heard Joe come up the stairs. Her mind darted frantically for possible defences. But against what? What if it wasn't just a lecture, what if he were going to fire her?

'Is your kid coming today?' She was thrown completely into confusion and so turned the question over suspiciously. What did he really want from her?

'Doesn't she usually drop by on pay-day?' he prodded.

Pay-day! How had she become confused, forgotten what day it was? Her first feeling was surprise, closely followed by a rush of chagrin. She hadn't noticed it usually was pay-day when Darcy came by and had just been pleased that she visited occasionally. Now, her face burning, she realized that whenever Darcy left she took most of her salary with her. Embarrassment and anger fought with panic that he would not pay her before Darcy came, so she would not be able to slip out a couple of twenties.

'Didn't you say that she sews pretty well?' Another question out of left field. Where the hell were they coming from? But she couldn't deny it. She'd bragged on Darcy's blue down jacket which she had borrowed one day.

'Yeah.'

He pulled a cardboard box into the room. 'I was going through my stuff and I wondered if she'd be interested in any of this. I'm just going to dump it otherwise.'

She still didn't understand, so he dug into the box to demonstrate. He held up a green sweater with holes in both elbows, and two thoughts rushed simultaneously through her mind. First, that she had never realized that Darcy and Joe were of a similar size and second, that she didn't know that her children looked so... so... destitute that it aroused the pity of strangers.

But before she could speak, or even form a thought, Darcy herself walked apologetically into the room and suddenly Connie saw her through Joe's eyes.

She was dressed in a bundle of odds and ends and all of them together were still too thin for the wind and snow. The army fatigues, the sweater, the hooded sweatshirt; they were all things that she'd had with her on the backpacking trip.

Connie tried justifying. Of course she hadn't meant to leave all Darcy's winter clothes behind! Who could find everything in that madhouse the three of them called a room? But somehow this time she could not excuse herself as she watched Darcy shift from one foot to another, trying to warm herself.

'You want these?' Joe asked, pleased to be dealing directly.

'Can I look?' She was very cool, as if nothing surprised her anymore, as if strange men offered her boxes of clothing everyday.

'You bet.'

As Darcy knelt beside the box Connie continued to stand paralysed, looking at her with a stranger's eyes. Why the hell wouldn't Joe leave? Was he enjoying humiliating her? Oh, no, it was because he hadn't paid her yet. And now he'd have to do it in front of Darcy, who had turned the box upside down. She held up one garment after another, handling them as if they were treasure. Long underwear with holes in the knees. Mismatched mittens. A red flannel shirt with tattered cuffs. She looked at Connie with a delighted smile, as if she expected her to feel the same way.

Couldn't she see that this was different than hand-me-downs and second-hand stores, that this was charity from someone who thought that she wasn't taking care of her own kids? What the hell was Connie supposed to say?

'Hey, aren't these great?' Darcy held up a pair of black wool sailor's pants with all thirteen front buttons missing.

'I've always wanted a pair, ever since...' she trailed off uncertainly, and then dug through the pile with renewed vigour. Connie finished the sentence in her mind. She had wanted a pair ever since Sadie had gotten some for cross-country skiing. In her new awareness other awkward silences forced themselves into her mind, times Darcy had stopped short for fear of saying something that would upset her.

She managed a weak smile in Darcy's general direction, pretending everything was okay. Finally, mercifully, Joe had his wallet out, was moving over towards her. One good thing about Joe was that he paid cash, under the table. If only he had done it before Darcy got there. Maybe she would be too engrossed in the clothes to notice...but, no, as if she had smelled the money she was there, watching silently as every bill changed hands. Following its path from Joe's hand to hers as if she were watching a tennis match. That goddamn Joe, again acting as if he wanted to humiliate her, counted it aloud, so that Darcy knew just how much she had, right down to the last cent. Why couldn't he just hand her the wad?

'How come you're out of school so early?' she asked Darcy to distract her. 'Don't you have basketball tonight?'

'No, I've got a free sixth period. Usually I just do my homework, but I thought I'd swing by tonight since you're right in the neighbourhood.'

Somehow from the tone of her voice Connie knew that she should have known about the free period. But then, she also should have figured that Darcy wasn't interested in her work, that she only stopped by on pay-day. For a moment she fought between two emotions - gratitude that at least Darcy was willing to talk in euphemisms in front of Joe, and anger that Darcy had come at all, as if she couldn't take care of things herself.

'When's your game this week?'

'No more games. Just the tournament.' Again the tone said she had been through this before. Connie gave up the effort. It wasn't distracting her from the money Joe was putting in her hand anyway. What if she didn't hand it to Darcy? Would she say anything in front of Joe if she just put it in her pocket?

Now Joe had to get in on the act.

'How are you rated?' he asked.

The grin over the wool pants had been nothing compared to the one that now split Darcy's face. 'First in the league,' she said. 'Number one. There's no reason that we shouldn't take the tournament if we don't choke.'

'I hear from your mom you're a real hotshot player, huh?'

Connie jerked. When had she told him that? She could hardly remember saying three words to the man socially, yet he seemed to know all about her family. Darcy's side glance before she answered told her that she too was surprised, and for some reason that made Connie swell with anger again

Darcy struggled between modesty and pride. 'I do okay', she said.

'Just okay?' Joe teased.

Her face reddened and she ducked her head shyly but did not answer. For no reason Connie remembered a day the winter before when Darcy had come into the house carrying a trophy, with Nikona behind her chanting, 'Best in the league! Best in the league!'

She had missed the last question between them, and it took her a moment to figure it out from Darcy's answer.

'Yeah, I'm anticipating a couple of good offers. I'll decide where I'm going then.'

Where was she talking about going?

'Have you been scouted?'

'No, they don't do that a lot anymore. I've got to send a video tape to the colleges I'm interested in. We're filming at the tournament.'

Connie opened and then closed her mouth silently. It would be better to talk about this at home. She'd had no idea that Darcy was still thinking of college when it was so obviously impossible. Joe had stopped counting and she knit her brows together. She was certain that there should be more, but was afraid to ask. Maybe he did know about those early afternoons. Automatically she folded the money.

'Mama, I've got the bills here. I thought if I could drop them off we wouldn't have to get money orders or stamps. And I could pick up groceries too.' She was trying to allow her to save face in front of Joe, and again that strange combination of gratitude and anger battled within Connie. It didn't matter how Darcy tried to dress it up now, Joe had shown her what his image of Connie Frasier as a mother was. Suddenly she was hit with a staggering wave of remorse. She could be better. She would. She would start by giving Darcy all the money this time, not keeping any for herself.

But even as she thought this she found herself sliding two twenties out of the stack, trying to keep one hidden beneath the other.

'Why don't I stop and get stuff for dinner tonight? You'll be tired, honey.' She looked away from Darcy's eyes, from the weary set of her face that said, Sure, Mama, you don't have to lie to me. I won't call your bluff in front of him.

Then finally they were both gone, Joe telling her to lock up behind her, and Connie was left alone in the empty house with only her thoughts.

*It is a warm summer night, late. Later than she meant to be, but she got lost twice on the drive out, trying to find the place where Annie is living. She is not drunk. Oh, maybe she had one or two little ones. But only for courage. Anyone would have done the same. It is only nervousness that makes her stumble on the porch steps. She hasn't seen her children or Annie for two weeks, and all the liquor that she has poured into that hole of loneliness has not been able to fill it.*

*She had thought to knock demandingly, to ask Annie what the hell she thought she was doing, to quote the law. But her knock is timid and for a moment, before it is answered, she wishes that she hadn't come.*

*Then she is hit with a square of light, and Annie is there at the screen with another woman whom Connie does not know.*

*Time has veiled the rest mercifully. She remembers Annie crying and pushing away from her embrace. She remembers the envelope of x-rays, the Doctor's report from the hospital. She doesn't remember her panic, praying that it was an accident. Please, god, I didn't hit my daughter and make her bleed, did I? Please, no. Sometimes she gets on my nerves and it's so hard not having enough money, but I love her so beneath it all. I didn't hit her. I didn't hit her, did I? Did I?*

She still didn't remember the truth of that night, but she knew that Annie thought she had hit Darcy. Darcy had been just a little girl. She never talked about it. No one knew if she remembered. But surely, thought Connie, lighting a cigarette with shaking hands, I'd remember if I hit my own child that hard. Wouldn't I? (But how did I get the bruises on my own face, and when did Darcy tell me about the basketball tournament?)

Maybe she hadn't been a good mother then. She had never tried to deny that. But the problem wasn't the drinking. Everyone used that so neatly, so they didn't have to look behind it. The problem was that she had been twenty years old with two kids. The problem was that she hadn't married out of love or even lust, but despair. The problem was that she hadn't wanted her husband to stay because she hated the way he treated her and her babies, but she couldn't let him go because she had no way to feed the three of them.

She could even be more honest than that. Maybe the drinking had been part of the problem. Then. She had seen it happen before, had seen a friend get into a bad place and try to drink or drug her way out. Maybe she had done that. In fact, she'd come right out and say that she had done that. But so had a lot of other people, and it didn't mean that everyone around them had put the screws on not to touch another bottle for life. No, you got through your bad times, worked them out. Then the drinking naturally went down when you didn't need it so much. It would have happened anyway, regardless of Annie or the detox programme. Just like it would happen now. Things would work out, the kids would calm down, money wouldn't be so tight. She wouldn't drink so much when she was less upset.

She began to clean her tools. Calmly. Rationally. Like the mature woman she was. One who recently had more than her share of upsets in life. Maybe her concern over them, and her parting of ways had made it seem as if she wasn't a good mother. She could change that. She would change that. She hadn't kept the money to drink at all. It was just that a grown woman needed a little cash on hand. She'd use it for groceries, make a proper dinner tonight.

She was a good mother.

It was storming again when Connie went outside. The snow might have made her change her mind had the supermarket not been right on the way home. Darcy bought bulk food at the Co-op by their house where once a month she helped clean out the store rooms for a membership discount. But the supermarket would be fine for tonight.

Connie blinked her eyes against the bright lights inside the store, trying but failing to remember what she had seen in the cupboards at home. Well then, chicken and rice. They hadn't had curry in a long time. She loaded her cart with the vegetables she needed, passing the wine department with the resolve of a good mother. Not because that was the problem, but because it irritated Lyn, and the two of them needed to get close to one another again.

'Connie!' At first she couldn't place the voice behind her, because it didn't belong in the supermarket. (It belonged in the bar, dark and smoky, and there was almost always someone there who would buy her a drink if she couldn't pay.)

The woman came closer and she saw it was Jeanette with whom she had been out several times. As always, she looked very sharp, this time in a pair of brushed corduroy pants and a cream coloured blouse, over which she wore a vest that was surely handwoven. She could afford to buy that kind of thing because, as Connie remembered dimly, she was a lawyer or possibly even a judge. Which just went to show how paranoid people were about drinking, because she had overheard other women referring to Jeanette as an alcoholic, and anyone could see that it wasn't true. An alcoholic couldn't look so nice or hold an important job. Of course, she had once seen Jeanette weeping wildly in the bathroom at the bar near the end of the evening, but people had to let go once in a while. (Maybe it had been twice. Maybe it had been every time.)

'I'm glad I ran into you. Nobody knew your number. We're having a little thing for Shelly's birthday tonight.' Jeanette gestured towards her cart, which was piled with avocados and chips and jugs of wine. (Oh, a little would taste so good now. No!)

Connie almost said yes immediately. She could see that Jeanette expected her to and wondered, strangely resentful, if she thought that she had nothing else to do in her life.

'Thanks anyway, but I'm going to spend some time with my kids tonight.'

'Well, darn. Sorry to miss you. But you know where my place is in case you change your mind.' Which was exactly what Connie had been thinking herself. But only after a couple of really quality hours with the kids.

It was dark by the time she got outside, and now the snow was really coming down. Even though she expressly forbade the kids to hitchhike she stuck out her thumb. It was too damn cold to walk the fifteen blocks. She could take care of herself in a way they couldn't. Her luck was good though, the man who picked her up didn't even try to talk to her over the loud music on the radio. She settled the bag of groceries more comfortably, nestling the bottle of wine between her legs. It was just a small one, like anyone might drink with her dinner and didn't she deserve it after saying no to Jeanette's invitation?

As the loud music enfolded her she planned the evening. First she would surprise the kids with a good dinner. A formal kind of thing on the table, as they used to do for special occasions on the farm, but had all been too busy for lately. Candles, good plates, cloth napkins. No, she had left all those things behind. But she would bathe and change her clothes, and they would take the time to talk about their lives. Then she'd clean the kitchen, even though someone besides the cook usually did that. Back home they did each job once a week, according to one of Sadie's meticulous charts. But there they didn't take into account outside jobs. Here she was the only one working, so it had been only fair that a couple of times she skipped house jobs.

Then there were a couple of small chores she would do, things the girls might even help with. Planing the warped bottom of the bathroom door so it would shut all the way. And there was an old table that they had found in the basement. She had heard them mention stripping it for a desk. If they did those things together after dinner then they could talk and laugh together the way they used to.

# TEN

Slap. The girl in the red tossed the ball ahead of her to Darcy, and the red team tore down the court in a fast break. A blue guard tripped over her own feet in the confusion and went down, but no one stopped. When they scrimmaged they played for real. Karen would be under the basket by now, Darcy could count on her. She almost passed the ball without looking carefully, then caught herself. Karen was her teammate back home. This year she was playing with red-headed Lee Ann, who was sometimes inspired, but not as predictable. But she was open now, and she leaped high to receive the ball. She pivoted and faked, drawing the blue guard just a little out of her zone and tossed the ball back. Darcy shot from the top of the key, a high arch that swished through the basket without even touching the rim.

'Hey! Darcy! Get out of there!' The coach's voice, high and thin, snapped her like a whip. Startled, she jumped and looked around. The rest of her team was down court while she stood day dreaming in the key. The blues were taking advantage of the hole she had left in the defense. She hustled down to fill it, but her mind was not on the game. It wasn't the first time it had happened. She had written about it that day in her English class.

'Dear Nikona,
    At first it seemed like basketball was a light in my life, and even like it was a big enough one so that it could light the rest of my day. I might not feel so good in the morning, but I could cheer myself up by thinking about practice. The closer it got the better the day got. Evenings weren't so bad, because it had just happened.
    But now it's like everything is grey. I feel so down and I seem to space out all the time, even when I'm playing ball. When I'm

on the court all I can think of is Lyn screaming at Mom and Mom screaming at Lyn, and me wanting to be somewhere else.'

A shrill whistle sounded from the side line. 'Okay, time to go home.' Almost as one they turned to scowl at Ms Ernst, the coach.

She laughed aloud. 'You're gluttons for punishment,' she said, as if it were the most delightful of things to be. 'You'd go all night long if I let you. No dinner. No TV. No sleep. The zombie basketball players. If only I could get you to warm up and cool down as well.' This last was directed towards two of the second string sophomores, who had sunk into exhausted squats. They were behind her, but nothing escaped her notice. 'If you can't be sensible on your own I'll send you on a couple of slow laps. Look at what a good job Sandy is doing.'

Sandy, the other centre, was a fair girl with streaks of blue and green in her hair. She gave everyone a very superior smile as she did a slow stretch.

'You get a gold star, honey. Just remember that when I start in on you later.'

Hilary, the trainer, had broken out bottles of water and orange slices and was passing them around as they all stretched half heartedly.

'Now, I suppose you've heard,' Ms Ernst looked at them over her glasses, 'that we have a tournament this week?'

The girls grinned and nudged one another. Lee Ann snapped her fingers and said, 'Damn! I've got to wash my hair that night!'

The older woman rolled her eyes. 'You guys are too cute. I don't know how I ever got stuck with you. No, never mind,' she held up her hand to forestall comment, 'I know, just lucky, right? Okay, to get on with it, we do have this tournament, and it does happen to determine state championship. Remember that? It's what we almost won the last three years, and what I think we can win this year, considering our record. At least we've got a good shot. Now, does anybody not know where Wheatville High is?'

'Isn't there an activity bus?'

'Not for this one. We've used up every bit of our budget. But if you don't have a ride check with me.'

'My father says that after this is over he is never going to another basketball game in his life,' Sandy mumbled around an orange slice. Darcy, sucking on a piece of grapefruit, was silent.

'Now, considering that you've worked so hard, and that I have a department meeting tomorrow I thought I would give you a break and we wouldn't have practice. Go home and let your families see what you look like. Yes, yes,' she patted down the ragged cheers, 'I considered having Mrs Page come in and watch you run a thousand laps wearing ankle weights, but I just couldn't give that pleasure away to someone else. Now,' she continued, eyeing them sternly, 'I would appreciate it greatly if everybody who punked out for the last game would sew the sleeves back into their jerseys and refrain from dressing up this time. You all looked great, your hair was not overstated, and I'm sure it gave us a great psychological advantage over Fairmont. But the refs did not think it was funny, and I think it made it hard for them to be absolutely fair. Okay, that's it.' As the girls began to pick up their sweat pants and trickle into the locker room she added, without looking up, 'You looked pretty good today.'

Pretty good? They grinned and punched one another's sweaty arms. If she would admit that much they must have been really hot.

The locker room was noisier than usual because of their high spirits. Darcy spent a long time under the shower listening to the shouts and laughter, reluctant to end the best part of her day. Finally, though, she forced herself out of the warm water and back to her locker. Sandy was standing there, looking woefully at her blue and silver game jersey. The sleeves had been taken out, and then tacked back in by hand.

'Look at this mess,' Sandy said, 'this looks awful. Whose bright idea was it to cut our sleeves out, anyway?'

'It was yours,' called Lee Ann, 'and if Darcy hadn't shown you how to take the seams out you'd have gone ahead and cut the material, and then you'd really be up a creek.'

'Oh, yeah.' Sandy made an even more mournful face.

'Yeah, and I am personally never going to forgive you for not telling me the plan sooner so that I could have grown the hair in my armpits out like everybody else.' This was from Joan, one of the starting guards.

'That was where our advantage was - we scared that other team. The refs were just mad because they thought we should be such little ladies.'

'Hey, Sandy,' called another of the girls, 'When's your hair going back to normal? What did your mom say when she saw it?'

'In about a month, and you don't want to know. She thought it was a great joke until she found out I accidently used the permanent dye. In fact, if you want to know the truth I'm still not sure she's not going to shave my head while I'm asleep. She's mentioned wigs several times in a way that makes me very nervous. But seriously, what am I going to do with this jersey? I don't want to pay fifteen bucks for a new one, and I sure can't fix it so that it looks the same.'

'Using matching thread might help a little,' suggested Lee Ann.

Darcy, who had pulled on her pants and t-shirt during the exchange, slicked her bangs back to look at the offending jersey. 'Look,' she said, 'no problem. Just toss the whole thing in my pack, and I'll fix it on the machine at home when I do mine.'

There was a great wave of laughter.

'Man, Darcy, you were just scammed,' Joan yelled. 'She's been hanging out by your locker with that shitty looking shirt for twenty minutes waiting for you to get out of the shower. You should be ashamed, Sandy.'

'No, no, I'm not running a con. Okay, so maybe I am a little. But I was planning on paying to have it done. No, really, Darcy.' Sandy waved aside the protest. 'I have to pay someone to do it. I mean, I hate to sew, and my mother has severe sewing machine anxiety. She breaks out in hives if she gets in the same room with one. Look, I'll rip you off, okay? I'll underpay you. Will that make you feel better about it?'

'Hey, Darcy,' yelled one of the second string forwards, 'are you a business? I'll pay you to fix my shirt, too. I think I have sewing machine anxiety too.'

'Pin the sleeves on and put them in my pack,' Darcy replied, throwing up her hands helplessly as the requests kept coming.

'I'll also give you a ride home so that you don't have to walk in this crap,' Sandy offered, in the tone of one who is bestowing a great favour. Again there was laughter.

'You still dragging that tailpipe, babe?' Lee Ann asked.

'No,' Sandy answered in a dignified voice. In an undertone she added to Darcy, 'Because I have it wired up with a coat hanger. And I got oil in my hair doing it too, so forget mechanics.'

'A ride sounds great.' Darcy pointed to her right ankle, which was taped. 'Just let me get this off.'

She tapped on the open door of the coach's office before she went in. 'I just want to get the scissors,' she told Ms Ernst, as she knelt in front of the big first aid kit.

The older woman looked up from her paper work. 'How's that ankle doing?'

'Good. Ugh, there's nothing nastier than sweating beneath

underwrap. Great, actually. See, you can hardly even tell the difference between them anymore. It's just preventative now.'

'Well, I'm not surprised it looks good. You've been taking good care of it.'

'You know it. I thought I was going to get frost bite from soaking it. I felt like I had a bucket permanently frozen onto my foot. It was lucky it happened at the beginning of soccer.'

'But weren't you disappointed when you had to drop off the team?'

'Nah. I'm not a good player. It was just a way to stay in condition.'

'Well, everybody is glad that you can play now. Remember, we're going to be video taping you at the game Thursday. Have you got your colleges picked?'

'Any place with a good engineering department. After that whoever will pay the most.'

'Darcy, darling,' Sandy's voice outside the door, 'was it tonight that we were planning on going home? Or are you going to kiss up for a while longer?'

Darcy tried to choke back a laugh and failed. Luckily Ms Ernst did the same.

'I don't know whether to kill her or just enjoy her, green hair and all.'

'It wouldn't do any good to kill her. My cousin is just as hyper and my aunt says that the only reason she didn't strangle her when she was ten was because she believed that kids like her would come back as the true living dead, and that would be even worse, because then they would *never* sleep.'

Ms Ernst laughed again. 'Please do me a big favour. Try to control her for the tournament. Don't let her come up with anything new for this game. Please.'

'We'll all try, but...' They both shrugged hopelessly as Darcy trailed off. She waved as she left the office.

Sandy's car was actually a '64 Chevy pick-up which had seen better days years before. But, as she said whenever the other girls teased, it got her places, the heater worked, and the front seat was wide enough to seat four.

Different players caught rides with Sandy off and on. Everyone on the team liked her, but most of them had to take a break from her now and then. Tonight Lee Ann and Joan climbed in beside Darcy.

'We're going to kick ass, we're going to kick ass, we're going to completely take this tournament,' Lee Ann sang, beating out a rhythm on the dashboard.

'Well, I'm nervous,' said Sandy. She wrenched on the wheel as if it were not only alive but fighting her.

'Honey,' said Joan — they had all picked up the endearment from the coach — 'you don't have to sweat, because they're not even going to let you on the court. Darcy's going to play the whole game. Maybe you'll get a few minutes at the very end when we're five thousand points ahead.'

'Six thousand,' amended Lee Ann, who was now tapping on the window.

Darcy squirmed uncomfortably. It was true that she got to play more than Sandy because she was better and in a way it wasn't fair. Sandy had been on the team ever since she was a sophomore, while Darcy had barely squeezed in under the wire for this year's try-outs. Sandy didn't seem to resent it, but there was no reason to draw attention to it.

But Sandy just laughed. 'Hey, that is just fine with me because by the end of this tournament I am going to be Darcy's manager. We're going to the Olympics together and don't be surprised if we don't have the time to even talk to you two on the way.' She pulled to a stop in front of Lee Ann's building and the red-headed forward got out.

'Come on, let's go,' Joan urged, as Sandy continued to sit at the curb, the engine idling.

'Hmm.' Sandy shook her head, craning to see over the two passengers. 'Want to see if she gets in okay. Oh, there she is.' She pointed with her chin to a second story window.

Darcy could see Lee Ann and two small red-headed sisters waving. 'Good, glad she made it up the hall,' said Joan. 'Now let's split.' Her voice was not quite complaining, but it was obvious that she thought Sandy was being silly. It was just as obvious that Sandy, who now had the radio on singing her own words to the popular song, didn't care what she thought.

Darcy was silent. One of the things that she liked about Sandy was her awareness, her little ways of looking out for her friends. She liked a lot of things about Sandy. She liked her loud, joking manner, and the way that she made fun of herself more than anyone else. She also liked the way Sandy got intent and serious in their chemistry class, pushing her hair back with one hand as she pored over the manual, asking sudden questions that were neat and to the point. Time after time she had felt them click in conversation, had looked over everyone else's head to catch Sandy's eye and share a joke no one else had seen. Why then, when Sandy was so obviously friend material, had she remained just a little aloof, not allowing herself to be drawn into the group of basketball players and choir members Sandy hung out with?

The answer was easy if she asked the same question about the other girls. The truth was she had forgotten how to make friends. There was no one at her old school whom she had known for years, no friendship whose origin was lost forever somewhere back in grade school. Then, too, living with Nikona and Lyn had spoiled her. For too long she had needed no one else. She pursed her lips at the prick of pain that came with the memory, and the loss.

They were at Joan's house now, and Darcy said goodbye absently. She noticed Joan's exaggerated wave out of the corner of her eye, but her mind was still on the friendship which she had been careful not to develop with Sandy. It wasn't that she was afraid of being rebuffed. She knew that if she asked Sandy to come up to the apartment now as they pulled up she would cut the engine without hesitation. They could go upstairs together... and what? She had heard Sandy chatter about her family; the two younger brothers who went to junior high, the mother who was going back to school, the balding father who taught. She had seen the four of them sitting on the risers at games, carrying on two or three conversations that everyone seemed to be able to follow simultaneously, yelling Sandy's name if she so much as touched the ball.

But Darcy had never told her much about her own family, or why no one ever came to watch her play. What if they went up and her mother was there, drunk and sullen, or sober and over-eager, ready to adopt Sandy as her own friend, to pour out her troubles if Darcy left the room for a moment? She'd brought one girl from her soccer team home. Only once. She closed her eyes, wincing, and remembered the letter she had written afterwards.

'I thought it would be safe, Nikki. We were walking to a scrimmage, the house was on the way. I had a whole bunch of homework. I just wanted to drop off my books and use the bathroom. Mom should have been at work. But she got off early. Probably just took off. When I got out she had Barbara cornered, was telling her a whole story about how awful you all had treated her, how even her daughter hated her now. We were only there for five minutes, but it seemed like forever. I couldn't defend her or excuse her.'

She hadn't been able to admit, even in a letter that would be sent to no one, that what she really wanted to do was put her down.

'You know, all those lectures your mom gave us when we were kids didn't totally go over my head. (They probably missed you completely, though, since you had your eyes rolled so far back I was afraid they'd get stuck.) I say to myself, "It's a sickness, it's nothing to be embarrassed about. She can't help it." But I am embarrassed. I don't know if Barbara told anyone else on the team. She was really nice, so she probably didn't. But I felt so paranoid. If anyone whispered or giggled I was sure it was about me. I was glad when I sprained my ankle and couldn't play and I was even more glad when we were thrown out of that apartment and I had to change schools. (I know I told you about how awful that was, but that was the one part that was good.)

'And I felt so angry. There was a chance that I could have a friend and she totally destroyed it. And, Nikki, I don't even think she was drunk. She was just acting weird. Sometimes I don't know when she's worse. I guess I'm mad because I feel like she can help it. All she has to do is stop. All she has to do is stop.'

Darcy opened her eyes. No, she couldn't ask Sandy in.

'What are you thinking about?' Darcy forced herself to smile, make her voice light.

'Nothing. Well, the tournament. How do you think we'll do?'

'You'll do great. I may crumple under pressure.'

'Right. The bigger the crowd, the more you love it.'

'Well it is true,' said Sandy thoughtfully, 'that I wanted to be in the theatre department, but the drama club was full. How do you feel about being videotaped?'

Darcy considered. 'I haven't really thought about it. I'm glad it's a tape instead of an essay. How do you feel? You're going to be on it, too.'

'Not to try to get a scholarship. I saw a video of my brother's soccer game last year, and the only time he was shown was when he tripped and his butt was in the air.'

Darcy shuddered, imagining trying to impress a university coach with that piece of footage. 'Let's hope we don't have the same cameraman.'

'Well, if all else fails we can set it to music and send it off to MTV!' Sandy tapped lightly on the dashboard, drums imitating basketball noises. After a moment of slapping and humming she said, 'I love basketball. I'd be totally content if I could play two games a week all year round. Hey, I've been meaning to ask you — when did you learn to play?'

'Oh, gee, a long time ago. Are you sure you want to hear this? It's more like a saga than a story.'

'Sure, I can take it.'

'Okay, you asked for it. When my cousin Nikona and I first started school...'

Sandy held up one hand. 'Let me just check and see if I have the cast straight. You lived with her and her mom, right?'

'Right, up until last year.'

'And you're the same age?'

'No, she's a year younger, but we're in the same grade.' It was on the tip of Darcy's tongue to explain that she hadn't been held back, but she let it slide. That was a whole other can of worms.

'So...?' Sandy prompted.

'So. We went into first grade and Nikki immediately tested and qualified for the gifted and talented programme. Real high IQ and what they call artistic and creative.'

'Great!'

'Yeah, on paper. But a kid like that doesn't always do so well in a regular classroom. Little bitty school, right? No special programmes, or maybe some years when you're lucky a teacher who comes in for a few hours every week. So here we are in first grade and while the rest of us are trying to figure out all the sounds 'a' makes, Nikona has zipped through the third grade reader and is wondering if there is life on other planets. So she's driving the teacher nuts and my Aunt Annie starts to worry about whether or not she's being challenged enough at school.'

'She's Nikona's mother?'

'Right. She had this booth at a Saturday market in a town that was about an hour away from where we lived.'

'A food booth?'

'No, she's a textile artist. She makes weavings and wall hangings — that kind of stuff. Anyway, there was a school in this town offering enrichment classes on Saturdays. So Aunt Annie decided that she would take Nikona with her on Saturdays and enrol her in a couple of these classes.'

'I thought this story was supposed to be about you and basketball.'

'It is. Be patient. I warned you that it was a mini-series. Now, being cooped up in a car for an hour with Nikona at this time was enough to drive an adult crazy. It's still somewhat of a strain. So...'

'She decided to take you along to keep her busy on the trip.'

'Right! But it wasn't very interesting for me to spend all day at the market, plus everyone was worried that I'd be warped if Nikona got all the special attention. So...'

'She signed you up for a basketball class.'

'Bingo! Because I liked sports, right? But there weren't any basketball classes for kids my age so she...' She stopped and gestured Sandy to fill in the blank.

'Lied about your age?'

'You got it! She said I was eight when I was really only six, and everybody thought I was an idiot savant or something — great potential as a ball player, but totally socially retarded.'

'Oh, I love it!'

'Wait, it gets even better. See, this class was for boys only, and they didn't have a girls' class. Well, Aunt Annie thought that was totally obnoxious so...'

'Don't tell me she told them you were a boy, too!'

'No, no, she wouldn't do that. No, she just enrolled me in the class anyway, you know, another blow for equality. But what she didn't realize was that no one caught on to it. They just assumed I was a boy. You know, kids are kind of sexless at that age anyway, and I was kind of gawky and skinny and had short hair. And Darcy can be a boy's name, too.'

'Only in English novels.'

'Well. So at the end of the class the teacher felt obligated to tell my aunt that on top of being a total jerk I had a severe problem with my sexual identity.'

Sandy was holding her sides and howling with laughter. Darcy held up her hands, enjoying the attention. It had been ages since she'd had an appreciative audience.

'Hey, this is just the beginning. I'll just give you chapter headings from here on in. "Jean puts up the world's shortest hoop!" "Louise spends two weeks teaching six-woman ball before she realizes that the rules have changed radically since she was in high school!" "Darcy's mom creates a stink at the grade school because there's no girls' team, and ends up coaching the damn thing herself for two years out of library books!'"

Sandy wiped her face. 'And the last chapter is that the three of you moved here for your senior year so that you could have a better shot at a full scholarship, right? I mean, no matter how good you are, you're going to tape much better if you're shown against a top ranked team, instead of some D league team in the sticks.'

Darcy furrowed her forehead in surprise. What made Sandy think that? Had she said anything to lead her? Or had she just created the explanation out of Darcy's elusiveness?

She opened her mouth to protest, then closed it again. If she corrected Sandy then she would have to explain what actually had happened.

'Yeah,' she mumbled, ashamed and relieved at the same time.

'And you're going to do it! We are going to look so hot on Thursday. I can hardly wait! But look, I've really got to go. If we keep on sitting here we're not only going to freeze, your neighbours are going to think that we're making out like that couple up there.' She nodded at a battered blue Datsun station wagon that was parked at the curb in front of them.

Darcy squinted to see through the snow. 'Oh, I think that's my little sister and her boyfriend.'

'Oh, it is?' Sandy looked at the car more intently. 'Shall we flash them?'

Darcy reached out a hand too late to stop her; she hit the horn twice and flashed the lights off and on three times. In the strobe effect Darcy could see the couple in front of them unclinching. The girl was indeed Lyn, and the third flash of light caught her in the act of pushing the boy away from her with her elbow.

'Darn it, Sandy.' The closeness was spoiled by Darcy's anticipation of Lyn's anger.

'Why? Doesn't she like to be teased?' Sandy sounded astonished, as if a sister who didn't like to be teased was totally out of her realm of comprehension.

'No, she doesn't like to be teased.' That's putting it mildly, Darcy thought. Yet, as she climbed out of the cab, waving aside Sandy's apologies, she couldn't help thinking back to when Lyn didn't mind being teased. You had to at least get used to it if you lived with Nikona or you'd spend your whole life being angry. She could remember the two of them zinging back and forth at each other about crushes, friends, clothes, and then ganging up to do the same to her.

By the time Darcy got to the porch Lyn had climbed out of the other car and was around the side of the house, yelling something Darcy could not hear into the wind, as if she were calling someone. Darcy waited for her in the doorway. The wind blew the words 'Here, kitty,' back to Darcy, but no cats appeared, and after a moment Lyn gave up.

Once they were inside Darcy began to apologize. 'Look I didn't ask her to do that. It's just that she's impossible to control...'

Lyn held up her hand. 'Don't apologize,' she said. 'You did me a favour. I was just trying to figure out how to get out of there before things got ugly. You wouldn't think that would be a problem when you're sitting in a car without a heater in the middle of a blizzard and there's a stick shift in your arm pit, would you? My only guess is that guys become totally immune to outside stimuli when they're in that condition. You could probably operate without anaesthetic. I have no other explanation for being able to do it in the front seat of a Datsun, otherwise.' She swept up the stairs ahead of Darcy as if she were on stage. There was something strange about it and it took Darcy a moment to clue in.

'You're using the wrong lines,' she said quietly, mounting the stairs behind her. 'I'm not Mom, remember? If you want to make me scream you're going to have to come up with a different script.' She didn't know what made her challenge Lyn when usually she let it all go past without comment. Maybe it was that taste of friendship with Sandy. Maybe she was just angry because Lyn was using her to try out a new role. 'Let's See If We Can Make Mom Fight' — a long running play starring Lyn Frasier as the hard, sexually experienced teenager. No roles for anyone else. Lyn stopped and gave her a long look. For a moment Darcy thought that she would be scathing and she winced in anticipation. But her sister only gave a short, harsh laugh.

'Right. I'll have to talk about killing puppies or outlawing basketball to get you, won't I? But it never hurts to practice.'

'It does!' Darcy thought. 'It hurts me to listen!' But she said nothing. Her courage had been used up by the two sentences. Instead she hoped that maybe their mother wasn't home and they could spend a quiet, if not companionable evening. She had six jerseys to fix and the money was something to look forward to. She hadn't had spending money in forever. There was no place, no taco stand or sandwich joint, that would hire her and promise her the time off she needed for basketball.

But then Lyn opened the door, and Darcy knew that the quiet evening was another dream.

She could swear that an actual coldness, colder than the air on the stairs, seemed to surge out of Lyn and back down to hit her. For a moment she closed her eyes and thought about the kitchen on the farm, where the three of them did their homework during the winter. She ran up the steps, hoping at least to be able to prevent out and out warfare.

'Hi, Mom!' she said brightly, putting out her feelers. Was she in a mean mood? Would she fight back when Lyn attacked? Or would she cry? Would she be heading out to spend the money from her pay? Unconsciously Darcy's hand strayed to the lump of bills in her pocket. It was all still there. The rent wasn't really due till the tenth. She didn't think that her mother had seen Joe slip her the fifty that he always held back and paid directly to her.

Lyn put her books and her purse on the couch. Without looking at anyone she picked up Connie's jacket with her thumb and forefinger, a gesture that conveyed high disgust, as if it were something not only dead but nasty.

'Kind of wet,' she observed to no one. 'Made quite a little puddle here on the couch. Of course it would dry right out if we had any heat.'

Oh jeez, couldn't she ever keep quiet? Couldn't she just go to their room if she didn't want to be around Mom? There were enough hassles to last the rest of their lives without Lyn trying to start one deliberately. Darcy knew that if she succeeded she would skilfully manipulate the fight to a peak, and then slam out, leaving her to pick up the pieces — pacify, or bow under the rage. Sometimes she wanted to just... the picture would not come, her thoughts were too angry. Close to panic she pushed them away before her stomach could boil up in familiar turmoil. She didn't really want to slap Lyn or her mother alongside the head, she told herself, didn't really feel the sharp anger. She turned her head slowly, carefully, willing herself calm.

But Connie was not in the mood to fight tonight. She scuttled over to Lyn and took the offending coat apologetically. It was almost more painful for Darcy to see her this way than the other. At least if you stripped away the lies and the bragging and the meanness there was something of her mother in the other, a core that was feisty and funny and took shit from no one. This mood reminded Darcy of a cringing puppy, and just because she didn't fight wouldn't mean Lyn would give up. Oh, Lyn'd much rather have temper because it gave her an excuse to display her own, but she'd settle for tears. With a sigh of resignation Darcy turned towards the kitchen. She couldn't stop it, she had tried before. Lyn's anger cut her off just as effectively as it did Connie.

She put the bundle of shirts and sleeves down on the small table, noticing that she needed to let down the leaves so she could dig out the grit. She would fix spaghetti tonight. Canned sauce, meatless, it was hot and quick. Suddenly her evening seemed to stretch out before her, hopelessly long and filled with chores. She groaned softly, considering skipping dinner. She was probably the only one who would eat anyway, and now her stomach was upset.

Her mother followed her into the kitchen and began fussing. 'Darcy,' she said, 'I said I'd make dinner tonight. I'm making dinner. I said I would. I've started.'

Actually, the only thing that she had started was the oven, but there was a chicken dripping blood on the counter next to a box of quick white rice. Automatically Darcy totted up the bill in her head, figuring the large per cent of the week's food budget that her mother had spent on the one meal. But still, it was out of the money Darcy hadn't counted on anyway and she had to give her credit for at least trying. It would take forever to cook, but maybe the grapefruit she had eaten after practice would hold her. If only her mother wouldn't keep going on and on about it.

'Yeah, Mom, I did hear you say it. I must have forgotten. That's great, I'm really hungry.'

'Is there any particular reason that someone is letting our limited supply of hot water go through the safety drain?' Lyn's disembodied voice floated frostily from the bathroom. 'I mean, does it have a religious significance that I'm not catching?'

Connie skittered into the bathroom and shut the water off, Darcy following. Her mom really was going for the big time tonight. Making dinner and taking a bath and no sign of going out later. But Lyn was giving no quarter, standing in the doorway and eyeing the bathwater coldly as if it were some distasteful pagan ritual.

'I just thought I'd let it run until...' Connie began explaining in a flustered voice. Then she looked at Lyn and threw her hands up hopelessly. 'Shit, you don't care, do you?' She fished a carefully saved cigarette butt out of her pocket and lit it. Darcy braced herself for a fresh attack, but Lyn just turned and stomped into the bedroom.

There was a crash, and both of them ran to see what had happened. A can of Stripease was laying on its side, the thick gunk oozing onto the floor. Already the varnish was starting to blister. The soles of Lyn's school shoes were coated with the stuff.

Lyn was livid. 'Great!' she shouted, 'Just great! How am I going to replace these if they're ruined? Can't you at least just keep out of the way if you can't do anything else?'

It was on the tip of Darcy's tongue to say, 'Can't you look where you're stomping?' but she bit it back. It would only fuel the rage that, at least so far, had not reached out to lash her. She pushed past Lyn to rummage through her clothes box, looking for something she could sacrifice. There was a green t-shirt from softball two years ago. It already had holes in it from battery acid. (A quick flash - Nikona leaning over to look into the engine of the truck, using tools under Sadie's sure instruction. I don't have time for this, Darcy screamed in her mind, 'Quit showing me things I can't have!') The shirt would do. She tore it easily, and tossed a piece to Lyn to use on her shoes.

But when she got back to the doorway Connie was already there, trying frantically to repair the damage, to shovel the Stripease back into the can with a blue and silver rag.

'Mom,' Darcy said, her voice tight and controlled, 'where did you get that?' Then louder, as her mother looked up quizzically, still scrubbing the floor. 'The rag, Mom. Where did you get the rag you're using?'

'Off the kitchen table. But what does that matter? I just wanted to get this mess cleaned up. I only left the can here for a second when I heard you coming. I just wanted to say hello.'

The last sad line made Darcy hurt for her. But there was nothing that she could do except try to save the shirt.

'It doesn't matter. But do me a favour, okay? You use this one, and let me have that one.' She reached for the rag, trying to trade, but for a moment her mother held on. Her voice, carefully controlled, rose. 'Mom, just give it to me!' She jerked hard. Out of the corner of her eyes she saw her mother tumble back on her heels, but she didn't stop to help her up.

Darcy stood for a full minute rubbing the jersey sleeve under the cold water in the bathroom, even though she could tell immediately that it would do no good. The shrivelled, stained material could never be put back onto the jersey. It would cost fifteen dollars to replace it, every cent the girls would pay her and more. She put her head against the mirror close to tears. As if it weren't enough, Lyn was still going at Connie in the other room.

'What were you trying to do? Why did you have that crap out here to begin with?' Her voice was furious; Connie's, when she answered, pleading.

'I just thought... I thought that maybe I'd strip that table tonight. You know, your desk. For a surprise.'

God, she sounded so beaten. Darcy would have given anything to stop Lyn from what she knew she was going to say. It wouldn't hurt for her to allow Connie to at least save a little face! But she was too tired to intervene and she knew that she couldn't stop Lyn even if she tried.

'What are you talking about? Have you freaked out completely? Look at the table. I stripped the top of it months ago.'

There was a murmur from her mother, low and pitiful. Darcy could not, did not want, to hear the answer. She was so suddenly tired. All she could do was to keep rubbing the sleeve fruitlessly under the cold water.

There was Lyn's voice again, shrill and ugly. 'No, it was not while you were gone! You were right here and you don't even remember, do you?'

Oh, Mom. Oh, Lyn. Why wasn't there somewhere else she could go to hide? Darcy dragged herself to the door of the bathroom, trying to protect herself once more with her lists, trying to organize the rest of the evening so that she could get through it, trying to still the little voice inside her that said bitterly over and over, 'Why doesn't anybody ever take care of me, why don't they take care of me?' First food. Then homework. Then the uniforms, the money spent before it was even collected.

Her mother and sister were still at it. They had moved from the bedroom to the living room, Lyn in her stocking feet, but with her coat still on, Connie with her arms crossed defensively, smoking a second butt. Darcy could see that Connie was close to tears, but she spoke calmly.

'You don't give anybody a break, do you? You know, everybody makes mistakes. I was trying, and everybody makes mistakes.' It was only two short sentences, but it was the first time she had ever indicated anything was wrong, that there was any reason she needed to try. For a moment Darcy held her breath, wondering if Connie would refer outright to the drinking. Could she, when Lyn and Darcy couldn't even say the word between them?

She couldn't. She took one last look at Lyn, whose mouth was set in an ugly, cruel line, then she turned and walked out the door, snatching up her coat on the way. Darcy wondered for a moment, listening to her pound down the stairs, if she had taken her keys. Then she dismissed it. She didn't care.

Darcy turned slowly towards Lyn. She wasn't planning on saying anything, so the words surprised even her when they came out. 'You had to do that, didn't you? You just couldn't keep your mouth shut.'

'Oh, yeah, sure!' The force of Lyn's venom made Darcy step back. 'I was supposed to just kiss ass like you, wasn't I?'

'I don't kiss ass, but I don't start fights when I don't need to either!'

'Oh, right! "Oh, Mommy I must have forgotten that you told me that you'd make dinner."' Lyn twisted her voice in cruel imitation of Darcy's. '"It's all my fault that for once you remembered something you promised to do. Oh, Mommy, I'm so sorry that I couldn't get over there in time to save my uniform." Oh, god, you do it all the time, you've always done it. You take the blame for everything you can. Even when we were kids you were always twisting it around so that you could take the rap for somebody else.'

'Yeah, and you were one of those people that I was taking the blame for. Remember that, huh? That you were the main one of those people, and, oh, you were glad for it then.'

'Well, she doesn't need it. She's supposed to be the mother, not you! I don't need it either! It's not as if you're doing a good job of it! You never make her do anything, you never stop her. You didn't stop her from bringing us here, you didn't say a word when we had to move. Basketball try-outs, that's all you cared about, whether we'd be in the right school district! You didn't say a word about how it felt to have the landlord ask us to leave because the neighbours were complaining about her puking on the stairs!'

Darcy was astonished out of her anger. 'What are you talking about? What could I do to make her do anything?'

'You could do... something! You could stop making it so easy for her! I'm not going to act like it's my fault that we're here or that it's my fault that she feels bad or that any of it's my fault! You do that if you want. You might as well, you're great at it! But I'm not going to!'

Lyn shoved her feet into her tennis shoes and slammed out the door. The way she tossed her head at the last moment made it seem like a rerun of their mother's exit.

# ELEVEN

It was not late when Lyn returned but the apartment was dark. She switched on the light in the living room, first using the light from the hall to see if Connie was on the couch. If she had been she would have turned the light on with a sharper click, slammed the door, just to remind her mother that she had been out at night and that she didn't know where she had been or what she had been doing.

Not that it had really been anything bad. She'd just hung around for a while trying to cool off and sort things out. She'd sat on the steps for a long time, listening to TV from the first floor apartment, trying to understand how in the same breath she could tell Darcy that she didn't need to be taken care of, then accuse her of not doing a good job. It hadn't really come clear. There was one old memory that came close to the same feeling -— slapping Darcy's hands away from the zipper on her coat so she could do it herself, and the next moment crying because she needed help. The memory held that same feeling of frustration and desire.

She'd walked down to the video arcade then and hung around until some guy got the idea that she was cruising. She couldn't call Rick. He was at work, and besides, lately a night date had meant only one thing to him. She couldn't deal with that now. For a moment she'd wished she had Robin's phone number, even knew her last name.

She had a headache, the bad kind that she always got after she fought with Darcy. Darcy could really be a wimp but Lyn knew inside that they were both just fighting the best way they knew how. Trying to survive. She didn't need to try and make Darcy bleed. She knew she could. She didn't have to prove it.

She could tell that she would not be able to sleep, tense as she was, so she wandered into the kitchen with her jacket still on. Everything was just as it had been when she left, right down to the raw chicken on the counter. Darcy must have shut down immediately and gone right to bed, as she had been doing more and more. Lyn opened the refrigerator and put the chicken in it. Cleaning up a little would be one way to say she was sorry without having to use words.

She turned off the oven and bent down to look under the counter for an empty jar in which to put the rice. There was a smaller bag sitting under the table and she hoisted it up.

'Well, look at this,' she said aloud, as she pulled out Connie's forgotten wine. Connie had been in too big a hurry and now Lyn didn't have to stay up after all. She reached for a glass, thinking that the wine was cheap compared to the kind that Rick usually got, but that it would have to do.

Half an hour later the food was put away, the dishes from breakfast and dinner the night before were clean and in the dish-rack. The chicken had been washed and rewrapped and was in the freezer. Lyn had even scrubbed the counters and swept the floor.

But she didn't wash her glass. She put it in the sink, with just a little wine in the bottom. She didn't need to hide anything. Darcy would think it was Connie's and Connie wouldn't remember. Then she climbed up on the counter to push the bottle into the very back of the unused high cupboard. Not that she would necessarily want it again. But just in case.

# TWELVE

Darcy's day felt strangely out of kilter. She couldn't remember the last time that there hadn't been practice after school. Weeks, maybe months. Not that it wasn't a lucky thing, because she needed to spend two hours at the plasma centre. She tried to avoid the place if she could, always afraid that she'd find her mother in the next chair. But the money they gave for two pints of plasma had paid for more than one emergency and there was no other way she could get the extra money for the jersey. She'd told the coach what had happened, or at least had told her that there had been an accident. The details were private. But now she had the money, and she had also caught up on all her homework while tied to the chair with the tubes and the needle.

The sun was shining outside as if it were summer and there were people on the wet sidewalks in shorts and tank tops, blithely ignoring the piled drifts of snow. The gutters were melted rivers damned up behind trash. The weather was crazy here. Like as not it would cloud up and snow again tonight. But she couldn't help being cheered up by the sun. Maybe things could work out somehow, maybe she could take Lyn with her when she went to college. Or, maybe...well, at any rate, she didn't have to think about it. She decided to treat herself with a visit to the women's bookstore.

She had never bought a book in the store that shared a beat up building with a deli and a head shop. She knew her classmates would think it an odd place to go for anything but a school assignment. But she liked to go in and hang out in the back where there was a couch, or in the basement where there was a library. Because so many of the books there were ones that were jammed in the shelves at home it made her feel comfortable, sitting there surrounded by, but not included in, the lives of the staff and customers. She knew that some of the women who worked the desk and were involved in the endless conversations about events and booktables were not much older than she was. If she wasn't so shy she might have been able to make friends. If she wasn't so shy and if she were willing to explain the whole mess of her life.

There was a big bulletin board in the front of the store. She always stopped there first. The notes were about women looking for places to live, or renters, jobs or rides. Darcy read them all pretending her life was normal, that she was just someone looking for an apartment. The sun was even warmer shining through the front window than it had been outside and she peeled off her flannel shirt and draped it over a chair with her sweatshirt and her school books. She moved on to the posters. They advertised concerts, conferences, poetry readings. One in particular caught her eye. On it was a photograph of four women sitting in a row on the steps of a long porch. The photographer had caught intently serious looks on three faces but the fourth woman was looking to the side with a totally astounded expression, as if something amazing had happened just out of camera range. The caption read, 'Raging Woman Theatre.' It gave a time and that day's date.

Darcy had seen the group before, though not on stage. They practised occasionally in the basement, paying no attention to anyone else who was down there. Darcy had been trapped twice when she was sitting in a corner. The first time she had been afraid to move across the floor to the stairs for fear they would try to swing her into their wild energy as she had seen them do with other observers. The second time she stayed by choice, laughing to herself. They made fun of everything. She had particularly liked a skit about old hippies that had reminded her of Aunt Annie and Louise.

Suddenly she was seized by an overwhelming desire to go out.

To be where there were lots of people having a good time, laughing, not fussing. She remembered a concert from years before when she had been no more than six or seven. It was not the first time she had been to a concert but it was the first time she had been allowed to sit through the whole thing. She had felt a touch of smugness, for Lyn and Nikona were still banished to the child care room, since they still couldn't be quiet for more than two songs in a row. She remembered the audience milling everywhere, her own family staying near but laughing and talking with friends from the city. She had been fascinated by the bright dress-up clothes, by Sadie's dangling earrings worn only for such occasions. She still could hear them click together as Sadie shook back her hair. She had not cared if the music ever started or not, for it had seemed enough just to sit and absorb the colours and the sounds.

Darcy fingered the eight dollars in her pocket, wanted to spend it on a ticket, thinking of other concerts and festivals. She wondered if there was work exchange. Sometimes there was. She could run a light board fairly well from working on plays at school and she had helped pick up and fold chairs after lots of events. Except then she had known people involved and someone else had made the arrangements.

She stole a look at the woman running the desk, who might or might not know about the performance. She was not even one of Darcy's favourites, a loud woman with frizzy hair whose main topic concerned a science fiction novel she was writing and how it was going to knock all the others off the market when it was published. With a sigh Darcy turned away from the wall, not bothering to read about the rest of the events to which she couldn't go. Maybe tomorrow she could at least come down and get the poster before anyone threw it away.

The bell on the front door jingled and a woman with a briefcase under one arm swept in. Her familiarity confused Darcy for a moment. Only when the woman began talking did she recognize her as the fourth woman in the theatre photo. Darcy had been thrown off by her work clothes, a grey suit with nylons and pumps. She had only seen her in a sweatshirt and patched jeans at rehearsal. But it was definitely her all the same. No way could Darcy mistake the broad, theatrical gestures that drew all eyes to her.

'Ah, Queen of the Busdrivers!' The woman greeted the staffer at the desk and swept her into a hug. 'Any more nasty little children throwing rocks at the back of your head?' She didn't wait for an answer, but with one arm still around the other woman, began rummaging through the middle drawer of the desk. She pulled out a large manilla envelope with 'Theatre' scrawled across it in purple marker. 'How are ticket sales?' she asked, peering into the envelope. 'Do you think we'll have a full house tonight?'

Darcy shuffled her feet, edging nearer to the two as they discussed sales. She hated talking to new people, especially ones that were likely to converse in tones that could be heard by everyone in the room. But memories of the Berkeley Women, of Holly Near and The Washington Sisters were tantalizingly sweet, as was the taste of theatre she had gotten in the basement. 'You're just being nostalgic,' she scolded herself, trying to think instead about some of the salsa groups Nikona followed instead of wallowing in the songs of her childhood. But damn it, she wanted to go out.

So when at last the woman turned away from the desk ready to swoop back out the door, she was ready.

'Do you have any work exchange?' She blurted it out and then stood, her face burning, ready to have the conversation shouted all over the store.

The woman, however, took a long look at her and answered in a soft, normal tone.

'Oh, hi! You've watched us down in the basement, haven't you?'

Darcy nodded and, encouraged, added, 'I can run a light board.'

The woman laughed. 'Where were you when we needed you last week? We've definitely got to get your phone number. But for tonight, how would you feel about picking up chairs?'

Darcy nodded eagerly. The woman dug a ticket out of the envelope. Then after a small pause, she handed her a second one.

'Do you have a friend, maybe?' she asked. 'One who also wouldn't mind picking up chairs?'

Darcy didn't answer but closed her hand tightly around both tickets. She would ask Sandy she thought excitedly, gathering her things. She would call her now from the phone on the corner. She slid her hand into her pocket to touch the tickets again.

But after she had looked up the number she hesitated. What was she thinking? The theatre did lesbian stuff, it would be a largely gay audience. How did she know Sandy would be okay with that? They had never discussed it. She never had to at home. Everybody in her old school already knew everything about everyone else in town. Her friend Rachel's mom, who was studying for the bar, had never been married, Matt's dad was thinking about getting an operation if his back didn't heal soon on its own, and Darcy and Nikona's mothers were lesbians. Everybody knew. So how did she bring it up to someone who hadn't know her since she was six?

Easier not to. Slowly she put down the phone. Sandy was out. That left Lyn or her mother. Neither of them would go, probably. But in the sunlight it was easy to be optimistic. She hurried towards home.

# THIRTEEN

'That isn't the point.' Lyn spoke in a soft voice, almost a whisper, and tried to keep the exasperation out of her voice. They had gone over this all afternoon, ever since they had left school. For that matter they had gone over and over it every single time they had been together for the past couple of weeks.

'It's not the point and it's not the best place in the world to talk about it either, Rick.' Lyn caught his hand and held it in hers, trying not to notice the sounds that Tony and Dawn were making in the front.

'It never is, is it!' He sounded petulant, like a child, but for a moment she was almost sympathetic. He obviously felt the same way that she did, as if he had been talking for hours, but nothing had been heard.

'Look,' she said, picking the last can of beer from the floor of the car. Her second wasn't quite empty, but she wanted to make sure that she claimed this one before Tony did. 'What is the big deal about this all of a sudden, anyway? I mean, we've been having a good time, we've been having fun and then all of a sudden it's like all we ever talk about is sex. You act like...' she had been about to say 'You're on heat, or something', but she stopped herself. She had told Robin that they might have to break up, but she didn't want to if it could be helped.

'What's going on?' she asked instead. She had a feeling that if she could find out what was motivating him it would explain a lot of things and she even had a good idea of what the honest answer might be.

'Nothing's going on.' He put his arms back around her and she allowed herself to be pulled close. He whispered in her ear, 'I just love you.'

This time she pulled away in earnest. She was sure he was quite sincere about what he was saying and it gave her a much more nervous feeling than she would have felt had sex been the only issue. 'No you don't,' she wanted to say. 'Let's just have fun together. You don't love me, because I sure as hell don't love you.'

'Have you been listening at all?' she asked aloud. 'I don't want to, and I'm not going to.' She popped the top of the can a little too violently and foam sprayed the back seat. The only thing she had to mop it up with was her knitted hat, so she ignored it.

'But why not? We can go over to Planned Parenthood and...'

'I do not want to go on the pill! Haven't you ever read anything? It's not good for women. Besides, that's not the point!'

He slammed his hand against the seat. 'Then what is the point?'

Well, that was the problem. She couldn't really tell him what the point was. Much as she wanted to she couldn't tell him that it just seemed far too weird to deal with sex on top of everything else. She was too young, the time wasn't right at all. No, that would definitely make her look like a total jerk if it got around, and somehow she was sure that it would.

'Why are you acting like this?' she said, trying to put him on the defensive for a change. Then, taking a shot in the dark, 'Are the other guys getting onto you about something?'

She knew from his silence, from his blush as he turned away, that she had hit the nail on the head. Again she felt a flash of empathy. He felt just as much pressure to be cool as she did. What a stupid way to have to prove yourself! Was he going to have to take pictures, or keep her panties in order to back up his claims? She knew that she should feel angry but she couldn't. She had no room to talk, she had used him first.

'Look,' she said, bending close, speaking like a conspirator, 'Let's just tell everybody that we're doing it. And I'll spread it around that you're really good.'

For a moment there was no sound except the slurping from the front seat. Then he began to laugh. Then they were both laughing, howling, clinging to each other, unable to stop.

'What is the problem with you two?' Dawn asked rather crossly. She had come up for air and was hanging over the back seat. She was one of the girlfriends that Lyn was always getting stuck with when they hung out with Rick's buddies. For the first time it occurred to her that they probably disliked the forced camaraderie as much as she did.

'Nothing.' Lyn waved it away. Then, knowing that Dawn was probably already ticked off she decided that she might as well make a break for it. 'I've got to go home.'

She didn't really, there was nothing for her at home. But though it felt good between her and Rick this minute she knew from experience that too much hanging out in the car could only lead to trouble.

Dawn sighed an exaggerated sigh as she turned but Rick backed her up.

'Yeah, I have to go too.' They cuddled naturally now as Tony started towards Lyn's house, both sipping from Lyn's beer. Dawn was silent and Lyn knew without looking that they must be passing through an area of town where there were street people. For some reason they fascinated Dawn morbidly.

'Let's get together tonight,' Rick suggested. Lyn tightened up, but he patted her arm gently. 'No, truce. Let's just hang out. I promise I'll be cool if you will.'

'Great,' Lyn said dryly, 'I'll try not to pressure you.'

'Thanks, I'll appreciate it.' He smiled at her and she was overwhelmed with a rush of genuine liking. 'I have to go to dinner with my folks but I don't think it should last too long. I can probably pick you up between seven and eight.'

'I'll wait downstairs.'

'No, don't do that it's too cold, and I don't know for sure when I'll be there. I'll come up.'

She agreed, knowing that if her mother was home she would wait on the stairs regardless. She hated the feeling she got when she turned away from the car and towards the house. An armed camp. That's what home felt like.

She saw in her mind, as if through a window, herself and Nikona washing the dinner dishes. As if the memory was separated from her by glass there was no sound, but behind them, at the big oak table, she could see Louise with her guitar, her head inclined towards Sadie who was playing fiddle. She remembered the tune, 'Petrunella', just as she remembered the bright quilt on the big frame that showed through the door going into the living room.

But the memory lasted only a moment, two steps at most, and then she was back on the dark, drafty staircase. Already she could feel her anger rising within her, alarming in its intensity and rapidity. Alarming too, because more and more it seemed to have assumed a life of its own.

'Come on,' she said aloud to herself, 'you don't even know if she's there. And if she is, you don't know if she's going to do anything.'

But the words which might have soothed her some months or even weeks before, had absolutely no effect on the choking emotion. Wretchedly she thought that she should have stayed in the car with the kids. Surely anything that might have happened there would have been better than this feeling. Darcy said, 'Just cool it', but she didn't understand the way it was, how lately it seemed as if the anger ran Lyn rather than running through her. Darcy didn't understand how exhausting it was and what an effort it cost her to appear merely sullen.

Then she brightened, remembering the wine she had stashed away the night before. Two, maybe three glasses of that and she would be under control. She would be able to work in her room and maybe even watch TV in the same room with Connie. Because she was sure somehow, that tonight her mother would be home.

She opened the front door and stepped in quietly, assessing the situation. There was nothing in the air that spoke of Darcy. But, damn it all, Connie was not only there, but in the kitchen messing with that chicken again. Blocking Lyn off from the cupboard. It wasn't that Lyn feared her disapproval. She just didn't want Connie to think that she emulated her. Lyn drank socially with her friends. Connie was a drunk.

She passed the door without saying anything. If she couldn't get into the kitchen now she would barricade herself in the bathroom, soaking in a hot bath, until she could. The fact that Connie was in the kitchen showed that she was in a repentant mood. If they were lucky the repentance might last a couple of days and a few things would get done around the house. Maybe she'd leave her laundry in a pile where Connie could see it. She'd gotten it done that way before.

She was sure that she would be safe in the bathroom, that Connie knew better than to try to talk to her with her lies. She would wait and grab Darcy when she got home.

Sure enough, Lyn had not been in the tub for more than five minutes when she heard the apartment door slam, and then Darcy's voice.

When had she stopped admiring Darcy for being so good, started wanting to slap her for it instead? She told herself that it was just the anger talking and that it would soon be under control, but still she could not help feeling a trickle of disdain as she listened to Darcy moving around the apartment, talking to Connie as if everything were fine. Darcy was so predictable. Lyn knew that she was hanging up her sweatshirt, putting away her books. In a moment, since Connie was dealing with dinner, she'd be making tomorrow's lunch to stick in the fridge.

But this time she didn't. Against all routine the door opened and Darcy stuck her head into the bathroom. For one awful moment Lyn thought it was Connie, come to trap her while she was naked and vulnerable, and she cursed the broken lock. She sighed with relief as only Darcy, bright-eyed with excitement, stepped into the room and pulled the door shut behind her.

'Did it ever occur to you that some people like to be private in the bathtub?' Lyn asked the question without too much hope. Darcy didn't have a very developed concept of personal modesty. She had never once been uptight about showering at school the way Lyn and Nikona had been at first.

'Huh?'

'Never mind. What do you want?' The night before she had resolved to be nicer to Darcy but now she found it hard to hold on to. Look at her outfit, her carelessly pushed back hair. Didn't she care if people made fun of her? No, her mind was on basketball and escaping to college. With an effort Lyn pulled herself away from that line of thought and tried to concentrate on what Darcy was saying.

'...so she came in and gave me these work exchange tickets, right? And here they are! It's not far from here, we can catch the bus, and they're just great! They're funny, you'll love them. Okay? But we gotta get ready soon.' Without being aware of it she had gone into her ankle exercises, rising first on one leg, then the other, then walking back and forth on her heels, two steps each way in the tiny space.

'Stop that. Is there any possibility this can wait?'

'Lyn! We've got to get ready if we're going to go.'

'Okay. Start over.'

'I have these tickets.' Darcy said very slowly. She sat down on the seat of the toilet as she spoke and pulled up the hem of her pants to look at her right calf. 'To a women's theatre production. Got it so far?' She rubbed at a spot of dirt on her leg with her thumb. 'All we have to do is help clear up chairs afterwards. I've seen them rehearse, they're really funny. You'd like them.' She dipped her hand in the tub for water to scrub her leg. Lyn slapped at her irritably.

'Don't do that. Take a bath later yourself if you're dirty. I can't come, I have a date.'

'Oh, come on.' Darcy took her shoe and sock off. 'You can go out any time. This would really be fun and we haven't done anything together in forever.'

For a moment Lyn was truly tempted, lured by the same memories that had lured Darcy; the crowds of excited women, laughing, talking, hugging. But there was no way for her to cut Rick off.

'No. I can't.'

'Oh, come on...' Darcy began again, whining like a three-year-old. She stuck her shoeless foot into the tub.

That was the last straw. Lyn shot up, dripping.

'Get the hell out of here! Just get out! I don't want to go!'

Darcy pulled her leg from the water and beat a hasty retreat. From the dumbfounded expression on her face Lyn could tell that she had no idea why she had lost her temper.

She was instantly sorry that she had yelled. No, she wasn't. Why did her sister have to act like such a goddamn Darcy all the time? She slumped back down in the tub, unable to enjoy the hot water any longer. She couldn't even apologize because she knew that Darcy would just take it as a signal to renew her pleading and then she'd probably just lose her temper again.

She could hear persuasive murmuring through the door and guessed that since she had refused Darcy was now turning her attention on Connie. For one absurd moment she wanted to rush out and grab the ticket from her hand. Even if she didn't want to go, she didn't want Connie to have it!

Instead she climbed out of the tub and slowly began drying herself. She stood over the heat vent, knowing and not caring that every moment she kept the door closed cut off the heat to the rest of the apartment.

She had hoped that Darcy and Connie would be gone by the time she finally got out of the bathroom but they were still standing around in the living room, fussing about coats. Both had dressed up for the occasion, though as often happened Darcy's outfit hadn't quite jelled. She was wearing her nicest jeans, which weren't really all that nice anymore. Tucked into them was a bright blue top with a patchwork yoke that belonged to Nikona. Frowning, Lyn turned away from her remembering Nikona's curly blonde hair against the blues and greens. Then she smoothed her face and turned back, taking care not to look at Connie. It wasn't Darcy's fault that she made her think of Nikki. She didn't need to spoil her evening. She lectured herself but at the same time she noticed that Darcy had layered the top over a silkscreened blue turtle-neck and that the purple printing showed around the neck whenever she moved. She had also attempted to smooth her shaggy hair but had only succeeded in drawing attention to its awkward length. Lyn gritted her teeth to keep from saying anything, even going so far as to retrieve the missing earring from the saucer in the bathroom and hook it in her sister's ear. She didn't look at Connie, even out of the corner of her eye, though she was aware of her bustling around on the other side of the room trying to decide on a combination of outer clothing. She couldn't resist saying aloud as if to no one in particular, 'I think Darcy's down jacket would look best.' Connie had left it in the bar weeks before. But there was no response. Darcy and Connie just went on talking around her as if it really made a difference whether Connie put on a sweater or a wool shirt, or both.

Only when Lyn made a full turn did she really look. Then she froze with rage.

Connie looked good. Part of her long hair was pulled back and clipped high on her head. The barrette was chipped and bent but the style suited her, showed off her green eyes and high cheekbones. Lyn used to look good with her hair that way too. Connie hadn't forgotten any of her own clothes. Her grey corduroy pants and dress boots hid how gaunt she had become.

She wore a green and grey print blouse, perfect for her colouring, her build. Of course it would be. It was Lyn's blouse. How she had sweated over the tiny pleats in the front. How dare Connie wear it! Yet even as she fought for words, trying to define her anger in terms of imposition, she knew that the real reason that she was angry was because Connie looked so like her old mother. If she'd picked up her banjo Lyn could have believed that she was on her way to a dance.

Lyn sucked in a hot breath, ready to battle. Then she became aware of Darcy hovering next to her, kind of aimlessly patting the air, as if somehow that would calm things down. Slowly she let the breath out, holding herself with all her might. It was Darcy's evening and she had already yelled at her when she had vowed to be kind. When she finally spoke it was between clenched teeth.

'That's my blouse.'

'Yeah. I would have asked but I thought you'd decided to live in the bathroom.' Connie didn't look up from buttoning her sleeve. She wasn't whining and flinching as Lyn had thought she would be earlier. But Lyn was too good at reading her moods to have been wrong. She had been right before. What must have happened was that Connie's mood had changed quickly and dramatically. It happened more and more often, particularly if she was trying not to drink. Her look when she finally raised her eyes was dark and warning. 'I don't have anything clean. You borrow my stuff all the time.'

Not any more, Lyn wanted to scream at her. Maybe six months ago, but not now. But she said nothing, just bit the inside of her cheek as the two of them finished fussing. Think of Darcy she ordered herself. Yet when her sister gave her a grateful look she scowled horribly at her, blaming her for her part in the whole show. And she couldn't resist speaking as they were going out the door in a voice so cold that it seemed to hang in the air between her and her mother.

'Do me a favour, okay? Don't get puke on it.'

Another night it would have been enough to make Connie cry, send her spinning with apologies. Not tonight.

'Don't you dare speak to me that way!' she answered. Her voice was level and showed a touch of her old authority.

Or what? Lyn thought. What are you going to do? Are you going to ground me? Do you really think I'll stay in? There's nothing you can do!

But Connie was speaking again. 'That reminds me. I don't want you to have anyone in while we're gone.'

'What?' For a moment Lyn was confused, unable to follow her thread of thought. Then she felt a kind of bitter triumph. She had scored then, all the times that she had put on her worldly act and talked sex, all the times that Connie had pretended not to be listening. Another point for Lyn! But she answered incredulously.

'Why would I want to have anyone over here? Who would I want to have see this dump?'

'I don't even want to hear it!' Connie's voice was hard and ugly, just short of a scream. 'I imagine that the same people that you hang out with would be thrilled to be here and I don't want it! Your sister never gives me any trouble. I can trust her not to bring her friends around when I'm not here.'

'Darcy doesn't have any friends!' Lyn hadn't meant to say it and was sorry the moment the words left her lips. But she couldn't hold back, it was riding her now. She sent Darcy a pleading look saying you'd better get her out of here because I can't control it now, while the words continued to pour out of her mouth as if of their own volition.

'Just what exactly are you saying about me? You want to come right out and use words for it?' Her mother was thinking exactly what she had set her up to think. Why then was she feeling a strange hurt? 'Or do you want to talk about what you are going to do if I do have someone over instead?'

'Don't do it, I am warning you!' Connie took a step forward and it seemed to Lyn as if her hand twitched.

Go ahead, she thought, hit me, I dare you. You're wrong if you think I won't hit back!

Darcy was pulling on Connie's arm, making a sound that was more like moaning than words. Connie turned angrily to brush her off and Lyn seized the moment to escape, running to her room and slamming the door behind her. She was still talking, half screaming. It took her a moment to recognize the words coming out of her own mouth.

'I will hurt her,' she was saying. 'I will hurt her, I will!'

# FOURTEEN

The church was filled with women, most of them out of their seats, milling and greeting friends. But Connie felt no festive excitement tugging at her. She had driven over fast, shaking with anger, and the way Darcy had clung to the edge of the seat without saying a word had somehow infuriated her more. She didn't want to get dressed up after a hard day at work. All she wanted to do was crash. Or maybe go out with her friends for just an hour or so. But here she was and all in the name of motherhood. Goddammit, the girl was eighteen years old!

When she was eighteen years old she was married and had a baby. Her mother certainly hadn't been hanging around her worrying about whether she was paying enough attention to her, about whether her clothes were warm enough. Darcy was practically an adult.

'Look, Mom! Look!' Darcy was excited, laughing as she pulled at Connie's sleeve and pointed at this and that through the crowd, now at a photography display mounted on a folding screen consisting mainly of pictures of sweaty, earnest rugby players, now a woman and little girl selling bright political buttons off a card table. Everyone was out for the show, dressed in their best, bright rainbow colours and hats and vests. To be truthful it made Connie a little nervous.

There were so many people, so much light, so much energy. She wished she were somewhere else where it was darker and more relaxed. But no, she was here, proving that she was the kind of mom who kept tabs on her kids, took time to do things with them.

Darcy was jerking at her again, babbling something about seats as she pointed into the sea of women. Connie nodded, yeah, yeah, not really listening.

'I'll meet you there,' she said brusquely, shaking her arm free.

She headed for the crowd at the back of the room, not looking back to see if Darcy were following, willing that she was not. It was not really Darcy with whom she was so crabby, though everything she had been thinking about dependency was true. She was still upset because when she had checked her wallet that morning at work she had found that it contained less than a dollar. She had started out with over thirty the night before and that was supposed to last until pay-day. All day long she had puzzled and fumed. What had happened to the money? Had she been ripped off? They had gone out to a couple of bars after the party for Shelly. She remembered laughing at the way the car was skidding in the snow; she remembered dancing until her face was sweating. She remembered the warm feeling that everyone with her was her friend and would be close to her until she died. But she didn't remember spending the money. Could she have spent that much just partying?

There was no way to find out. All she knew was that the money was gone and she hadn't had a drink all day.

'Hey, Connie!' She was jostled in the side.

'Hey, Vi! Long time!'

'Last night you mean. I didn't expect to see you out again tonight, I thought you'd be going to bed early. I wouldn't be here myself if I didn't have a friend in the show.'

'My kid dragged me here.' She pointed at Darcy, half a head taller than everyone else, with her chin.

'I didn't know you had kids, Connie.' Vi was not focusing totally on her, but waving at friends in the crowd. Still, the resentment Connie had been feeling burst out bitterly.

'Do I have kids? I have one who is the Queen Martyr of the world. I have another one that needs a good slap in the mouth. Everything that I've done for eighteen years has been for those kids. Where I've lived, who I've hung out with, the jobs I've had. Everything, they've always come first...'

'Well, yeah,' Vi broke in. 'Look, there's Vickie, she's saving a seat. Catch you later, okay?' She squirmed through an opening in the crowd.

Connie was aware that she'd been brushed off but she didn't really care. A lot of childless women didn't want to hear about the pressures of being a mother. What mattered was that she was near the knot of women now and as she had hoped, the focal point was a beer table. Two women behind it were pouring drinks as fast as they could. And right in front of the table — lucky for her! — was her good friend Raylene. Or at least even if she wasn't actually her friend, they had talked in the bar several times. Quite a few times as a matter of fact. (At least that's what she thought, but the memories were kind of blurry and Raylene's face blended into those of other women with short, dark hair.) At any rate and this she remembered clearly, Raylene had bought her a drink before. Maybe she would do it again.

'It's not begging!' she muttered to herself, trying to smooth out her blouse before she approached the table. 'Everybody does it. I'll buy when I can. It's so much easier for them. They only have to pay for themselves. I'll buy when I get some money!' She tried to walk confidently, hating to ask or even hint, but wanting the drink more than her pride.

To her great relief Raylene (it was Raylene, wasn't it?) recognized her immediately and swept her into a big bear hug. She was wearing a blue t-shirt that said 'Outlaws' on it as were the women behind the makeshift bar. She was wired, almost shaking with a party mood.

'Hey!' she called to one of the women, 'A beer for my buddy Connie.' For a moment she held Connie crushed to her side, forgotten, as she scanned the room behind her. Then with a laugh she recalled herself and set her back on her feet, fluffing her with her big hands like a pillow.

'Gotta support the team,' she told Connie. She had been drinking for some time. Her eyes, her voice, her excitement told Connie that. For a moment, as she watched her pay for the beer out of a wad of bills Connie was so consumed with jealousy that she almost told her to keep her goddamn beer. Almost, but not quite.

Ray reached for the beer too soon so that some of the foam sloshed onto the table. She wiped at it with her hand, then laughed at herself and dried her hand on Connie's shoulder with a gesture that was totally sexual but also absolutely impersonal, as if she were merely sending the energy randomly. In a moment, Connie remembered — a little more of the bar scene surfacing — Ray would turn her attention on someone else. But that was fine because now Connie had the one beer, rescued off the table and that one beer, gulped down before she went back to find Darcy, would hold her the rest of the evening.

'Please don't do that.'

It wasn't the words, which at first Connie thought came out of some traitorous tape in her mind, that stopped her — it was the strong hand tugging on her sleeve. Angrily she tried to shake her daughter off, spilling half of her drink on the two of them in the process.

*'Please, Mama, don't.' Who knows how long the little girl has been tugging on the back of the twenty-year-old woman's shirt as she sits at the kitchen table, her head in her hands. It seems to Connie that the child was born knowing the phrase, which she repeats as monotonously as the baby cries in the next room. Or maybe she doesn't say it so much anymore, since Connie just can't keep her temper since the baby was born. Not that she wants to hurt her older daughter or scare her. Never that! It's just that the children are always there, always wanting.*

*Well, the mother wants too. She wants to be held, wants to be loved, wants to be out of her marriage, wants to be free. She wants to be someone that Annie is proud of, like she used to be, instead of someone she scolds when she comes to visit, with her own baby fresh and clean. Connie wants too!*

*But she never gets any of the things she wants. At least she cuddles and plays with Darcy, tells her stories whenever she feels good enough, tells her she loves her. She gives them what they want, if she can. But she won't do what her daughter wants this time. It's a little too much to be told what to do by a three-year-old whenever she picks up a bottle. She brushes the child away with the back of her hand, resisting the urge that comes upon her at the last moment to make the hand a fist, to put force behind it. She wants too, and as she swings the bottle up to her lips again she knows that out of all the things she wants that it is the only one she can have.*

Angrily Connie shook the girl off her arm, glancing around quickly to see if anyone was watching this little incident. Or rather, she tried to shake her off. Darcy was strong and she clung like a leech. With great presence of mind Connie gulped the last of her beer before she finally jerked her arm free.

'Don't grab me!' she hissed between her teeth, 'And don't tell me what to do!' She thought of her wallet which she knew didn't contain enough change for a second beer. Goddammit anyway! All she had

JANE SEVERANCE

wanted was one drink! She tried to turn away, intending to crush
her cup down on the table in disgust, but Darcy misinterpreted her
move and grasped her again, holding tight to her arm.

'Please don't, Mama.'

Connie drew her breath in slowly, carefully. Now she was really
angry. She hated being clung onto. All around her women were
drinking carelessly, slamming it down, letting it dribble and foam,
laughing and buying another if the first was spilled. Every one of them
having a good time, none with a grown child latched on like a parasite.
She tried to hold her temper but she really meant it when she said,
'Let go of my arm!' And to show that she wasn't just talking she gave
Darcy a little shove to shake her off.

Maybe the shove was too hard because, though she didn't exactly
knock her down, she did send her reeling into two women standing
behind them. She looked away from them, focusing on Darcy. The
whole thing was her fault and if she wanted to apologize she could.
She should have dropped Connie's arm the first time she was told.

Darcy righted herself without looking around. Her eyes never left
Connie's face. 'Please, Mama...' she began again.

'What are you talking about?' Connie hissed at her, ignoring the
small pool of silence that was beginning to spread around them. 'It's
none of your business what I do. I'm not hurting you!'

For a moment Darcy didn't answer back. Connie was still furious
but she also felt a little smug. Let Miss Please-Don't answer that one.

But then Darcy spoke and her eyes slid from Connie's face down
to the floor.

'Please don't embarrass me again tonight.'

Somehow all of Lyn's snide comments had not been half so bad
as this one, this single remark of Darcy's that alluded to her drinking.
Could Darcy really not even look at her? When had she ever
embarrassed her? Connie tried to summon up a little self-righteous
anger. Suddenly all she could think of was a time that she had spoken
in a play in high school and her father had clapped far too long and
loud, shouting until the rest of the cast, waiting to continue, had started
to fidget and whisper. Then, before she could shake the memory of
the man who had died driving drunk sixteen years before, she thought
of the only basketball game she had made it to that season. It had
been a little late, she had stopped on the way to unwind. She
remembered being proud of being the mother of the best player on
the team. She remembered cornering the coach to brag after the game

and having that brag turn into a rambling complaint about her life. She remembered Darcy taking her gently by the elbow (had they changed into street clothes already?) and leading her out the door, even though she was sure the other girls were getting ready to go out. Suddenly the two scenes blended into one and she could not recall at which she had felt the pain, at which she had caused it.

But even as she allowed herself to be pulled towards the chairs, she knew it was not Darcy's pleading that kept her from buying another beer but the fact that she had no money.

The house lights dimmed as they sat near the back, careful not to look at one another. Darcy sat stiff, wooden, staring at the stage. Connie took several deep breaths, trying to banish the memory, to bring things back into perspective.

'It's just a quarrel,' she said to herself. 'It's no big deal.' She thought of a time years ago, when she had watched Annie storm out of her house after quarrelling with her mother over the length of her dress. Carefully she did not remember losing her temper and shouting at her father when he was drunk and not ducking quickly enough to avoid a blow on the side of the head.

The audience surrounding her roared with laughter, and she realized that she'd missed the whole first part of the opening sketch. She tried to focus on it but almost immediately was side-tracked by her own thoughts.

Every single person she cared about was pulling on her in one way or another. Wanting something from her, wanting her to be different. No one cared how she felt. That was what had happened on the farm while the girls were camping. She knew that Darcy and Lyn blamed her for picking them up the way she had, but they couldn't understand the way she felt, the way she was being pulled apart. They didn't stop to think that a lot of women wouldn't have worried about their kids, would have just taken off without them. After all, she knew they'd be well cared for. But she wasn't like that. They didn't think about that when they were pulling at her with their 'Don't, Mama' or their cold remarks. They didn't think about how she'd always had them with her, that she'd done the best she could. Yes, there were times when she couldn't find jobs, when nothing had gone right, but she'd done the goddamn best she could. It was Annie who had separated them that time, pulling then just as she was now. Well, how did Annie feel about it now, knowing that she could no longer boss and threaten her? She felt a flash of an old feeling that she hadn't thought about for years, a kind of confused wondering over whether she loved Annie for rescuing her, or whether she hated her for being what she was not, what she, continually rescued, could never be.

The lights dimmed. The scene on the stage was changing. There was soft murmuring from the audience. A woman sitting in front of them said louder than a whisper, 'Oh, shit, they're going to get heavy, I know it. Why do they always do this?'

'Shh,' her friend hushed her without looking at her.

Connie sneaked a peek at Darcy who was staring at the stage with her mouth hanging open, as if the empty props were just as enthralling as any live action. Okay, she told herself sternly, Darcy's fine, you're fine. It's stupid to sit here and think about what's past instead of enjoying the show when you're going to have to pick up chairs later either way. Resolutely she focused on the stage.

Two women were entering a room defined only by folding chairs and a lamp. Their arms were around one another and they were laughing and reaching out to touch the fingertips of their free hands. Immediately, before they said a word, they conveyed to the audience that they had been somewhere together flirting, having a wonderful time and that they were now overflowing with sexual energy. One reached out to grasp the other's waist, swung her close, and then toppled her into a chair.

'Long time,' she said, stroking her face.

'Too long. I missed you. Little things.'

'Yeah, having your lunch packed.'

'More than that. Jokes that nobody else would understand. Starting to call you from work when it was getting to be too much.'

'Me, too. Wanting to tell you about books, to have you there when the house made noises at night.'

Connie squirmed in her seat as they continued, telling the audience through their conversation that they had lived together for several years and that it was the first time they had seen each other since breaking up fourteen months before.

'Oh, no, it's this one,' moaned the woman in front of them. Her friend elbowed her in the ribs, shushing her again.

Against her will Connie was drawn into the fantasy being created on the stage. One of the women had more acting experience. Her lines and gestures were smooth and on time. The other was nervous. She didn't always project enough and she kept looking out at the audience as if to check and see if they were still there. But she flowed with a raw energy that kept every eye in the house on her. She broke out of an embrace and stood awkwardly, toying with her jacket, running her hands through her hair, projecting unease to the house. At first Connie couldn't tell if this were her character or if she were suddenly herself, lost on stage without a script. Then her old lover tried to approach her again and she backed off. Her voice cracked as she suggested coffee, TV, anything. What had made her change her mind so suddenly? For a moment the two women parried with words, the one growing more confused, the other more evasive.

'What's wrong?' the second woman finally asked.

The first rubbed her palms against the front of her sweater before she answered. 'It's just that,' stealing a peek at the audience, 'it's just that, well, I told you that I stopped drinking since we broke up. It's just that this is the first time that I've ever done it when I haven't been drunk. Not just with you. Ever.'

It was then that Connie lost the dialogue. It was still there in the background, skimming over her relentlessly like a song — the fight that followed, the lover yelling that there was a first time for everyone and why did she have to make such a goddamn big deal out of it? — but in the background. Suddenly Connie felt... full up. Thinking in slow and precise sentences with great spaces between the words, the way Nikona had first talked. She felt burst open, as if the women on stage had unknowingly tapped the spot that spilled her memories out like a split watermelon for everyone to see.

Oh, but the second woman on stage was wrong, asking 'Why are you fussing? It doesn't make any difference.' Because it did, so much. Everything. The first time she had gone to the grocery store sober and had panicked, realizing she didn't know where things were or what to choose. She had known those things drunk. The first time she had gone to a party and realized, halfway in the door, that she was going to have to make conversation, not just spiel off whatever came to mind and laugh if it didn't come out right. And the first time that the girls both went away at once and she felt like a ship without an anchor, panicked because she didn't know if, after so many years of staying sober for other people, she could do it for herself.

There was a choking sound beside her. The woman in the next chair was crying with one hand clamped tight over her mouth. On the shoulder of her brown vest she wore a rainbow painted button saying, 'Sober, Strong and Free.' With her other hand she was making a gesture that Connie recognized, clenching her fist over and over around a bottle that wasn't there.

The woman on stage was shouting now, accusing the other of playing old games, leading her on.

'Go ahead and have a drink then if that's what you have to do! But don't jerk me around!'

The first woman shook her head back and forth. She was hunched into herself, her chin resting on her chest.

'It is different,' she said. 'It is. It is.'

First times, Connie thought frantically, first times. I don't have the strength for them any more. I don't have the strength to look my daughters clean in the face and see how they feel, to rebuild. I can't do it again!

In the back of the hall what had first been a low buzzing had turned into a commotion. She heard several voices indistinctly, then a crash and a shout above the others.

'I don't have to stay for this downer!!'

Sounds of scuffling chairs, angry voices. Grabbing her sweatshirt Connie stood and fell rather, than pushed past Darcy. She thought that she heard her say something, grab at her sleeve, but she neither turned nor slowed. She just stumbled as fast as she could up the aisle after Ray.

# FIFTEEN

Someone was knocking at the door. Lyn's waking thoughts were slow and disjointed at first.

Someone was knocking hard on the door. Where was she and why were the lights from outside, which showed through the pinhole pricks in the plastic, in the wrong places? Oh, she was on the couch. She had fallen asleep on her mother's bed. After Rick left? Or maybe they had fallen asleep together? His coat was gone. All the lights had been turned off so that meant that Darcy had probably come home while she slept.

She got up and turned on the bathroom light and by it checked the bedroom, the lump of Darcy in the sleeping bag on the floor. She shook her head. She still felt muzzy. The clock on the stove told her that it was late, only a couple of hours before Darcy would be getting up. She shook her head again and turned on the burner under the kettle. Had Rick gone home without saying goodbye?

All the while the banging on the door kept up, sometimes almost dying down, sometimes increasing. And her mother's voice, threatening, pleading. Lyn stood and stared at the door.

*It is not often that the big sister goes off and leaves her by herself, but today she is gone, nowhere in the house. This is very bad, because they are fighting. Hidden, she hears screaming voices that don't seem to belong to the father who sometimes reads her gently to sleep, the mother with whom she plays 'This little pig.' Occasionally. Is it possible that the parents have been replaced by monsters, that they are the ones screaming in the other room? Oddly, this thought is comforting. You are supposed to feel frightened of monsters.*

*Either way she does not dare to go and peek. The big sister has impressed this on her. Saying it over and over. Hide! When they're like this hide, don't draw attention to yourself, allow yourself to be used as a pawn. They've practiced, playing it almost like a game.*

*The bedroom that the four of them share, the girls' bunks pushed against the back wall, isn't good enough. They are in the front room now but in their furies they often rage all over the whole apartment. But Lyn has practiced and no soldier could sneak across enemy territory more stealthily than she sneaks across the kitchen floor.*

*There is something very comforting and safe feeling about the place under the kitchen sink. She likes the dark, closed in feeling. It is good to have Darcy there to snuggle against, but the trade-off for being alone is that there is more room. Alone she can curl up and think of other things, tuning out the storm beating around her. Under the sink is safe.*

*She curls up and dozes. When she wakes it is quiet in the apartment. No yelling to tell her to stay hidden and also no crying. Her mother is not frightening when she is crying, just sad and she wants to hold Lyn too tight and cry on her. Lyn has a stuffed rabbit that she sleeps with at night. Sometimes she hugs it so tightly it rips at the seams; other times she forgets it and leaves it under the bed. Sometimes she gets angry and kicks it across the room, even though it didn't do anything. In an unclear way she thinks that she is her mother's stuffed rabbit.*

*But when Lyn goes to open the two knee high doors, which usually come unclicked immediately, something is wrong. A chair has been pushed up against the doors during the quarrel, pushed and wedged. She can't get out. SHE CANNOT GET OUT. What was comforting only a moment before has become terrifying as she struggles with the doors that will only move an inch or two. She struggles silently, unable to call. Then, with her face crammed up to the opening between the doors, one eye looking at the empty kitchen she whispers her one word — 'Sissy' — over and over. Near her, near enough to touch, is a red puddle, and she works the fingers of one hand into it, then brings them up to her mouth, sucking for comfort. Over and over. This is the way that Darcy finally finds her, pressed against the door so firmly that there are two sharp creases on her face, her fingers and mouth stained red with wine.*

Lyn didn't remember the incident. She had been too young. Her early memories were all sham, based on stories which Darcy had told her, that she had built up in her mind and then called her own. This was not something Darcy would have told her about.

Still, maybe there was a part of her buried deep that did remember. Certainly she felt satisfied, almost avenged, as she waited for her water to boil and watched the doorknob turn fruitlessly back and forth.

It didn't last long of course. There was hardly time to savour it at all before Darcy came staggering out of the bedroom, wearing the old long underwear Joe had given her with the seat still ripped out. She was disoriented, rubbing her eyes with the heel of her hand but homing in on the noise.

'For Christ's sake,' she said. Darcy rarely swore unless in this half asleep state, and then, as was happening now, her groggy voice never quite matched the words she was using. 'What the hell? What's wrong with you? Do you want us to get kicked out again? Do you want me to have to change schools again?'

'Oh, no, not in the middle of basketball season.' Lyn's voice was dripping with wasted sarcasm. Darcy reached around her to flip the lock. When she pulled the door open Connie, still holding onto the knob with one hand, fell into the room.

'Oh, shit,' said Darcy, still sounding as if she were mouthing someone else's script in her sleep.

Indifferently, Lyn looked over her shoulder. Connie was still pounding at the door and demanding entry, not yet realizing it was open. She looked as if she had been in a fight. Or fallen down a flight of stairs. Or walked into a door or hit her head on a toilet. Off the top of her head Lyn could think of a number of things that she might have done without even being aware of them.

She skipped off to the bathroom as Darcy reached out to pull Connie to her feet. Who knew, Darcy might really lose her mind and try to drag her in there to clean her up and by that time Lyn wanted to be safe in bed.

It was only in the bathroom as she stripped off her clothes, that she discovered that she was bleeding. Not a lot, just a little. She sat down on the toilet with a thump.

'Okay,' she said aloud, 'don't freak out. Your period is early. That's all. It happens.'

Only it didn't happen. Not to her. Not two weeks early, not in three years.

'Think about this,' she ordered herself. What had happened?

The first part of the evening was clear in her mind. Not until Connie's ultimatum had she thought about asking Rick in. Connie didn't want her to invite guests? Fine, she'd have party then. Let's see how she liked that! She'd show her just how much she listened to her.

It wasn't until Lyn was cleaning up, which consisted of throwing everything loose, from Connie's blankets to Darcy's textbooks, into the one closet that the other idea had occurred to her. Connie had practically accused her of having sex with Rick. So why didn't she just do it? Lyn could think of nothing that would upset her mother more. She knew that she regretted her own choice to be sexually active while still in high school, to get married and — though in all fairness Lyn had never heard her say it — to have children at such a young age. Lyn was too smart to get herself messed up with the second two, but Connie didn't have to know that. In fact, thought Lyn, she didn't really even have to go all the way. Even to spite Connie she still didn't want to deal with the problems she had tried to discuss with Rick. She just had to make it look like she had, and she thought that could be arranged fairly easily.

But that wasn't what had happened. Rick had arrived not long after that, and he had started apologizing the moment she had opened the door.

'Lyn, I'm really sorry. I thought about it a lot during dinner and I can't believe I was such a jerk. You were right on the nose, Gary and those guys have been on me for weeks about it. You know, "Did ya score yet, are ya still a virgin?" I just got really tired of it. But what a shitty reason to put pressure on you. Now you'll never believe me if I say that I want to do it because I care for you.'

Sitting in the bathroom she felt the same hot flush of shame that had washed over her then. He was a nice boy, he cared about her and treated her well and yet she had been planning on using him as a weapon in the war between her mother and herself, on seducing him only for the sake of getting caught. Suddenly the plan had seemed so tawdry and ugly she couldn't believe it was hers.

It hadn't helped her self-respect any when she found out he had brought her presents. There was a box of chocolate eclairs from their favourite bakery and a bottle of bourbon. They had opened both and that's when things started getting hazy.

She remembered playing cards. She remembered watching TV. She remembered talking a lot, talking more and more as it got later and later. But that was all. She didn't remember anything that would account for the blood. If they had made love wouldn't there be more of a mess? More importantly, wouldn't she remember it?

But she didn't and the only thing to do at this point seemed to be to shrug and decide that she'd just started her period early.

While she had been musing she had heard the couch moaning, Darcy shuffling into the bedroom, so she figured it was safe to come out. She wanted to check and see if Rick had taken the bottle with him or if there was anything left she could put up with her emergency stash.

The overhead light was not on and Lyn had blundered halfway into the room before she realized Connie was not, as she had thought, asleep on the couch. She was standing in the middle of the floor with her back to Lyn, looking at the painting that Lyn had hung on the otherwise bare wall during her cleaning frenzy. It had been at the bottom of the closet. Lyn had not seen it for several years, but remembered it hanging on the wall of Aunt Annie's bedroom when she was a child. In the watercolour a woman wearing a long green skirt squatted beside the ocean, looking into a tidepool. Her skirt was bunched up around her thighs and it seemed to spill over them and become part of the water at her feet, just as her blonde hair, pinned up at one point but now falling down, seemed to become part of the clouds behind her. Lyn remembered thinking at around five or six, that she would look like that when she grew up. It had a wire on the back and she had slapped it on a nail already sticking out of the wall.

Lyn caught herself with a jerk, ready to flee if Connie turned. But Connie didn't move. Darcy had dressed her in a nightgown belonging to Jean and the sleeves came down over her hands, the bottom puddled around her. Her hair had been twisted back into a single braid that hung over her shoulder. Her face was clean now but there was a scrape on one side and her upper lip was swelling. Dwarfed by the gown she looked like a pitiful neglected child.

Lyn saw it all by the light streaming in from the hall. Moreover, she saw that as Connie looked at the picture she was weeping. Tears ran silently down her face and dripped off her chin onto the nightgown.

Lyn looked at the painting again and suddenly she saw what Connie saw. No wonder she had thought that the painting looked like her. Though obviously done by an amateur hand, the woman was Connie. Connie maybe seventeen or eighteen years before, when she was a little older than Darcy. With an almost painful stab of perception Lyn understood that Connie was not crying for the lost youth, or even the lost freedom of the young woman in the painting. She was not crying because the painting evoked one certain memory. She was crying because the woman in the painting radiated a well-being, a wholeness she no longer had.

For the first time in months, the first time in fact, since she had begun in her mind to replace 'Mother' with 'Connie', Lyn felt something akin to pity. She had assumed, since Connie would not stop drinking that somehow she was getting satisfaction out of the life she was living. Now, just for a moment, she wondered if perhaps Connie could not stop. With another dart of insight, the kind that she and her mother had shared often before, Lyn knew that Connie knew that her own actions had killed the woman in the painting.

Lyn didn't know exactly what filled her head as she watched Connie. It was something like forgiveness. At least the anger was gone and for a moment she almost wanted to take her mother by the hand and lead her away from the picture.

Then Connie moved and Lyn saw that she had been standing with one foot in the middle of the last eclair. Chocolate and whipped cream clung to her and as she side-stepped, unaware, she left a great, dark footprint on the carpet.

Lyn turned and went into her room and shut the door.

# SIXTEEN

Darcy was cold. She was dreaming that Nikona had gotten up early, before it was even light out and before she left the room she had opened all the windows. The wind was blowing the snow onto the floor and no matter how hard Darcy tried she could not reach down to pull up her covers. All she could do was to huddle up and shiver.

She woke with a start, her head popping up off the kitchen table. Oh, of course she was cold and cramped. She hadn't been able to get back to sleep after her mother had come in so she had come to sit at the table with her notebook. She must have fallen asleep as she wrote.

Lyn had the water on in the bathroom, which meant that it was too late for her to run. Darcy flexed her stiff fingers, thinking about the letter she had been writing to Nikona.

'...and I can't change her. I realized that finally as I was folding those stupid chairs. I can't change her, I can't make it be the way it was no matter what I do. So maybe I should just do what makes me happy.'

The last words she had written seemed to spring up at her. She read them again, running her hands through her snarled hair. She had lain with her head on the notebook and parts of three or four sentences had come off backward onto her cheek.

Lyn came storming into the kitchen and against her will Darcy winced, knowing that it only pissed her off more, knowing that she had nothing to feel guilty about to begin with. Still, she didn't want to feel Lyn's wrath.

'So,' Lyn said scathingly, 'things didn't go like you planned, did they?' She was carrying a handful of make-up and as she spoke she checked each bottle carefully and then threw it into the trash with a bang, muttering, 'Empty, empty.'

Darcy opened her mouth to deny it. Lyn would just be more angry at Connie if she heard the story. But she was tired of being a buffer! Instead, answering just the words and not the tone, she said,

'No, They didn't. I wish you'd gone. No, I really wish that I'd gone by myself. She...'

'You don't have to tell me,' Lyn interrupted. 'I've been there. Just tell me one thing — were they selling beer? No, don't even tell me that! I'll just give you two possibilities. She either got drunk and made an ass out of herself and left you to walk home, or she got nasty and made an ass out of herself and left you to walk home. Did you forget that you talked me into a couple of these fun evenings before I decided I'd had enough? Why do you still do this to yourself? What did you expect?'

Darcy was startled. It was the first time Lyn had come out and said the words. She began to answer without thinking. 'At home...'

'At home! What do you mean, "At home"? This is it, Darcy, this is home now! You know what you're like? You know what ghost pains are, Darcy? That's when somebody loses an arm or a leg, has it cut off and thrown away but still feels pain there. They still feel an ache or an itch in their finger or toe. That's what you feel, Darcy, ghost pains! Home's thrown in the garbage, it's gone for good but you're still reaching down to scratch it!'

The words hurt but somehow they were almost like what she had said to Nikona in the letter. Slowly, carefully, she tried to answer.

'I wanted her to be the same. I wanted her to be fun and caring, I wanted her to be herself again. Damn it, you're not the only one who misses her! Just because you've always been her favourite doesn't mean that she didn't care for me at all, that we never did anything together. She's my mother, too!'

'Yeah, but you've never been able to forgive her for any of that shit from when you were a kid. No wonder you were never close!'

'And you can't forgive her for anything that's happening now! At least I can talk with her, be with her when she's sober!'

'Yeah, but it's not the way it was, is it?'

'No.' They had both been yelling, but Darcy's answer was quiet, and for a moment total. Then she began to fumble for words.

'No, it's not the same. I can't trust her now. It doesn't matter where I get her, it doesn't matter how I act or what I do. She doesn't change. Or, if she does it won't be because of anything I do. I guess that's been our mistake all along. We need to decide how we can live with things the way they are.'

'What are you talking about? You mean you just want to tell her, "Hey, that's cool, you just do whatever you want to, pull any kind of shit you want. Don't worry about it, we'll adapt." No way! I'm not going to do that just because you're afraid to stand up for yourself!'

'Can't you see that it doesn't matter? Whether you like it or not, it doesn't matter at all. Do you think that the way that you act has made her change anything at all? So why should I set myself up, wanting her to do something when I really know that she never will?'

As always when confronted by one of Darcy's logical arguments Lyn wanted to scream, to do anything to break down the wall of reason. Facing it drained her in a way that screaming and shouting with Nikona didn't. But screaming arguments made Darcy recoil, draw in on herself, even if she wasn't involved and Lyn knew that a direct shriek would end things immediately.

'That's easy for you to say,' she said, her voice so tightly under control that she was almost panting. 'You just have to wait out a year. Not a whole year even, and then you'll graduate and go off to college. But what about me? Huh? What about that? I'll still be stuck here with all your theories about living with her the way she is. I'll have at least two more years alone.'

She had struck a nerve. Darcy fairly squirmed with guilt. But she tried to answer calmly. 'I didn't say to accept her as she was, I said maybe we shouldn't set ourselves up by expecting anything different.'

'It all means the same thing! All it means is that you'll be gone and I'll be here! It's not fair! It's not fair that you're older than me, that you're gifted and I'm not.' Lyn was closer to tears than she would have liked to admit. She turned her head so that she would not keep rereading the sentence printed backwards on Darcy's cheek, 'Nikki, I've got to leave.'

'No, it's not fair. But is it fair of you to ask me to stay? Lyn, I'm already behind a whole year in school because of you...'

'Because of her!'

'Fine, okay, blame her, but it was you I did it for. I loved school, I loved it, but I couldn't stay because I was too worried about you being home alone all the time. I begged my teacher to let me bring you, and when she wouldn't let me I stayed home with you. Do you think I didn't want to be out of that house as much then as I do now?'

'So you did it once. It didn't hurt. Do it again, just for one year at least. Please!'

'And then what? You'll still only be a junior. I can't! None of the college teams will pick me up. Everyone on those teams is young and I can't afford to be another year behind. I can't afford to get out of practice. I'm looking for a free ride, Lyn, they don't just give those to anybody. If you can just stick it out a couple of years until I can help you...'

'Four years, Darcy. It takes four years to graduate and team players try to make it five. You're so anxious to run that you've gotten your facts confused.' Lyn had hit another sore spot; she could tell from the way Darcy lifted her head and blew her breath out so hard that both cheeks went slack.

'I am not anxious to leave you,' she said, carefully spacing each word. 'I may be anxious to run, but not to leave you. I have probably thought about this, worried about this, more than you ever will. I can't see any other way. And why do you care anyway? All I am to you is a dishwasher, a buffer. You're just afraid that if I'm gone you'll have to talk to her, that you'll have to make sure the rent gets paid or buy groceries.'

Music went on suddenly and loudly next door and Lyn knew that the neighbours were trying to keep from sharing the quarrel. What could she say to Darcy? That as tough as she pretended to be she was still afraid to be without the big sister who had cared for her so long? That wherever she was, whatever she was doing, she used the thought of Darcy at home, solid and predictable, to keep her anchored emotionally? That she was her lifeline? They were all true things, even though at the moment she wanted more than anything to smack Darcy a good one, and might have if she hadn't been brought up in a household where one woman hitting another was considered a cardinal sin.

She sputtered for words, trying to remember what the argument was about, instead of just letting weeks of rag explode. How did she explain to Darcy how she felt about their relationship? Could she understand that sometimes it seemed to Lyn that her sister was an extension of herself, like an arm or leg? You might punish it, over-use it disgracefully without ever thinking to stop and say thanks, but it didn't mean you wouldn't scream like holy hell if someone suggested cutting it off. It was nothing she could explain.

Then with a startlingly quick gesture, Darcy turned from the sink and wrapped her arms around her in a hold that was too tight and forceful to be called a hug. As she struggled to free herself Lyn had a quick flash of Jean holding Sadie in a dark, ugly mood, ignoring her struggles and curses as she rocked her, crooning of how they all loved her. Darcy did not croon or rock, just said once in a tight voice, 'Don't do this to me.'

Just for a moment Lyn relaxed, only long enough for them to both know that there was a truce. Darcy unwrapped her arms and went back to the sink, embarrassed.

To cover her own mixed feelings Lyn slapped her hand against the kitchen wall.

'You can turn it down now,' she shouted above the music, 'we're through.'

She expected an answer from the neighbours they had rarely seen but a man's voice came back.

'Great, glad to hear it.' Then, 'Why doesn't she go to the community college here in town?'

It was too much after the tension of the fight. The girls looked at one another and broke into hysterical laughter. Then in unison they turned and shouted at the wall, 'Because there's no basketball team!'

With a jerk Lyn looked at the clock and realized that it was late. They would both have to hurry. Things were still far from being settled but at least it didn't feel like they were fighting one another. As Lyn gathered her things hastily Darcy slapped a lunch sack in her hands. Her own but Lyn knew that she needed the gesture of reconciliation. Then she was down stairs, running for the bus.

# SEVENTEEN

When Joe stuck his head into the room around lunch time Connie thought at first that it was going to be some kid of replay of Monday. Certainly the words were almost the same.

'Hey, Connie, see me before you leave for lunch, please.'

She jumped. She never got used to the way he popped in and out without warning, never waiting for an answer and she had a strong feeling that he knew it and enjoyed it.

But she couldn't really focus on her irritation, just as she hadn't really been able to focus on her work. She was thinking about that morning.

What had the kids thought? That their yelling wouldn't wake her? Or that she somehow wouldn't understand that they were tearing each other to pieces over the idea of living with her? Did they think she just wouldn't care? She had been too hurt to do anything but lay under the blankets, pretending to be asleep, until after they left. All long it had pulsed inside her like an ugly, unclean wound.

Nothing was comforting. She tried, half-heartedly, to send herself into a rage against Joe, thinking how lucky he was to get her skills at the price he paid. But it didn't do any good. All she could think over and over was, 'Don't they know how much I love them?'

Once again her thoughts carried her past time. Joe reappeared while she was still cleaning her spackle knives. She gave a little squeal and held one up in front of her as if for protection, then lowered it, feeling like a fool. It didn't put Joe at ease either. He stood there for a moment awkwardly, then blurted out,

'Connie, I'm going to have to let you go.'

At first it seemed blunt, so ugly, that she thought she couldn't have heard it right. She heard a clattering on the floor and looked down slowly to see that she had dropped her knife. For just a moment she was able to muster up a flash of anger, thinking, 'Okay, to hell with you asshole! I'm better than this anyway!' But then it was killed by the memory of looking for work. Oh, god, it had been so hard. Not just because she hadn't done it for years. But dragging herself around, trying to say the right thing, to sell, but not oversell, herself. Trying not to let the desperation show in her face.

'No!' she choked out, not even bothering to ask why. Just 'No!'

Joe looked away towards the half-finished wall, towards the woodwork that needed repairs. Anywhere but her face.

'Yeah,' he finally said. He held up both large hands to cut her off. 'Look Connie, you're a great worker when you're sober. If you want to know the truth, you're a pretty good worker when you're drunk. If you'd just stay on the job. But every time I turn around you've cut out early or you've called in sick. I've got other places to look at and I can't use somebody who needs full-time supervision, whose hours I can't trust.' He pulled a piece of paper out of his pocket and held it close to her face.

'Look!' he said, waving it so that she couldn't, 'This is the past month.'

She was too confused to think. Panic gripped her chest and to her dismay she realized that she had started to cry. She had always, always looked down on women who cried to get their own way, but now at the thought of endless contractors who would turn her down because she was a woman, and too old a woman at that, she could not keep the tears from streaming down her face. When she spoke there was a whine in her voice.

'No, really, I'll...' she took a deep breath trying to control the desperate note so that she could list her good qualities. 'I'm a good worker. You said that yourself! George...'

'George is here,' Joe said, in a tone so final that she knew that all other arguments were futile. He had his wallet out, counting out the pay for the two days.

Silently, still crying, she reached for the money. But at the last minute he pulled it back,

'Should I drop this by with your daughter?'

That was when she really wanted to hit him. Somewhere, back far beyond the pain, she knew he had a point about her not being there. He did have a business to run. But for that comment she would have gladly laid his head open with a hammer.

'What do you care?' she shouted, snatching the bills from his hands. 'If you gave a shit you wouldn't do this to them!'

Even as she heard the words she was saying she was ashamed but she was also desperate.

'Hey, listen! Don't you give me that!' Now Joe was angry too. 'I kept you on a lot longer than I should have because of those kids. How do you think I felt seeing your daughter come here on pay-day in her summer clothes, trying to hold back some money so you wouldn't booze it away? But they're not my kids. It's not my job to take care of them!'

He was shaking and he half turned as if to walk away. Then he turned back, pulling a piece of paper out of his pocket.

'Look, if you ever decide that you want help...' he began.

'I don't need your advice!' As she screamed it, saliva dripping out of the corner of her mouth, she knew that even now she would do anything, anything that he asked if he would just keep her on. She felt as she had at the theatre performance, the fear of starting new sweeping her so intensely that she swayed on her feet. He pushed the paper into her hands and she didn't have the strength to resist or even drop it. She didn't know how she made it past him, down the stairs and into the street. She remembered none of it, not until she found herself at the bus stop, clutching her things in her bare hands as it started to snow.

She fumbled with the money, dropping the coins onto the sidewalk. Oh, god, more than anything else she wanted a drink. Just one drink, that was all she needed to pull herself together. No. It wasn't what she needed. That was why she had been fired, why the kids didn't want to be with her. No.

There was a phone booth behind her. Annie. She needed to talk to someone. Oh, if only she could talk to Annie. It didn't matter what had gone on between them, surely Annie wouldn't turn her away. She was sober. She dialled the number with shaking hands. It was a bad time of day to catch anyone home. But if anyone was there, it would be Annie in her workroom.

'Honeywomen Apiary and Beecatching. Threestar Textile Art; sculptures, clothing, mending, alterations and quilting.' The answering machine clicked on but that didn't mean no one was home. Annie often used it to screen her calls during the day. Connie pressed the phone tighter to her ear, listening to Sadie's voice. She had done this before. But this time she would wait until the message came to an end. She would!

'A Cut Above Carpentry; roofing, remolding and painting. Harvest Moon string band; contra and square dance calling. Dee, Annie's going to leave for the market at 7.30 a.m., Saturday, be here if you want a ride. Jake, we've... '

No. She couldn't. Connie hung up the phone. What could she say to any one of them about the way she'd messed things up again? Slowly she walked back to the bench and seated herself, her head in her hands.

# EIGHTEEN

'Hey, babe, I'm so glad to see you here.' It was totally uncool, and unlike the opening she had planned but for once Lyn couldn't control herself. She had been watching the clock with one eye all morning. Ten took forever to arrive. Then she was the first one out of the room, not waiting to peel off her coveralls or for the boys to invite her for a snack.

'Hey babe yourself.' Robin was sitting on the floor, eating peanuts and sunflower seeds out of a ziplock bag and reading a magazine. 'Is something wrong?'

'Oh, it's just... last night...'

'Not your mom again?'

'No. I mean, yes, always her, but that's not what happened. Rick and I...'

She had meant to tell the story, cool, with a touch of humour. She had wanted to be able to laugh with Robin about not even knowing if she had experienced what was supposed to be the high point of her life. But that wasn't how she blurted it out. It came in a jumble and she found herself on the edge of tears for no reason she could name.

'Have you talked to Rick?'

'I tried. I mean, I looked for him this morning before school but he didn't show. That's no big deal, he's late a lot. And what am I going to say to him? "Hi, last night was great, incidently, what did we do?"'

Robin did not reply for a moment. There was a furrow between her eyes and she did not look at Lyn as she played with the plastic bag. Zip, unzip. Zip, unzip. When she finally spoke her voice was serious.

'So, you had a blackout?'

It was so unexpected, so stupid, so totally off the point that Lyn was taken aback. No, she hadn't had a blackout! Blackouts were what her mother had when she couldn't remember where the truck was in the morning. She had just been tired, tense, and a couple of drinks had relaxed her more than she had planned.

'No, I didn't have a blackout.' She spoke from between clenched teeth.

'But that's what it's called when you've been drinking and you can't remember,' Robin persisted. 'Has it happened before? Does it happen a lot?' Her face was drawn and serious and it seemed to Lyn that she was trying to make everything into her fault, just the way Darcy did.

'No!' she said, not realizing she was shouting until she heard her voice echo off the wall. Her arm came up for emphasis and she accidently knocked the bag out of Robin's hand. Nuts and seeds flew everywhere. She did not apologize. Suddenly she was glad. Maybe it would make Robin realize just how off the wall she was being.

'Well,' Robin said, 'if you go over to the Planned Parenthood Clinic they can probably tell you if you need to worry. Have you bathed since last night?'

Lyn shook her head uncertainly.

Robin caught the hesitation. 'Look, Lyn,' she said in a very careful voice, 'I'm not just being a jerk. But blackouts are a serious sign. Don't you know that you and I are in a very high risk group? I'm worried about what you're doing to yourself.'

'Doing to myself!' Lyn spluttered. 'You should... you of all people know about all that stuff that has been done to me this year. My mother...'

'Yeah,' Robin interrupted, 'you blame your mom 'cause you're drinking and she blames your aunt. In Alateen...'

'Alateen you, Robin!' Lyn shouted the word as if it were a profanity. 'I didn't come here for a lecture! I came for advice and if you don't have it then just say so!'

'Okay.' Robin held up her hands. 'If you can't see it, I can't make you. Advice. Talk to Rick and see if you even need to worry. Then go to the Planned Parenthood Clinic. Maybe you can get the morning-after pill. I think they're used to this kind of thing. It'll cost you some money. I don't know how much, maybe ten or twenty bucks.'

'Thanks. I've got to go now.' Lyn didn't look at Robin as she walked out of the room.

# NINETEEN

The room was already packed when Connie got there but the door was still open which she took to mean the meeting had not yet started. Both things were good. The last thing that she wanted was to be noticed.

She eased herself in, trying not to make it look like scuttling, but at the same time not meeting the eyes of any of the men and women who were standing around gossiping. Folding chairs had been pulled into a circle and without looking above the seats she found one that was empty and more importantly, near the door.

She sat down and played with the piece of paper in her hands, rolling it, then unrolling it. She had already done it so many times that the edges were tattered. She couldn't believe she was here, couldn't believe she hadn't stuffed the paper down Joe's throat when he had first given it to her. Instead, here she was, slowly destroying it. The words, now too crumpled to read, said:

Gay AA
Detroit Street Center
1p.m. weekdays.

She had no idea why she was there. Maybe it was no more than the fact that she knew where the center was, had passed it many times on her way home from work. Or maybe it was just because she was cold and too scared to go anywhere else. Not looking for a job because she might be rejected, not home because she might drink herself into a pit, out of which she would not be able to climb.

People were sitting down now, responding to some signal that she hadn't seen. Shyly she raised her eyes just a little, enough to catch some faces. To her surprise there were several women there that she knew. She furrowed her brow. What kind of help was she going to get from women like Ruthie who she had seen shitfaced at parties more than once? Talk about the blind leading the blind. And Kay, an alcoholic? That was a laugh! My god, the woman was a doctor, she was so together that it was frightening. What would she have to say to Connie? She probably wouldn't even talk to her.

She looked across the circle and then quickly away. But not quickly enough, not before one of the women had caught her eye and smiled. Cautiously Connie looked back. The woman was looking at her. She smiled again and gave her the thumbs up sign. Who the hell was she? For one awful moment Connie was afraid it was someone with whom she had gone home and since forgotten. Then the button she was wearing on her jacket clued Connie in. It was the woman whom they had been seated next to at the theatre production, the one who had wept with her hand over her mouth. Connie looked away without smiling back.

A short man with a full beard was opening the meeting, passing around a book while they took turns reading the laws or regulations or something. Oh, they called them steps. Now that she was listening Connie noticed them posted on big signs on the walls. She didn't know much about AA. In fact she had once kind of laughed about it with a friend, joking about women who traded being addicted to alcohol into being addicted to going to meetings. At least it doesn't cost money, her friend had said and she had answered, yeah, but you can't do it in your own house or keep it under the bed. That had struck them both as funny and they had laughed themselves sick.

Nervously she started to light up a cigarette. The woman next to

- 113 -

her nudged her in the ribs.

'No smoking meeting,' she whispered in a not unfriendly way and with her head she indicated the door. Connie could see two or three people already standing in the hall with cigarettes. She started to put the pack away and then stopped with it out totally unable to make up her mind what to do. She looked down and her hand was shaking. She couldn't believe it, she was almost ready to burst into tears because they wouldn't let her smoke where she wanted to.

She took hold of herself firmly, made herself listen to the man who was speaking. That was what she had come there for, wasn't it? But she wasn't able to answer the question because she didn't know why she had come. The man was telling some story she didn't quite understand since she had missed the first part of it. Again she asked herself who he was to have anything to tell her. It sounded like he had a good job, none of the crises she faced daily. Well of course he could stay sober, who couldn't under those kind of circumstances? Now it was a woman's turn.

'Hi,' she said, 'I'm Noreen and I'm an alcoholic.'

'Hi, Noreen,' everyone chorused back to her.

What was that all about? Had they done that to everyone? Dimly now Connie did remember that there had been some kind of call and response as each person spoke. Did that mean she would have to do that if she ever had anything to say? Carefully, she listened. Yes, they did it every time. She became more and more indignant, anger with a combination of fear. She wouldn't say that, she couldn't. No one was talking except by choice but that didn't make any difference to Connie. Somehow she had convinced herself that at any moment they were going to turn on her, all these people who were either perfect or fuck ups themselves and make her say, 'My name is Connie and I'm an alcoholic.'

Not her. She stood up casually, as if she were just going out for a smoke. She picked up her day pack as if it were just an afterthought, as if maybe her matches or lighter was in it. Intellectually she knew that no one there would try to stop her. Emotionally she was terrifed that if they knew she was leaving, everyone would leap up and grab her, hold her and shout worthless advice in her face. She had to work at keeping her walk slow. She hoped everyone was focused on the woman speaking, on the story she was telling about how badly she had wanted a drink over the weekend. She breathed a great sigh of relief when she finally gained the door.

'Hi.'

Connie was already at the top of the stairs when the woman spoke. Startled, she jerked her head around, keeping her hand on the banister as if to a life line.

'Want a smoke?' It was the woman from the theatre production, speaking as if they were old friends. She didn't wait for Connie to answer but stuck a cigarette in her mouth, lit it, and handed it across. Without letting go of the stair railing, Connie took it very, very carefully, as if it were something that might break if mishandled. She waited for the woman to say something about the way she had run out in the middle of the show. But she said nothing, merely lit a cigarette for herself and then smoked it peacefully, sometimes appearing to be listening to the meeting, sometimes humming and bobbing her head to her own tune. Gradually Connie's grip relaxed. Finally, when her cigarette was almost done, it was she who spoke first.

'I just lost my job,' she blurted, and then blushed because she had told it to a stranger just the way that Nikona used to tell people in the street family matters. But the woman didn't seem to think that it was at all strange.

'What a drag,' she said and the sympathy in her voice seemed real.

'Yeah,' Connie replied simply. She thought of Joe and the final tone of his voice. Dammit, he could have given her a warning first, couldn't he? She was a good enough worker for that. But then she wondered uneasily if perhaps he hadn't. There was some memory nagging at the back of her mind which read something like that, something he had said she had gotten angry about, muttering the rest of the afternoon that he should mind his own business.

'You ready to go back in?' the woman asked, nodding towards their seats. Connie looked back in the room, at all the faces that were turned earnestly towards the speaker. It was a woman, talking in a rather loud voice.

'Well, I've been sober five years and...'

So what, thought Connie, suddenly angry. I was sober twelve years. Twelve! By myself! Then she felt very weak and frightened, for it was as if the past six months had wiped out that total. She didn't get to add on thirteen and fourteen. She had to start at day one, just like everyone else and the thought of how many days it would take to make another twelve years was too overwhelming.

'No,' she whispered.

The woman smiled and began to softly hum again, soundlessly tapping her fingers against the door frame.

'Aren't you going back in?' Connie asked after a moment.

She smiled and said, 'I'll stay out and keep you company.' Then, just as panic was rising in Connie's chest again, panic that she would not be allowed to leave as she pleased, she added, 'I've spent a lot of meetings in the hall myself.'

She turned back towards the door and Connie took an experimental step on the stairs, testing to see if she were really there just to watch her. But nothing happened, her name was not called, she felt no hand on her arm. She hesitated for a moment, then cautiously she sat down on the top step and lit another cigarette.

# TWENTY

'Darcy, see me in my office please.' Ms Ernst spoke to her as they were straggling off the court, more exhausted even than usual.

The other girls gave her sympathetic looks but only Sandy said anything as she walked past.

'You're going to get your butt chewed,' she whispered as she pulled off her sweat soaked pinny and gave it to Hilary, the trainer.

'Thank you, Queen of Tact!' Darcy hissed after her. Sandy was probably right. She had looked lousy. She might as well get it over with.

'Ms Ernst,' she began when she walked into the office. 'I'm sorry. I know...'

'It's not that,' cut in the older woman. 'Oh, yeah,' she added at Darcy's puzzled look, 'you looked pretty bad out there today. But I figure you already know that, right?'

Darcy nodded miserably.

'Hey, it's okay. Everybody has a bad day. You going to be able to pull yourself together for tomorrow?'

'Yeah.'

'I just wanted to remind you that we're going to be taping. Do your best and if it doesn't click we can try again Friday. It's a double elimination, so we're guaranteed at least two games.'

'I hope we play a lot more than two!'

'Me, too. I think we will. Have you got a ride? Remember, I want everybody there and dressed down forty-five minutes early.'

'Yeah, I can get there.' She hadn't actually asked one of the other girls but she knew that Joan would pick her up if Sandy couldn't. She turned and started to leave.

'Darcy.' The coach put a hand on her shoulder. 'You know, I haven't just been oblivious all season. I've seen that you've been under a lot of stress from home. I didn't say anything because I didn't want to butt in. I'm not trying to now. But if there's anything I can do to help...'

'Thanks.' Now she really wanted to get out but Ms Ernst held her a moment longer.

'You can take this or leave it, but is there somewhere you could go after school tommorrow? Maybe to the library, or a friend's? Just so that you'd be sure to have a good long restful period before the game starts?'

It was not a bad idea but Darcy was so embarrassed she was close to tears. To cover she said the first thing that came to her head.

'They're not taping in color are they?'

'I don't think so. Why?' Ms Ernst was also obviously relieved to change topics.

'I just thought, the green hair...' Both laughed. 'Speaking of Sandy. ...' The coach inclined her head towards the locker room where they could hear shouting.

'Anybody, anybody,' Sandy was hollering as Darcy came through the door. 'I will challenge anybody here to a game of Centipede.'

She was trying to dress, but her shirt was twisted behind her, and she shook both arms wildly, trying to free herself without looking at it. Darcy reached out and took hold of one cuff. Sandy pulled free and turned in one motion.

'Okay, here's the plan.' She was still shouting though Darcy was right in front of her. 'Mexican food two hours before the game at La Fiesta. Then...'

'Turn it down, Sandy,' requested Lee Ann with her hands over her ears.

Sandy smiled and folded her hands primly. 'Very well,' she said in a sugary voice, barely about a whisper. 'We are all going to go over to Wheatridge early tommorrow. First we are going to pig out on Mexican food. Then, while we recover we are going to visit the biggest video arcade you've ever seen. Nickle games. I can kick your butt at anything you name.'

'You've got to come, Darcy. The last time we were there they threw Sandy out for creating a scene.' Joan was laughing. 'But we figure they won't recognize her with the hair.'

'That wasn't my fault. It was some rude, macho boys who didn't take losing well and we won't talk about it.' Sandy's volume was going back up. 'Are you with us or not?'

It sounded tempting, and just what Ms Ernst had suggested, but Darcy didn't have to check her wallet to know that she'd have to refuse.

'And be involved in a brawl? Forget that.' While they were there she would hit the plasma center one more time. Money that she would use for going out after the tournament, no matter what. Then, next week she'd start looking for an after school job.

Sandy didn't pressure her. In her own odd way she had a great deal of tact.

'Fine for you then, but if we win we're going swing dancing and you can't say no to that, so get ready.'

Whistling a fast country 'n' western number, she grabbed Joan by the hand and twirled her under her arm.

'That's particularly nice without the shirt, Sandy,' Darcy heard someone comment as she went over to her own locker. It was only after she was in the shower that Darcy realized that she would now have to make different plans to get to the tournament.

# TWENTY-ONE

'How come you didn't say goodbye to me last night?'

Dammit, it wasn't the way Lyn had meant to start. She was doing the the same thing she had done with Robin, blurting out the first thing on her tongue. It was just that she had been so upset all day long!

Rick gave her a look she could not read. He opened the driver's door and flipped the seat up so that he could put his books on the back floor before answering her.

'I did say goodbye, Lyn. Don't you remember?'

'Yeah, sure. Just kidding.' God, why was she lying? She just couldn't bring herself to tell him that she couldn't remember anything at all. It seemed so...sleazy.

'Really?' From the tone of his voice she knew that he suspected that she wasn't telling the truth and for some reason it made her angry.

'Yeah, really.' Heavy on the sarcasm, but he didn't bite. 'Well, you know, Lyn, if you really do remember I'm surprised that you're even over here talking to me.'

Now she had really backed herself into a corner. She tried to wing it. 'Well, I forgive you.' She smiled hoping it was the right thing to say.

'You forgive me? That's a laugh!' He slammed the car door with a vehemence she had never seen him display before. 'That's a laugh,' he repeated. 'Come on, Lyn, tell the truth. You don't remember. What else don't you remember?'

'Well, I had to skip class and spend all morning over at the Planned Parenthood clinic, if that's what you mean!' She hadn't meant to tell him that either, not that way.

He nodded his head slowly up and down. 'That was a good idea.'

Then her guess had been right. Of course, she already knew it, the physician who'd examined her had said as much before he gave her the tablets.

'How'd you pay for it?'

'I used my shop fee,' she said sullenly. Still nodding pensively he reached for his wallet. She wanted to tear up the twenty he held out to her. It was too much like being paid for the act. But there was no other way she could get back the money Darcy had doled out to her, so she snatched the bill and stuffed it in her pocket. It made her even more angry that he had offered it without being asked, that he was behaving decently when she wanted to scream at him.

'Well?'

'Well, what? Sounds like you're all taken care of, you don't need me anymore. I mean, your plan didn't work last night, right? Better think of something else.'

She didn't know what he was talking about and he knew she didn't know. He was just trying to force her to say it. Instead she said, 'You knew I didn't want to do it!'

He spun around so fast that she flinched.

'Yeah, you're right, Lyn, I did know you didn't want to do it. So you can just imagine how surprised I was when after three drinks you were all "Let's take off our clothes and do it right on the couch and to hell with handling it emotionally after all!"'

'You used...' she stopped herself before she said it, knowing it was not true.

'I used you! Oh, that is a good one Lyn! That's really great! Why don't you just admit that you don't remember what happened, because it's obvious!'

'All right!' she said, hating him for making her admit it, 'So I don't remember! I'm surprised you do either, you were drinking, too.'

'Hey, we don't even talk about what you were doing and what I was doing in the same breath, Lyn. I had one drink. You finished the bottle.'

She had never seen him like this. He was shaking but she didn't know if it was anger or something else.

'I'm sorry.' She tried to back down, not sure exactly what she was apologizing for, but sensing that it was for something more than just getting sloppy. Time to inject a note of humor. 'So we had a wonderful time, right? Birds sang, the earth moved. Tell me all about it.'

He turned away from her and folded his arms on the top of the car. 'We didn't have a great time, Lyn. I don't even see how you can even talk about being used.' He laughed, short and bitterly. 'I'll tell you what though, it sure made me realize what a jerk I'd been to want to have sex just so I could tell the boys. Boy, I'll never do that to another girl. It hurts too much.'

She didn't like the way it was sounding, that he was referring to other girls.

'What...'

'But at least I cared for you, Lyn! You weren't somebody I just picked up to score with! But I guess you didn't care back, did you?'

'What are you talking about? I was the one that had to go over to the clinic! What kind of caring is that?'

He turned quickly and she saw that he was on the verge of tears. She had never seen him cry before.

'So what? So fucking what? Big deal compared to finding out that your girlfriend made love to you just to try and piss her mother off! How do you think that feels, Lyn, to be lying there trying to at least pretend that the first time is something special even though I have to ignore the fact that you're totally fucked up, and to have you spill all the details of that little plan, including how ticked off you are because she didn't come home on time! And you're pissed off because you think I didn't say goodbye! That spoiled your first time. Well, it was my first time, too, Lyn.'

Roughly he wiped the tears on his cheeks with her jacket sleeve.

More kids were coming out to the parking lot and some were looking their way, eager to be entertained by someone else's drama. Rick pulled a handkerchief out of his pants pocket.

'Rick, I'm so... it was only because I had too much to drink, I didn't know what...'

Horrified, she stopped. She sounded just like her mother. He shook his head. 'Oh, and that makes everything alright? It's an all encompassing excuse for whatever you don't want to be responsible for? So, like if you'd been driving and had hit a kid his parents would just be cool if you said that?'

'But I wasn't driving!'

He rode over her objection. 'You know what I really want to know, Lyn? Is that the whole reason you date me? Just as a gesture? You didn't want to dye your hair purple so you thought you'd get at the old lady by going out with a jerk?'

'No!' She was telling the truth. She did like him and for some reason it was only within the last few minutes that she had realized how much. But how could she explain her initial reason without it sounding just as bad? She looked over Rick's shoulder and saw Gary and Dawn coming, hand in hand. Of course, it was Rick's turn to drive today.

'Come and get me tonight, Rick. Let's talk some more. Let me explain.' By that time she would have had a chance to get her thoughts together.

'Explain what? This sounds good.' Gary opened the passenger door and threw his pack into the back. 'I hope you guys aren't going to dink around having a fight or anything because my mom is going to kick my butt if I'm not home right away. She wants me to stay with my little brother while she gets her hair done.'

'Don't worry about it. Just get in.' Rick didn't look at him as he spoke. His eyes were still on Lyn's face.

'I don't think so, Lyn. I really don't feel good about this. I think I want some space to think it over.'

'Please...' Lyn began, but she clamped her teeth shut on the rest. She wouldn't beg, she wouldn't whine, she wouldn't cry. Her eyes filled with tears even as she made the vow, and blindly she turned away from him, trying to orient herself so that she could get to her bus.

Rick put his hand on her arm. 'I'm not going to dump you just like that. Get in, I'll take you home.'

She shook her head rapidly, keeping her face down. 'No! I'll take the bus. I'd rather.'

'The buses left five minutes ago. It's me or walking across town.'

Of course it wasn't really. But Lyn couldn't face the two transfers that the hour long city bus trip would take. Silently she walked around the car and got into the front seat.

'Did we have a fight here? Do the lovebirds need to kiss and make up?' Gary had been smoking dope, he always was obnoxious when he was high. 'Come on, Ricky, don't be like this.'

'Shut the fuck up, Gary!' She could see that she had offended him and he was in her welding class. She didn't care. Dawn, who had been in the act of offering her a joint, hesitated, but Lyn snatched it from her fingers and took a long, savage drag.

Rick turned on the rock station loud, but the music didn't cover up the fact that no one was speaking. Gary and Dawn whispered in the back, probably talking about how bitchy they both were and they didn't offer the joint again, which made Lyn even angrier. It wasn't until they were just around the corner from Lyn's that Dawn spoke.

'Look at this weird kid,' she said, nudging Gary.

A lot of Dawn's comments were about the way that other people looked, and they always increased when she was high. Often Lyn ignored them. She couldn't say then or ever, what alerted her, what made her think 'Oh no, oh please, oh no.' But even before she turned she knew that her sudden guess was right. Her glance was quick, just enough to take in Darcy in her usual potpourri of garments; sweater over sweatshirt over plaid flannel shirt, each showing a bit beneath the other. A long blue skirt that had dragged in the slush and men's overshoes protecting her court shoes. Her hair spiked up only on one side. A big jack-o-lantern, everybody-is-my-friend grin as she walked towards them, all ready to say hi to Lyn. She was raising one hand already and Lyn saw a red mitten attached to a string that went through her coat, dangling from her sleeve.

'Hey,' Rick said, still looking in the mirror, 'Lyn, isn't that your...'

'No!' Lyn spat. 'Come on, let's go!'

'Yeah, Rick, let's go. She's weird!' For once she and Dawn were united.

'I'm sure...' Rick persisted.

'Get going. I don't know her!' Even as Lyn shouted the words she knew that Darcy must hear. As Rick stepped on the gas she could not refrain from looking back in the mirror, from watching Darcy's face drain and her figure grow smaller and smaller.

# TWENTY-TWO

The first thing that hit Lyn when she entered the building was the smell of soup and bread mingling. They were comforting smells. They brought back swift images of Aunt Annie kneading dough, Jean waving the cleaver dangerously as she talked and chopped and a more general feeling of dreamy well-being, because in spite of any daily crises everyone was going to be fed.

Then she remembered that it was Darcy cooking at the top of the stairs. She hadn't gone in the house when Rick had dropped her off. Darcy would be right behind her. How could she face her after what she had said? She had walked. She didn't know for how long, but it was dark now.

She couldn't call the words back, she couldn't even promise her sister that it wouldn't happen again. She wanted to, but would it be the truth? Darcy had no idea how tentative she felt her hold at the school was, how easily she envisioned becoming an outcast. She couldn't take that if it happened. School was her only safe place.

Explaining it wouldn't help. Darcy wouldn't understand her wanting to have friends who might see her sister as a liability, any more than Dawn would ever understand that Darcy often scavenged useful things from the stores' dumpsters. With a heavy sigh Lyn mounted the stairs. Her shoes and coat were soaked by the snow. She hadn't realized how cold she was until coming in out of the wind. She felt numb, inside and out.

She wanted to be angry at Darcy. She had really tried. Even though her anger had begun to scare her sometimes it was preferable to feeling guilty. But she hadn't been able to fan up a fire against either Darcy or Rick.

She turned the doorknob slowly. The smells were really strong in the apartment. Hopefully she looked toward the kitchen. Maybe Darcy hadn't heard her at all.

One look at the set of Darcy's shoulders and the sour expression on her face was enough to tell Lyn that she had. And if that hadn't she would have known something was wrong by the one soup bowl and one plate that sat on the kitchen table. Darcy never just cooked for herself. Even after six months of refusals she tried to coax Lyn and Connie's appetites. Until tonight.

'Hi,' Lyn finally breathed cautiously. Darcy looked up with her eyebrows raised in surprise.

'Are you talking to me?' she asked, touching herself on her chest with her left hand while she stirred the soup with her right. 'You don't know me, do you?'

Lyn blew her breath out, not knowing how to answer. Maybe she'd change first. As she moved towards the bedroom Darcy called after her, 'You did me a favor, you know! It won't be hard to leave now!'

Okay. So Darcy wasn't going to make it easy. As she stripped off her wet clothes Lyn ran her mind around the problem. Would an apology do it? She didn't think so. Darcy was slow to offend, but once she had been hurt she hung onto it. Besides, Lyn couldn't say what she wanted to hear, couldn't say, 'I'm sorry, I'll never do it again, I'll introduce you proudly next time.' She was proud sometimes, dammit! But why did Darcy have to be such a space cadet, such a slob? Something like anger flared up and she examined it closely. Would she be able to use it? No, it refused to flame.

It was cold. She put her tights and wool socks on beneath her overalls, as well as two flannel shirts and her one heavy sweater. But still she felt cold. She decided to sit for a minute in the bathroom even though she knew she was really just killing time.

She couldn't see how an apology or confrontation was going to work but at the same time she couldn't stand living with another cold war in the house. She just wouldn't be able to take it. Maybe there was a third way.

Back in their room she searched for her cribbage board. The trick she was thinking of was a cheap one, one she had never used before. But she had seen Nikona do it enough times to think she might be able to pull it off. Nikona had an impossible time with apologies. If the thing weren't too bad Darcy could sometimes be lured into a game and be charmed back into a good mood without anything ever being discussed up front. Cribbage wasn't the ideal game with which to do it, but they didn't have a Scrabble board.

Her board was nowhere to be seen, so she picked up the red velvet bag that held Darcy's. Something crackled beneath her fingers as she slipped her hand through the mouth of the bag. It was over three hundred dollars in twenties. Her first thought was that somehow Darcy had been hoarding and she was furious. She needn't have taken that twenty from Rick at all! Then she realized that it was the rent and grocery money exactly, stashed till Darcy could get to the landlord's office. She put it back into the bag and continued to search until she found her own board.

In the living room Lyn seated herself in the battered armchair directly across from the kitchen door. She looked in hoping to see another bowl set out, any sign Darcy was thawing. No, she was still stirring the soup with one hand, using the other to prop her trig book open on the counter. She appeared to be absorbed in it. She still had on her collection of shirts and sweaters and had added a purple knit cap pulled low over her ears. Lyn could not will her to turn around. With a sigh she dealt a six card hand to herself and the imaginary partner whom she hoped would turn into Darcy.

Through the thin kitchen wall she could hear the neighbors playing an old Weavers album. Louise had the same record at home. As Lyn discarded her first two cards she found herself singing along under her breath. She reached for the second hand and as she looked up she caught Darcy singing too. Hopefully she smiled; it was a chance to laugh together, share memories. But Darcy just turned back to her book. Not, however, before giving the board a long disgusted look that said she knew just what Lyn was up to and that she could forget it.

Lyn's face burned but she continued playing both hands nonchalantly as if it were something she did all the time. She might as well save face now since it was clear that she was going to have to grovel later, if not to Darcy, then to Rick. But she didn't even want to think about it.

She had made a mistake cribbing her point and had to go back. How long was it since she had played cribbage? It seemed forever. Was it... surely it wasn't clear back on their camping trip? That was the last time that she remembered. The pollen from the goldenrod had been thick in the air then. Unconsciously she breathed deeply as if she still smelled it, and suddenly the complete memory came rushing back to her.

*She remembered the smell of the wild flowers, and the campfire smell that came off her own clothes as she ran down the hill, elated at the thought of seeing her mother, at sleeping in a real bed, at eating food that had been chosen because of how it tasted rather than how much it weighed. Then suddenly there was another smell, one she thought she had forgotten, which made the bile rise in her throat not only then but now, in memory. She had* come to a halt so quickly that she had fallen on the loose rocks, but even in her skid she managed to turn herself so that she stayed beyond her mother's outstretched arms. How Darcy had known she never could tell, for she had come down slower, was surely too far away to be clued in by the smell as Lyn had. Yet it was she who had spoken first.

'You're drinking,' she'd said, a statement, not a question. 'Mama, you've been drinking again.' Her voice as she spoke was totally flat and emotionless.

Lyn remembered the rest in flashes, the way you remember the highlights of a film. She could see Connie's face when Darcy had spoken, the way the smile of greeting turned into an ugly, angry grimace, the way that she had lifted her arm as if she would slap her the moment she got close enough. She remembered her own choking panic in the cab of the truck when she first realized that they were going the wrong way. She remembered Darcy questioning her mother anxiously and getting no tangible answers, getting nothing until Connie took her hands off the wheel to shake her by the front of her shirt. That was answer enough. From it they learned not to question, to accept as clues the little titbits of information Connie dropped inadvertently. Only because Lyn had reached around them to grab the wheel had they not gone off the road that time.

Then there were the increasing stops at rest areas so that Connie could sneak away to 'brush her hair' searching the glove box to see if Connie's name was on the title of the truck everyone on the farm had used; sleeping two nights in the cab while they looked for an apartment that was cheap enough.

All those things she remembered. But why? Why was she thinking about it? Usually she avoided this particular memory if she could. It made her feel sick, like the horror flicks Nikona had dragged her to twice. More, it made her feel angry.

She stopped playing, holding her cards very still. Angry. Yes. She felt angry. Below them she heard a key turning in the front door, fumbling footsteps across the hall. Without realizing it she gave a sigh of relief as she sunk back into the chair, the cards forgotten. She didn't need to feel guilty anymore. She listened to the faltering steps coming up the stairs.

'She made me move,' she thought, 'she took me away from my family. She lied when she said she loved me. She doesn't care about me. She doesn't care about me. She doesn't care about me.' The apartment door opened.

# TWENTY-THREE

Connie couldn't remember when she had ever been so tired before. After the meeting she had panicked. She never should have gone job hunting dressed in her work clothes, with plaster in her hair, still so close to crying that she could not keep the begging tone out of her voice. But all she could think of was having to tell the kids she had no job, of being thrown out of another apartment.

But at least she still had most of the money that Joe had given her. She could say that much. She had tried, she hadn't crept into a bar and spent the afternoon, much as she had wanted to. She wasn't drunk. And she didn't have to tell the kids tonight; she could put off telling them until the news was about changing jobs, rather than being fired.

She fumbled for her keys, shifting the bottle of wine that she held to her hip.

Darcy had scratched the first trigonometry problem out on paper three times, but she was no nearer to getting the answer. It was busy work, just as stirring the soup was busy work. Something to keep her mind off the stab of pain she had felt when Lyn had turned away from her, shouting for the whole world to hear, 'I don't know her!'

She was better at feeling pain than anger. That was her main feeling, a dull, throbbing pain. A sense of betrayal. But there was some anger too, and she felt a flash as she looked at Lyn trying to use Nikona's card trick on her. Did Lyn think she was an idiot? Did she think she would set herself up again and again forever? Or did she think that she was so damn easy to live with? Didn't she realize that sometimes Darcy was embarrassed by the make-up, the hair, the whole Miss Teen-model act? It wasn't something she particularly wanted her friends to see, but she'd never said a word. Nikona, now she would have had a ball with it. Darcy could see her squinting into the mirror, imitating Lyn, dabbing lip gloss on with her little finger, stabbing at her eyelashes with her mascara. But Darcy hadn't said a word. If that was the way Lyn wanted to play it, more power to her. So who the hell did she think she was, putting Darcy down?

Her thoughts were interrupted. Something was going on, the air felt different. She glanced at Lyn who had stopped playing and was sitting with her head cocked towards the door. Darcy listened, too.

It was their mother on the stairs and Lyn was going to start a fight. Darcy could tell from the look in her eyes, from the very way she held her head.

'Why does she have to do this?' It was the first thing that came into Darcy's head. Then she thought, 'No. I don't have to be a part of it anymore. I won't be. They can fight it out together. I'm leaving soon.' She picked up her bowl.

But as Connie finally got the door open she stopped. Connie looked more than tired, more than drunk. She looked ill. Her clothes were soaked and there were dark circles under her eyes. She did not greet either of them. She just staggered to the middle of the room and stood. Darcy had seen her like this before. Left alone she might continue standing, might stay there until she fell and then she'd be sick on top of everything else. With a sigh Darcy put her bowl down. She went into the bathroom and started the hot water running, giving Lyn a warning look as she passed. There was little hope that she could check her. Her eyes were bright and the way she looked at Connie made Darcy shiver. She was like a fox with a rabbit. Well, Darcy would try to keep her off long enough to get Connie warmed up. That was fair. But after that she was strictly on her own.

She took her mother by the elbow, none too gently. 'Come on,' she said, 'let's get something hot inside you.' Her tone was meant to be placating but she could not entirely keep out the disgust. Most of it was directed towards herself. She had gotten right into the centre of things again. But what else could she do? She couldn't just leave Connie to fall on the floor with Lyn hovering above her like a carrion crow, ready to peck her eyes out before she was even dead.

She turned the kettle on, planning as she reached into the cupboard. Tea with an extra spoonful of sugar because coffee might keep her awake, and that was the last thing they needed. While they waited for the tub to fill she'd try to get her to feed herself. Darcy picked up her own bowl and filled it in one motion.

'Here,' she said. She tried to push the bowl and spoon into Connie's hands, but she was still clutching her paper sack. Gently Darcy took it from her and set it on the table, then pulled off her soaking, mismatched gloves. She tried again.

With a jerk Connie pushed her away, shaking her head. Darcy's heart sank. On top of everything else Connie was going to fight her. But no, she just wanted to struggle out of her wet jacket. That meant she was thinking. Darcy relaxed a little. She pulled at the jacket from behind, shooting another look at Lyn.

It was probably too much to hope for, but maybe she would be able to get Connie settled in the tub with her dinner and could disappear herself before the fireworks. That damn Lyn! She turned off the burner beneath the soup and pushed the pot to the back of the stove before turning back to Connie, who was now struggling with her sodden shoes.

# TWENTY-FOUR

'She brought me here. She doesn't care about me. If it wasn't for her Darcy and I could still be friends and I wouldn't be fighting with Rick.'

Lyn was still sharpening her anger, honing it like a knife. She thought suddenly of Robin and how she got support not to be angry with her mother. Lyn would never give that up. It was the only thing she had.

She could see Darcy and Connie in the light of the kitchen framed by the door as if she were looking at them on a cheap TV. That was how removed she felt. Totally unconnected except for the cord of throbbing anger that went from her to Connie, that followed her every move. Behind them she could see into the lighted window of the apartment next door and she watched the mother and small son in that kitchen with the same detachment that she watched the mother and daughter in her own.

She didn't know where the anger was going to lead her, but she found herself on her feet, drawn into the kitchen as if the line between herself and her mother was shrinking. The woman in the next kitchen was chopping vegetables, talking to the little boy at the same time. Their mouths moved, but Lyn could hear no sound. It seemed that the same was true of Darcy and Connie. She could see what they were doing, but she could not hear what they were saying. Connie was searching the counter top, and shelves irritably, not stopping to pick up the things that she accidently pushed onto the floor. There, she had found what she wanted, the one paring knife. She used it to saw at the knotted rubber band on the end of her braid. Darcy tried to give Lyn another warning look, but she turned her head, thinking only of Connie.

'She doesn't care, but I'll make her pay attention!'

She didn't know what was going to happen until she looked up and caught the horror and dismay on Darcy's face. Only then did she look at her own hands and find herself holding the bag with the wine. At that moment she had a last flash of control, of knowing that she could put the bag down, could leave the scene before it even began. Instead she lifted it higher and did not just drop it, but smashed it hard against the enamel edge of the sink.

The crash of the breaking glass seemed to last forever, and so did the wine, pouring out, puddling around their feet. It was impossible that it could all have been contained in one bottle and Lyn watched in fascination as the crash echoed.

Then suddenly, just as everything had been slowed, everything seemed to move more quickly than usual. Lyn tried to say the line that had come to her as she lifted the sack.

'Oh, sorry, I must have bumped the table.' She had meant to say it slow and cool and with a smug grin. But instead she stuttered the last part far too quickly because she could see from the look in Connie's eyes that this time she had gone too far, she had really made her mad. In fact this time Connie, who had never struck her within memory, had her right hand raised, coming at her as if she were going to slap her alongside the head.

Automatically Lyn's own hand flew up and she caught Connie's wrist and thrust her backward. It was easy. She found herself thinking that a year ago they would have been well matched, but that now she could beat her easily. But she didn't. She had no compunction about holding her off, but she couldn't bring herself to actually strike her. It wasn't just because hitting one's mother was taboo. She had been raised in a household where it was never, never, alright for one woman to hit another. Even childish fights had been treated gravely if hitting was involved, bringing lectures about solidarity and the ways they would be oppressed as women without further oppressing one another. There were times when it had bored all three of them and they had made fun of it behind the adults' backs, but she still could not go immediately against it.

In her own rage, however, the teacher did not remember as well as the student. Connie flailed at Lyn with her other hand, hitting her in the chest. Unbalanced, Lyn fell back against the shelves, catching one board across her back, another across her shoulders.

Two of the jars fell without breaking. One, filled with generic macaroni, rolled beneath Lyn's feet and she stumbled as she tried to right herself. She still held Connie's wrist, automatically keeping it away from her. As she glanced up at their two hands together she saw that Connie still clutched the knife. She also saw by the way that she moved her hand, that she had forgotten it. Lyn could have shaken it free easily. But she did not.

'She had a god-damn knife!' she said in her head. She had no idea to whom she would tell the story, but it would be told to her advantage.

She struggled upright, warding off the blows Connie was landing on her ribs and arms, trying vainly to catch her free hand. Now the full thrust of her anger was on her and she let herself go with it, knowing this was the moment, and that she would be able to lose herself totally. She was caught in a savage rush of pain and pleasure; then suddenly she found herself looking at the whole scene as if from a rather disinterested third eye. She saw as if she were hovering near the ceiling: her mother and herself struggling together; though in her mind she simply labelled them 'the woman' and 'the girl'. The girl shimmered so with emotion that it seemed strange that the woman wasn't burnt as she struck with her haphazard blows. She didn't strike the woman back, but she shouted a string of curses and accusations so ugly that the spittle that ran down from her mouth seemed sour.

Vaguely her projected self became aware of the third person in the kitchen, the older girl whose face contorted with pain as she watched the fight. Emotionlessly, still listening to the torrent of curses, still monitoring the quick string of rationalization bouncing through her mind, she watched the struggling pair fall sideways together and entangle the other girl. Without being able to place it Lyn became aware of a high keening that filled the room. At the same time she noticed that the woman struck the girl randomly and hopelessly, not like a mother beating a child, or one adult against another, but more in the way that someone will hit a defective machine, knowing it will change nothing.

Then Lyn looked beyond the woman, out the window into the apartment next door. The mother had left the room, but the little boy was still on his stool. He clutched the counter, his fingers and face bloodless, and stared through the two panes of glass with a look of horror. In that instant the two parts of her, the disinterested observer and the anger-driven body snapped back together with a jolt that made her head rock.

*She doesn't remember a time. She doesn't remember an incident. The adults are only shadows and loud voices, Darcy a small soft shape and a smell that means 'sissy'. She herself changes; she is not always the same size and there is no clear picture in her mind of the way she looks. But she remembers the feeling. Total powerlessness as she watches others struggle. She knows that her face must have matched this little boy's.*

The sound was filling the kitchen. Lyn had noticed it before, but only now did she place it as screaming. Darcy was tangled between the two of them, pinned, pushing against Lyn with her free arm. Pushing, pinching, slapping. Hurting her, in fact, far more than Connie's weak punches. Lyn suddenly felt stupid, as if the hot light from within had burned her brain dry and it took her an eternity of fifteen seconds to figure out how to pull away from the screaming and hitting simply by sitting down. Connie came to the floor with her.

She let go of Connie's wrist suddenly and the knife fell, scratching Connie's own cheek. But Lyn was oblivious to the pounding from next door, to the wine soaking her pants, to everything but Darcy. Why had she screamed? Then she smelled the charring, saw the cloth seared to the burner where they had pushed her backwards.

She turned from one side to the other, mouthing apologies in the same unknowing way that she had mouthed accusations. She needed cold water, but the sink was piled with dirty dishes right up to the faucet and the dirty dish rag was hidden among them. Her next thought was ice, but the door to the freezer had been frozen shut since they had moved in. Helplessly she held out her hands to Darcy as if her touch could drain away the pain.

But Darcy pushed past her, heading for the window, gasping open-mouthed. As she bent to jerk it open Lyn, wincing, saw the charred hole in her sweat shirt, the gash of blistered flesh that showed. Darcy scooped a double handful of snow off the window-sill and awkwardly tried to hold it to her back. Lyn moved in to help, but Darcy forestalled her.

'Darcy,' she said, 'I only want to help you.'

'Help me?' Darcy replied in a bitter tone that Lyn had never heard before. 'Then do the dishes.'

# TWENTY-FIVE

The sun was just coming up when Lyn came out the front door. The street lights were still on, but there were already plenty of people out.

It was cold out. It seemed as if she had never gotten warm all night long. She had lain awake, shivering, long after Darcy had gone to sleep. Or pretended to be asleep. She didn't know which. Several times, convinced that she too must be awake, Lyn had almost called out to her, reached across the narrow strip of floor to touch her on the shoulder. She had not because she had not been able to imagine what would happen next.

Oh, she had thought about it while she was washing the dishes. Not just washing the dishes, but mopping the floor, digging at the cracks in the counter with a knife. She didn't know if she were working to appease Darcy or simply to keep from facing her. Finally though, both the kitchen and the wine were finished.

That was when she had ventured into their room. Even then, it was the thought of her mother returning, taking up with her where they had left off, that had driven her. At first she had been afraid that Darcy would want to talk to her, relieved when she had lain still with her back turned. Then, as the night wore on she had wished that she would talk. Lyn couldn't seem to initiate it, but she would have welcomed anything that would have chased from her mind the picture of Darcy's face as she screamed in pain, the smell of her flannel shirt.

She tried all the tricks she knew to keep from thinking about it. She tried to recall pleasant memories, but they would not come. All she could get were scenes of Darcy caring for her, standing up for her. Failing the past she had tried for the future. That was worse. When playing the game with Nikona she had never run out of jobs, adventures, plans. But lying alone in the dark, listening for her mother on the stairs, she could not imagine herself anywhere but the same apartment, hurting and angry with no one to talk to, her sister gone, her mother due back at any moment.

She didn't fall asleep till long after midnight and was woken what seemed like only a few minutes later by Darcy's alarm. Her heart was pounding in a way that told her she had been having a nightmare. Dry-mouthed, she lay without moving as Darcy got dressed. Then, as soon as the door closed behind her she had flown out of her sleeping bag and dressed hastily. The long night between them made the thought of confrontation even harder. How could she say any of the things she needed to say to her sister without hurting her more? She had berated herself during the night thinking now that it was too late, that she should have tried to form a unit with her, that they could have comforted one another instead of their dance of attack and appeasement. But could they have, really? Now Lyn had become convinced that they couldn't, that she couldn't have survived if she had acted differently. It was her anger that had kept her going. If she had tried to meld with Darcy, always accommodating, never complaining, she didn't know if she would have made it. But as she hurried around to the dumpster, clutching the coffee can full of dry cat food, she thought that there must have been another way.

'Kitties,' she called in a high voice, 'my kitty-kitty-kitties!'

But there was no answering mew, no sound of tiny feet running. Frowning she stood on the side walk and shaded her eyes so that she could make a quick scan. No kitties on the dumpster. No kitties up on the fire-escape or on the top of the neighbours' high wooden fence. She twisted her mouth up, trying to decide if it was worth risking her school clothes to tiptoe through the mud to the dumpster.

No, they would come if they heard her. They must be off adventuring somewhere. She turned back to the house, giving one last call.

'Kitties!' This time, to her surprise, she heard a faint answering mew. She called again and again the mew came back. Now she was able to place it. It came from the opposite end of the block. She walked that way briskly, still calling.

As she came closer she could tell that it was the little girl answering her, could see her dancing back and forth on the sidewalk by a red Dodge.

'Well, why are you being such a bad girl?' she called fondly, forgetting for a moment her turmoil. 'Why aren't you coming when Mama calls you? Why...'

She broke off abruptly. She had thought she was alone, but there was stirring by the front of the car, and three children, the oldest around twelve, stepped back onto the sidewalk. They had been crouched in the street between the parked cars. Each was carrying a back-pack and they were obviously on their way to school.

'Is that your kitten?' the girl asked in a high voice. Embarrassed, Lyn simply nodded. She put her hands down for the little cat, but she would not come to her. She continued to mew and dance frantically.

'Is the other one your kitty, too?'

Lyn looked up. 'Yeah. Where is...' Then she froze. Now she could see what the children had been looking at. Out in the street, thrown to the side, was the body of the little grey male.

'Poor kitty,' said the boy, his voice full of the compassion only a child can have. Even the twelve-year-old had already been somewhat dulled.

'He got run over,' she said, her voice sad, but also matter-of-fact. 'That's why Mom says we have to keep Frisky in the house. You should have kept him in the house,' she told Lyn.

'He wouldn't come in,' Lyn said, as if in a dream, unable to take her eyes off the mangled body. She was aware that the children were looking between her and the cats with something like a question in their eyes and she knew what they were thinking. They were just little kittens and she was a big girl, almost a grown woman. She could have made him come inside. They were right. She should have brought them in bodily. But how did she explain that she was waiting until they wanted to come in, until they would do it of their own free will? It seemed foolish now to think that they had enough sense in their little heads to have been allowed that choice.

'But that kitty's still alive,' said the little boy. 'Maybe you could take him to the doctor.'

Startled, Lyn looked quickly from him to the cat and, to her horror, she found that what he had said was true. The kitten was still moving one paw, opening his mouth piteously as if trying to mew. Lyn stood paralyzed. She knew that the kitten could not possibly live, that it was up to her to put it out of its pain. But she couldn't move to touch it. She had always been much too tender-hearted when it came to animals. As a little girl she would often cry, even over the death of a chicken, and everyone still shouted, 'Don't look, Lyn!' when they approached a roadkill in the car. She couldn't do it, she couldn't. She took a faltering step backwards. The three children regarded her solemnly out of three identical sets of eyes and she suddenly wanted to smash them all, to destroy their witness to her cowardice.

'My mom had to shoot her dog once,' said the oldest girl meaningfully 'because he was really old and hurt.'

Lyn just shook her head, still watching the little struggles.

'There's that lady!' shrilled the littlest girl suddenly.

'Oh, good. She'll help us!' said the boy and instantly the three were off running down the sidewalk. The look that the eldest girl threw over her shoulder showed clearly the disdain in which she held Lyn.

She wanted to be gone, to be safe inside where she couldn't see it anymore. But the children had blocked the way back to the house. She couldn't walk past them and the adult they had found to do her job. And besides, she felt sick, weak-kneed. The best she could do was to wobble a few yards down the side walk in the opposite direction. She squatted down in the dirty snow between the next two cars along the curb, putting her head against her knees, praying that it would all be over in just a few minutes. The girl kitten rubbed up against her, strangely plaintive and affectionate and she let her climb into her lap.

'...hit by a car, my mom says...'

'...but maybe the cat doctor...'

'...just ran away and didn't do anything and it was her cat...'

'Oh, poor kitty.' The adult voice cut over the children's babble. 'Poor little thing.' Beneath the car Lyn watched a large pair of hands gently pick up the battered little body and then quickly, efficiently twist its neck and head in separate directions. She almost cried out, but the thing was over immediately and the kitten lay still in the hands which cradled it gently, much more tolerable in death than it had been in its last minutes of life.

'Poor kitty.' It was the little boy again and Lyn could see his small hand coming down to stroke the fur she had not been able to bring herself to touch.

The girl was more indignant. 'That big girl didn't even do anything! We saw a dog on the road once that had been hit but it didn't die and my mom said that people who left animals like that didn't deserve to live themselves...'

'No.' The adult voice calmed her. 'Didn't you say that it was her kitty? Maybe she was too sad to do it.'

'But she should have!'

'But we can't always do what we should do. She did her best. Maybe she went to get help or to cry a little before she came back.'

'My mom,' the older girl told her confidingly, as if sharing a bit of information of great importance, 'says that crying is for babies.'

'Oh, but she didn't mean when your kitty is killed.' The woman was positive. 'She meant when you fall down or you're trying to get your own way. She's right, you stop crying over those things when you get big. But everybody cries when someone or something they love dies. It's one way to feel better.'

Lyn closed her eyes, and the talking receded before the picture of her mother digging a hole beside the giant lilac bush that grew in front of the farm house with a shovel that had part of the handle broken off. Herself, barefoot, snotty-nosed from crying, about eleven, sitting on the step some fifty feet away raging to Nikona.

'I hate her! I hate her! She didn't have to kill him!'

Nikona was picking at the hem of her shorts, making a fringe. She answered without looking at Lyn. 'You know she did. The skunk bit Tabby and the skunk had rabies. You saw the skunk, Lyn.'

She knew. She had read *Old Yeller*, had wept when they put away the dog that had saved their lives, had agreed with Travis who had frantically suggested that they just pen him up and watch him a while, that maybe he wouldn't develop the disease. But her mom hadn't listened to that suggestion anymore than Travis had.

'I hate...' she started again, but stopped. Her mother had put the shovel down and picked up the body of the cat. She was cradling him gently, stroking his head and ears with one hand just as she used to do when he was alive. Against her will Lyn remembered that it was her mother who had brought him home as a kitten, wet and almost drowned from being lost in a ditch and that it was her bed he chose to sleep on.

She saw Sadie's head coming between them suddenly as she squatted on the porch behind them. There was flour on her face and her hands. She watched silently for a moment, then said, 'You know, Lyn, your mom always tries to do what's right, even if it's really hard.'

Silently they watched her mother place the cat in the grave. As she picked up the shovel she looked up at them and the sun sparkled off the tears on her face in rainbow colours, as if hitting a prism.

The picture faded slowly. Lyn could hear the woman and the children talking again.

'But you should try to find her. Maybe burying her kitten is important to her. That's another way to feel better, you know, is to be able to say goodbye.'

Lyn leaned back against the grill of the car, not caring what it would do to her coat. She could only see the legs of the woman stepping back onto the sidewalk, but she knew that it was her mother. It was not just that she had recognized her voice, but even more by the way she had spoken to the children. That was the way she had always spoken to them as children, as if their feelings were of grave importance.

She had another flashback — the same memory maybe thirty minutes later. She saw the sun setting behind her mother's head as she sat on the step beside Nikona, saw the slump of her shoulders as if she were tired beyond belief. She gestured towards the new grave.

'You know,' she said, 'some day Tabby will change in the ground, and he'll become part of that lilac bush. Won't it be wonderful to look out at the flowers in the spring and see how beautiful he helped make them?'

'Hey.' It was the older girl. 'Do you want this?' She sounded less judgmental than she had before, though her tone still held enough reserve to let them all know that Lyn had not acted the way she thought proper. In one hand she was holding out the kitten, wrapped carefully in Connie's muffler, a rainbow scarf that was one of Aunt Annie's seconds. For just a flash Lyn saw Aunt Annie sitting peacefully at the back of her loom, listening to music as she drew the multicoloured yarn through the heddles. Then the picture was gone.

'Yes,' she said, reaching out her hand. With only his little head showing the kitten no longer looked grotesque. As Lyn took him the little girl kitten gave a mew of delight. She licked his face several times and then settled down next to him in Lyn's arms, purring. Lyn could see that the oldest child was as upset by this as she was, but the boy reached out a finger and gently rubbed the live kitten's head.

'That's okay,' he told her, 'saying goodbye is one way that you feel better.'

Then, without saying goodbye themselves, as if they had suddenly forgotten what had drawn them there, the children turned and left. Lyn could hear them for perhaps half a block. They were talking about school. The kitten was forgotten.

She looked back towards her house. Her mother was still out on the sidewalk, her back turned, black silhouetted against the sun. She was just getting home. For a moment Lyn wanted to call to her, to ask her to help her bury the kitten. But it was as if she was looking at an old, old photograph. She was touched by the scene, but the woman in the picture was too far away to reach. She simply stood watching as her mother locked the doors of the truck and went around to the front of the house.

# TWENTY-SIX

Lyn was not dressed for the snow. Normally it wouldn't have mattered that much. Rick would have picked her up, or at the most, she would have walked to the corner to meet the school bus. But she had gotten wet when she had hidden between the cars. Her shoes and pants were soaked up to her knees. She had shivered during the bus trip, and, now at school, she went eagerly towards the building.

There were not nearly as many students standing outside as usual. Even so, Lyn could not help but glance at the stone wall where she and Rick usually hung out with their friends. Embarrassed, she immediately turned away, but then looked again more cautiously. Rick was standing there along with Gary and Dave. He had caught her look. There was nothing she could do but nod. He returned the greeting coolly. Her face burning, Lyn hurried inside. She had hoped that maybe things would be back to normal when she saw him. Obviously she had hoped in vain.

The halls were overcrowded and noisy. Everyone was having one last chat, one last soda, even trying to sneak one last smoke before the bell rang. The monitors could not chase them out in the cold, so they were contenting themselves with just trying to keep the uproar down. One of them frowned at Lyn as she hurried by to the lower level, almost running, but she didn't notice.

Because of the cold some of the boys were already working. Lyn didn't speak to any of them, but she eyed them curiously as, with stiff fingers, she fumbled with her locker. She had never really thought of them as her friends. She had thought of them as Rick's friends, or friends of Rick's friends to whom she had been determinedly grafted for protection. Now what would they do if she and Rick broke up? Would they divorce themselves from her too? Maybe not all. Randy from the woodshop was her friend and she was also sure about Brian, the senior assistant who had helped her often. But she didn't know about the rest. She had walked a fine line with them, trying to flatter but not flirt. Nikona would have described it more bluntly. She would have called it 'sucking up'.

Finally she got the lock open and pulled out her wadded-up work clothes. She would change completely. Her teeth had stopped chattering but her hands and feet were still numb.

She was so anxious to be warm that she went through the swinging door much too fast and her wet shoes slipped on the tile. To stop herself from falling she dropped her tennis shoes and caught the edge of one of the sinks. As she bent to retrieve them the door swung open again and looking behind her, she saw Robin come in.

For a moment she froze in her upside down position. She remembered how angry she had been with Robin the day before. But yesterday seemed like forever ago and more clearly she remembered earlier when she had felt so alone and had wished for Robin's phone number.

She stood up slowly, planning on making a neutral statement, on showing Robin that she was willing to forgive her if she didn't push her anymore. But when she opened her mouth it was just as it had been yesterday. Worse, because everything she had been keeping inside seemed to well up in one great sob. She struggled to hold it back, but that almost seemed to make things worse. She meant to turn and try to compose herself. But instead she found herself weeping and Robins's arms were around her.

Lyn didn't know how long she cried, or what she had babbled between sobs. Coming back was very slow. She felt as if she were convalescing. She found herself sitting on the floor. Robin was rubbing one of her feet between her hands. The wet cuffs of her pants were rolled up. In one hand, though she had no idea how it had gotten there, she held a banana. Her wet coat was on the floor and Robin's sweatshirt was draped around her shoulders.

She sniffed and wiped her nose on her cuff. Robin looked up.

'Hey,' she said, 'you look like you're back in the real world. Now maybe you can eat that instead of trying to poke yourself in the eye with it.' Lyn hesitated, and Robin chided her gently. 'Everybody gets hysterical if they don't eat, Lyn. They make the president have a special snack before he steps into a summit meeting.'

Lyn peeled the top down and took a small bite. It was the best banana she had ever tasted. She suddenly became aware of exactly how long it had been since she had eaten and she gobbled the rest.

'Moderation in all things,' Robin observed. 'Puking is not an improvement over starving. There's more food.' She nodded towards a sack by Lyn's side.

As she pulled out a sandwich Lyn knew that she was eating Robin's lunch, just as she knew that she had taken the long wool socks that Lyn was now wearing off her own feet. But she didn't have the strength to refuse either.

'Did I say anything that made any sense?' she asked cautiously.

'I gather that nobody likes you, everybody hates you, and you'd go and eat worms, except that the ground is frozen.'

Lyn couldn't help but laugh, or snort, really, since her mouth was full. But even in the middle of the laugh she felt a stab of pain. The ground was frozen, and she hadn't been able to dig a hole to bury the kitten. She hadn't wanted to put him in the dumpster, so she had temporarily stashed him beneath it, in his old home. The female had jumped out of her arms and also run beneath and though Lyn had called until her bus was almost at the corner, she had not come out.

'Okay, seriously. You lost your boyfriend, you had sex and it wasn't even fun, you hate your mother, you were a shit to your sister and now she's going to leave you all alone. Girl, you are a mess, aren't you?'

Lyn nodded agreement. But, still, things didn't seem quite as bad as they had a few moments before.

'I just don't know what to say to my sister. I feel so bad — not just about burning her, but everything and I don't know how to show her, how to show her so that she'll believe it, that I'm really sorry.'

Robin was silent for a moment. Lyn was working on a bag full of cookies now and she reached in to get one for herself.

'Maybe,' she said finally, 'you should let her go.'

'But didn't I tell you? She *is* going.' Lyn peeled her wet pants off and pulled on her coveralls. 'Do you think anybody will take these if I put them on the heater to dry?'

'Who? Nobody ever comes in here but us and the girl carpenters and they're all cool.'

'Yeah, I heard what you said. She's going. But, you know, it's kind of like when you have to leave your kid at the day care centre. You're going to have to go to work even if she screams and cries and you have to peel her little fingers off your arm. But it must feel a lot better if the kid waves at you and you know she's going to have a good time.'

'But I don't want her to go,' Lyn protested, 'I'm not going to have a good time.'

'No, but in the end she's going to go even if you scream and cry. It just seems like one way of saying you're sorry. It sounds like she's already paid a lot of dues for you.'

Lyn frowned into the mirror, trying to repair her hair with her fingertips. She didn't like what Robin was saying. She didn't want to sacrifice herself. It was Darcy's job to sacrifice. Robin moved over next to her. She untied her red scarf and let down her long hair, then took a brush out of her pack.

'When I was about twelve,' she said, 'my older brother, Gordon...'

'I didn't know you had a brother.'

'I don't see him a lot anymore. He's at college now and before that he wasn't living in the area. When he was thirteen he went to live with his dad. He and his new wife were going to go to court and try for custody. They settled out. If you want to know the truth, I think that money was involved, but nobody would ever tell us.'

'Why didn't they take you, too?'

'Well, he's really only my half brother. His dad isn't my dad. Actually, I think they would have taken me if they could have. They're really good people. It wasn't like my mom was pounding on us or anything like that, but their house was definitely a better place to be. But I was so angry at Gordie! We had been buddies, we had stuck together and up for each other and I felt as if he had defected and left me behind.'

'Well, he had!'

'Yeah, but he was thirteen and didn't have much of a choice. And even if he had, why shouldn't he choose what was best for him? I wasn't his responsibility. I wasn't his kid.'

'But he was older. He should have stuck with you.'

'You can't always. You said that yourself during the crying routine. You felt like you couldn't stick with Darcy, that if you didn't fight you'd lose it. Well, she can't stick with you now. And I'll tell you another thing about my brother. I was furious with him. And the madder I got, the more I drove him away. Pretty soon he didn't even want to call me on the phone or have me over for the weekend because I made him feel guilty. It wasn't until I could back off a little and begin to try and accept the fact that he'd needed to get out for himself that he could be there for me at all. Then, eventually, we were there a lot for each other. We talked on the phone a lot, we visited a lot. We were still pretty tight until his step-mom got transferred.'

'That must have been awful.'

'It was. But his dad was so good. He really helped me learn about surviving with my mom and he made sure that I had other contacts. He was the one that got me started in this Alateen group. Half the time I don't even go to the meetings, but I hang out with kids I've met there a lot. It's really good to be able to say, "My mom was drinking today", and not to have to explain it or how it makes you feel. They know. That was one of the wonderful things about Gordie. He knew.'

Lyn felt sick to her stomach. She didn't want to live alone with her mother. She thought that Robin was wrong, that even now Darcy might stay if she made a big enough fuss. But how would her sister feel about her in five, ten years if she did that?

'Let her go,' Robin advised, 'you can tough it out for a couple of years. Get a job, it will get you out of the house and you can save up some money to leave as soon as you're out of high school.'

She had finished brushing her hair and it stood out in waves past her shoulders. She began to twist it up. Lyn watched her in the mirror, chewing the inside of her cheek thoughtfully.

'I didn't know you had a brother,' she said again finally.

'There's a lot of things you don't know about me. We haven't had a lot of time to talk.' Robin said it simply, but Lyn felt a twinge of her pain. Maybe Robin had been able to accept Lyn's limitations of their friendship, but that didn't mean that it hadn't hurt.

Robin was looking at her watch. 'I've seriously got to go. I'm really anxious for another morning with the pig pack.' She cracked the door, preparing to slip out first as she always did.

Lyn caught the handle and pulled it wide. 'I don't think I scoffed your whole lunch,' she said. 'Come on, let's finish these last cookies before we get to class.'

Then, when Robin gave her an inquiring sideways look she added, 'Sometimes you can stick together.'

# TWENTY-SEVEN

There was only a short practice planned. They were to scrimmage mostly, something to get them jazzed up for the game that night. Darcy stood at the door of the gym, holding her shoes in her hands. Most of her team-mates were already on the floor, but no one was warming up. There was a radio sitting on the floor by the bleachers turned to a country 'n' western station and all the girls were swing dancing. Some were dancing with each other and some had partners from the boys' wrestling team whom they had waylaid on their way to practice.

The only one not participating was Hilary. She was standing at the end of the court talking seriously to another girl whom Darcy didn't know. There was a video camera set up on a tripod between them. Hilary uncrossed her arms to motion in Darcy's direction and Darcy knew that the girl must be from one of the media classes and that they were practicing for the tape that night.

Sandy saw her coming onto the floor and she gave her partner a whirl that sent her spinning into another couple.

'Here she is folks, star of screen and stage and candidate for the next Olympics. Our own Queen Nerd!' She swooped towards the camera, as if to turn it on Darcy, but both girls gave her such hostile stares that she contented herself with creating a camera out of her hands and making a whirring noise.

For a moment Darcy wanted to push her away, even to slap her away. It seemed so unfair that she was happy and carefree and loud about being that way while Darcy's world was falling apart, not just in little pieces, but with large crashes. Yet another part of her longed to be bathed and covered with Sandy's light.

Sandy pulled up short in front of her. She reached out a hand as if to bring her into the dancing, then changed her mind and dropped it.

'Changed your mind about this afternoon?' she asked. 'We'd be thrilled to squire the star centre.'

For a long moment Darcy was tempted. To hell with the plasma centre and the truck keys she'd wrangled out of her mom before school.

'We're leaving right after practice.'

No, she couldn't. Her clean uniform was at home in her room with the keys. Maybe she could get Sandy to swing by, to wait while she made a sandwich to take with her? But her mother might be home. No, she'd stick to her original plan. She'd go out with the gang tomorrow, after they had made the semi-finals.

She shook her head, unexpectedly choking, hoping that Sandy, unpredictable, would not choose this particular time to hug her, dissolve her into tears. But Sandy kept her distance speaking in a controlled voice.

'Tonight's your night, Tiger. Take it.'

'She's right,' Darcy said softly aloud, watching her rejoin the dancers. 'I'm going to do it, Nikki. Tonight's my night. Tonight I'm the star. Tonight I don't worry about anyone but myself.'

As she sat down to put on her shoes she repeated over and over, as if saying it enough times would make her believe it.

# TWENTY-EIGHT

'I saw you with that girl from the mechanics class today.'

Lyn jerked her head up. All day long she had been waiting for someone to say those words to her, had been wincing in anticipation. But she hadn't expected them to come from Rick.

'Yeah.' It was all she could think of to say. Her bus had pulled up to the curb and the other riders were jostling to be first in line.

'That was nice to see. She needs a friend. I was wondering if you'd ever do it.'

'You mean...'

'Of course I knew. It wasn't hard to figure. Nobody spends that much time in the bathroom unless she's sick. It was either her or food poisoning.'

'I really like her. I want to spend time with her.' Lyn blurted the words out quickly before she could chicken out.

'Good. Maybe we can ask her to go out with us sometime. I mean,' he hesitated, 'if things work out.'

'I've got to catch my bus.' Lyn took a step towards the curb, then one back towards him. She was torn. She needed to see Darcy, to tell her what she had decided. But she needed to talk to Rick, too.

'I'll give you a ride home. If you want one. I even dumped Gary.'

She made up her mind. She knew that Darcy's team was playing the late game, that she would be home for several hours before she left. She could talk to Rick and still catch her before she left.

'Hey!' the driver called, 'Are you getting on or not?'

Lyn stepped back and shook her head, waving him on. Then she followed Rick through the snow to the parking lot.

# TWENTY-NINE

It took Connie a long time to get started. She was still sitting on the couch smoking an hour after Darcy had taken her keys and gone to school. She wished she hadn't given them to her. It meant so much time lost waiting for buses, that many more jobs she might miss because she couldn't get there in time. But she hadn't been able to think of any reason to tell Darcy that she needed the truck.

The thought of staying home wrapped up in one of the sleeping bags while she watched day-time TV, was enticing. Just for one day. But then she thought again of telling Darcy there was no pay cheque and panic clutched her heart. She cursed Joe, but at the same time she wondered if she could go back and talk to him, promising reform. Something told her she couldn't, that she would only be shamed again.

She tried to dress carefully. She didn't want that to be a problem today. Getting ready was harder than she'd anticipated. She couldn't remember how she used to twist her hair up for dress occasions, couldn't remember wearing it in any way but braided up tightly to keep out the sawdust. Washing her face, putting in her earrings, brushing her hair all felt awkward, though she was sure she had done them the day before. Still, they no longer seemed automatic.

Dressing was even harder. She pulled first one, then another article of clothing out of the cardboard box behind the couch which she used for a dresser. She tried to remember what she usually wore to dress up, what she liked. But she only became more and more confused and her hands began to sweat as she started thinking of the jobs she wasn't getting. Finally, around one, she decided to wear something of Lyn's. She could remember the combinations she had seen on her, and though they had looked a little strange to her surely Lyn's judgment could be trusted.

It was only accidental that she saw the keys at all. When she spotted them on the desk, half under Darcy's jersey, she left off adjusting her blouse and pounced on them eagerly. Driving would save her so much time. She could get the truck back in plenty of time.

# THIRTY

It was totally dark. No, that wasn't true. There was a thin line of light by her head which was resting against her doubled knees, and a parallel line at her feet. Darcy knew that it was the kitchen light shining around the door of the cupboard through the crack too narrow for her to see. She also knew, as one knows in dreams, that it was not she who was sitting, frozen with panic, in the space under the sink, the back of her neck resting against the U-bend of the drainpipe. It was not she who had ceased to struggle more than an hour before, and was now simply sitting thinking nothing, like an animal. It was not she who had accepted being trapped.

No, in her dream she was far away from the kitchen, from the apartment where her mother slept a good part of the day. She was back at school. This part of the dream was a dramatic contrast to the black squared by the thin light. This part of the dream was in full, vibrant colour, and not only bursting with colour, but joyous sound and smell, too. She was back at school! She was safe! And the wonderful part of it was that she knew that this time she could stay, not just for half the day, but for the whole day and the night and the next day and the next after that. She never had to go back home again.

She knew about the darkness, the locked doors of the cupboard. She knew about Lyn frozen with fear, her back and legs cramping, unable to release herself. She knew that if she did not return to the apartment to open the doors that Lyn would stay there forever. But if Darcy returned she might be caught again. So she pushed the dark image, the rank smell out of her mind.

She was at school.

Darcy woke with a start. Her left arm hurt. It hurt terribly and she started to jerk it away from the pain, stopping just in time as she remembered that she had a needle in her vein, connecting her to a tube that was in turn connected to a bag full of her own red blood cells. She had dozed on the first round while her blood was being returned to her, the plasma removed from it with a centrifuge. But there had never been pain when she had done this before.

Gingerly she lifted a corner of the gauze pad that was placed over the inside of her arm where the needle was inserted. She didn't like to look at the needle. She supposed no one did, that's why the technicians covered them. But she had sneaked a peek enough times to know what was normal.

What she saw definitely was not. There was blood welling up around the needle, dripping off her arm onto the chair. Darcy gave a little gasp and dropped the gauze. Wildly she looked around for one of the techs, but everyone seemed busy adjusting bags, clearing tubes. She couldn't catch an eye. The pain was much worse now that she had looked and she could feel her scalp sweating. Still, she could not bring herself to summon anyone with a scream. She waved her free arm in the direction of the desk, though no one was there.

'What's the problem?'

She looked around hopefully. But it was only the old man in the chair next to her. He must have been hooked up while she was sleeping. He couldn't have been there long, because his blood was still draining into the pint bag hanging by the side of his chair.

'Uh, my arm... there's something wrong.'

She felt a little nervous about the winos who frequented the centre and usually buried herself in a book to avoid conversation. But she was almost frantic now.

As she had done he lifted the square of gauze. 'Oh, not good,' he said, and he reached up and pinched her input tube shut so that no more blood was draining into her arm. 'Hey, problem over here!' he roared without looking up to address anyone in particular. Darcy squirmed in embarrassment, but at the same time she was relieved when two of the white uniformed staff appeared almost instantly.

'Oh, shit,' said the floor nurse as she looked at the arm. She was the one in charge of sticking small veins, like Darcy's. She had a brusque manner that was difficult to warm to. Crossly she added, 'You can let go, Roscoe. We have the situation under control. You shouldn't be messing with anyone else's tubes anyway.'

'Going to have to pull it,' offered the young male tech, who was a favourite of Darcy's.

'I know that!'

Darcy had no idea what had happened, or who had caused the problem, but the woman was not happy about it. 'You know you're not supposed to sleep while you're here.'

It took Darcy a moment to realize she was being addressed. 'I didn't mean... I just nodded....' She could think of nothing to say in her defense. At any rate, the woman was not listening to explanations. She had turned to the technician and was berating him for not discovering the problem earlier.

'It's not his fault that she's leaking and she certainly didn't cause it by falling asleep. That was caused by a bad stick and didn't you stick her yourself?' It was the man in the next chair who spoke. He could only have been guessing about the stick, but there was a light in his eyes as he spoke as if he enjoyed the prospect of stirring things up.

The woman had deftly pulled the needle out of Darcy's arm, and then turned on him, banishing it like a sword. A little blood ran out the end, but the underling swiftly clipped off the tube behind her back.

'You...' she sputtered, 'You... I'll... If you give me anymore trouble....' She was having trouble threatening him. It was the one advantage of being an indigent, there was really nothing you could take away.

The orderly leaned towards Darcy as the two fenced words, almost shouting. The rest of the donors had settled in to watch the exchange as if it were an engrossing TV show.

'Bad stick,' he told her. 'Your needle slipped and the blood was leaking under your skin instead of going back into your vein. You're going to have a hell of a bruise.'

'But I can go home now?'

'Oh no, we never let you go home until you've got all your red cells back. She'll have to stick you in the other arm. I'd do it for you, but....' He spread his hands without finishing the sentence, a gesture she understood to mean that her veins were too small, that he was afraid one would roll out from beneath his needle. They both turned to watch the shouting match which had expanded to include several other patients. The floor nurse was not popular.

Suddenly, however, she turned her back and returned to Darcy's side and just as abruptly everyone was silent though there was a pleased, excited hum in the air, as if something pleasant had taken place.

'Let's see your other arm,' she said to Darcy in a professional voice, taking her hand as she spoke. She swiftly tied a piece of rubber tubing around her upper arm and began patting and stroking her skin to find the vein. This was the part, over and above the stick, that Darcy found the most unpleasant. She turned her eyes away and likewise tried to turn her mind.

As if it had been waiting, as if only the pain had kep it away, the dream sprang back, full force, into her mind.

# THIRTY-ONE

Connie stood with her back against the brick wall of the building, too upset to remember where she had parked the truck, too upset even to light the cigarette dangling between her lips. A man roke off from the downtown foot traffic that flowed past and approached her.

'Hey, pretty mama...' he started, but one furious look made him veer away without another word.

Her lips twitched as she spoke under her breath. Saying the things she should have said, things she could only think of now, after she was out of that man's office. She still couldn't believe what he had said to her! She had done everything she was supposed to do. She had dressed up. She had gone to the unemployment office. She had sat quietly through the interview, balancing her answers so she was neither begging, nor overly assertive. She still couldn't believe that even before she was through talking about her experience, he had leaned across the desk, right into her face and after taking a big, rude, sniff, had said, 'Sorry. I never hire anybody who smells like whiskey this early.'

And that was it. That was the end. She had been ushered out in mid-sentence.

'I supposed you never needed a shot for courage, did you?' she asked him scathingly beneath her breath as she stood on the street corner in the snow. 'I suppose you never...' but she didn't want to talk to him anymore. She wanted to talk to Louise. Not a heavy talk, not about her problems. Just a warm, slow conversation about jobs they had done together, projects they would like to do someday. She wanted to hear Louise sing to herself, and to have her tell the stories behind the songs in a chant-like way, almost as if they were songs themselves. She hardly knew that she was in the phone booth until she heard the coins clinking in the slot.

'Threestar Textile Art. Annie Whiley, alterations, mending, quilting.' The tape was different than it had been the day before. It was no longer the voice of Sadie, sounding slightly irritated, but Nikona speaking. Connie relaxed for a moment at the sound of her, then tensed back up again. It had been almost as hard to leave Nikona as it would have been to leave Lyn or Darcy, for Nikona was like her daughter, too.

Connie remembered things about Nikona's childhood that she did not remember about Darcy's, like the first words she had spoken. She was surprised that Nikona was being allowed to tape. Too often she slipped her own jokes in with the legitimate businesses. The two that showed up the most were 'Cosmic gardening - let us help if you and your vegetables aren't communicating' and 'Assertive aerobics - for the truly right-on woman of the eighties.' But the tape went on without a twist. 'A Cut Above Carpentry, roofing, remolding and painting.'

She had been so busy listening for the joke that she had let the message run through. Now would come the tone. Connie was suddenly seized with a senseless panic, as if she could be identified simply by being on the line. Louise wouldn't be home, she wouldn't want to talk to her. But at the same time she could not bring herself simply to hang up. She clung to the receiver, sweat dripping off her face in the cold air, somehow dreading the silence that would follow, the tone more than the familiar voice on the recording: maybe because she knew that she could not breach it with a message.

But even though she was certain that Nikona had gone through all the businesses there was no sign off, no tone and she wondered if the machine was acting up again. Then, unexpectedly, a new recorded voice came on the line. Annie.

'Lyn? Darcy? Please call back tonight or leave a message where we can reach you. At school? We...'

The recording was cut off. 'Hello?' Jean demanded, 'Hello?'

Then, as Connie still clutched the receiver in silence, 'Who is this? Hello!' Her voice rose frantically as gently, carefully, Connie replaced the phone and just as carefully, walked away.

# THIRTY-TWO

'No, I won't. No, I won't!'

The wind tore the words from Darcy's lips and whipped them back behind her to a young woman who was also struggling home in the snow. She looked at Darcy's back strangely for a moment, then shrugged and continued in the opposite direction. 'No, I won't,' Darcy muttered one more time. Then, 'It was only a dream. She'll be fine by herself, it was only a goddamn dream!'

The snow was too deep for her to run, but she was hurrying along the drifted sidewalk as best as she could. The second stick at the plasma centre had taken extra time and then the bag had drained slowly. They were closing, cleaning up around her before she was done. Still, she had the precious nine dollars shoved in her pocket and luckily she had allowed herself plenty of time to get to the game. She would just make it.

She found that she had slowed and to hurry herself she again said aloud, 'It was only a dream.' Dammit, it was as if there was one part of her that wanted to miss the game. It was only a dream, Lyn was not locked away, waiting to be saved, but right now it seemed more real than walking against the wind, her face bent before the snow. That seemed like a real dream, something in which she could get lost forever. She looked up for a moment, checking the path before her, taking a quick glance around the street. Every house on either side had at least one door dark, framed by light and she slowed again, feeling a new twinge.

'I won't stay!' she screamed into the wind. 'I don't have to take care of her, it was only a dream!' But the wind blew her words away, so it was as if she'd made no protest at all. Someone had left the front door ajar. Not so safe, but at least she didn't have to find the key with her numb fingers. She thumped up the stairs, not bothering to kick the snow off her boots. She'd grab her things and turn right around. She had planned on a snack, but it was getting too close to game time. Ms Ernst was particular about being on time for the warm-up. She dumped her books on the couch and sprinted into the bedroom without turning the living room light on.

The keys were gone. At first her mind could not believe what her eyes told her. They couldn't be gone, she had put them on the table that morning. She spent several frantic moments searching the floor and shaking out the pieces of her uniform. The keys were gone.

An awful thought occurred to her. She ran back into the living room and heaved the one big window open. The black plastic rippled against the window and she took a handful and tore the centre out. A great rush of wind blew past her into the room, and the jagged banners of plastic that remained around the edge of the window flapped around her head as she stuck it out. She craned her neck as far as she could in both directions. The red truck was not where it had been parked when she left in the morning.

'She's taken it!' she cried aloud. 'Damn her! Damn her!'

Why hadn't she foreseen it? Because she still didn't want to believe she had to treat her mother like a thief.

She pulled the window back down. Even as she was berating herself she was stripping her street clothes off, her mind darting frantically. She'd change right here. It was too late for her to catch any of her team-mates. She'd run down to the store on the corner and call a cab. Nine dollars wouldn't nearly cover the ride to Westminster, but she'd go in and beg the coach for the rest. She didn't care how it looked, she was not going to let her mother spoil this night for her! Just stay home, a little part of her advised, it's your job to stay home and take care of Lyn. She shook the voice away. It was only a dream, only bad luck. She *would* go to the game.

She had torn off her boots to slip on her shorts and blue warmups. Now she sat to pull them back on. As she tied her laces the door downstairs slammed and she stiffened, like a dog who is not yet sure whether or not to bark. It was not the man downstairs. Someone was coming up. A slight falter in the step told her it was her mother.

A quick trip to the window confirmed it. The truck was parked in its regular place beneath the street light.

But she felt no relief. If anything the rage inside her grew. Her mother had not cared a bit, not a bit about anything she had told her. It was nothing to her if she were too late to play, if the video was taped or not. Her anger mounted until it frightened her. Swiftly she turned from the window, seeking some way to dilute the unfamiliar feeling before her mother came in. The peacemaker, the little girl inside her who had seen too many fights, skittered about frantically, looking for a hiding place. She had to calm down, she had no business being so mad.

The door flew open. She did not greet her mother, did not even look full at her for fear of what she might say.

'Mom, I need the keys, I've got to go right now, you promised I could have them.' She said the words all in one breath, speaking without moving her lips, holding out her hand.

There was no response. Connie fumbled with the bolt and then gave it up and instead hooked the cheap chain. Darcy glanced at her from the corners of her eyes. The keys were dangling tantalizingly in her right hand. She was moving her mouth as if she were talking to someone not in the room.

'Mom, please.' Darcy tried again. This time her teeth, as well as her lips were clenched, and the 'please' sounded like a curse. 'Please,

please, please,' she said inside. 'Please don't let her fight me. Please don't let me blow up.' The little voice in the corner, stronger now that her attention was elsewhere said 'Stay home. Lyn needs you.'

'No!' she said aloud, momentarily distracted.

Her mother jumped and snow fell off her shoulders and head.

'What did you say to me?' The set of her mouth was hard and ugly. She didn't wait for Darcy to answer. 'I can't believe it! I can't fucking believe that they would even put that on the machine!' She threw her arms up for emphasis, and the keys clattered against the wall.

Darcy's eyes were drawn to them. She didn't take in what her mother was saying, not until after she had said, 'I need the keys now!' one more time. Then she shut her eyes and bit her top lip. Her mother was cursing. Her mother never swore, not unless she was getting ready to be totally out of control. Of course Darcy knew immediately who 'they' were. Connie reserved that special tone of anger for the women back on the farm. She was convinced they had betrayed her and it was best not to talk about it. But Darcy could not resist.

'What do you mean, "message"? Did you call home? Is there a message for us?'

'"Is there a message for us?" It's not your home and don't tell me you haven't heard it! You've been going behind my back!'

'I haven't! What did it say?'

'You know what it said. Connie twisted her face in ugly mimicry of Annie's. '"Lyn, Darcy..." You know the rest!'

'How would I have heard it?' Darcy cried. 'I've never called, you told us...'

She stopped dead. 'She lied,' she thought, 'she lied to us!' Oh, she had always suspected that the stories weren't true. But to be told like this! She hadn't needed to go through the months of isolation. Her family was looking for her. Her mother had lied.

She found that she was breathing hard in anger, panting as if from a sprint. She couldn't think about it now. What she needed to do was get the keys so that she could get to the game. She would think about it all later. She knew she could not speak calmly, so she simply reached across her mother's body towards her right hand. But just as she was about to close her fingers over the ring her mother jerked her arm backwards, in a movement so sudden that she upset herself and tumbled to her knees.

As she scrambled to her feet Darcy caught a glimpse of her face and her heart sank. She had a flash of last year's C League basketball tournament, of her mother squeezed in the stands between Aunt Annie and Louise laughing, her face flushed with excitement. It did did seem possible that this face, distorted with anger, could be the same one. She opened her mouth to speak, thinking that she was only going to ask for the keys again. But what she actually said was, 'I want my mother.'

It was the wrong thing to say. She knew it before the words were even out of her mouth. Her mother's face twisted up even more.

'What are you talking about? It's always been you with Annie, hasn't it? Hasn't it!'

'No!' That wasn't what she had meant. All she wanted was to see her own mother — the woman who had come to the basketball game, who had read *The Wizard of Oz* to her at least twenty times, who had taught her to sew. But there was no sense trying to explain it to the woman in front of her. Besides, she was already screaming over the top of her monosyllabic answer.

'You're not going anywhere! If it wasn't for you I...'

Darcy tried not to listen to the rest. There had been a time when she had tried to listen fairly, to sort out what was real and what was not. But that had been months ago. She had stopped at the same time that she had stopped listening to her mother's apologies. It didn't matter how heartfelt any of it was. It was just drunk talk. All of it was drunk talk.

So she had no warning. It just happened. Suddenly her mother, in mid-torrent, cracked her alongside the head so hard that it reeled her back two steps.

There was utter silence. They looked at each other, twin mirrors of horror both equally shocked, both realizing that the point of no return had been reached. Her mother slowly raised her hand, staring at it incredulously as if it had done the thing independent of her will, while Darcy, equally slowly, equally incredulous, put her hand to her temple where her mother's ring had hit her.

She looked at the blood that her fingers brought away, totally disbelieving, yet at the same time totally unsurprised. Her mother had never hit her. Not like that. Oh, she knew from Aunt Annie that her mother had given her the scar that stood out now in dark relief above the cut, but she didn't remember that. She herself had always preferred to think that she had fallen or pulled something over on herself and that it was simply the sight of blood that had sent her out of the house in panic.

Her mother's face, already crumpling with tears, swam before her. Darcy didn't know the name of the feeling raging up inside her and she was afraid to look at it for fear of what she would discover. For a moment she locked her hands together in front of her.

'My mother doesn't hate me, she's only sick. My mother loves me, she's just sick.' Softly she repeated the litany that Aunt Annie had taught to the five-year-old crying on the steps. 'She doesn't hate me, she's just sick, And I don't, I don't, I don't hate my mother.' Carefully, slowly, she again reached for the keys hanging in her mother's limp hand.

*They have come back from the store and she is to help carry the sacks up the steps. It is a thankless task, for the only place they visited is the one with the rows and rows of bottles that make her mother's face light up and crumple with despair at the same time. No food. Maybe this time her hands will be strong enough to use the can opener on the stash that Aunt Annie left. As she hoists the bag to her hip she hopes so.*

*She hardly notices Lyn clinging to the hem of her blouse just where she wants to rest the bag. 'Pretty,' Lyn had whispered in the store, eyeing the child-sized bottle on the bottom shelf, and Darcy had slapped her hands hard, saying 'No, no, no!' So hard that she thought that for once her mother might intercede. But she was arguing with the store man, and didn't notice when Darcy dragged Lyn out to the steps where they sat and listened to the coming storm.*

*She is used to Lyn being in the way. But a bad thing happens near the top of the stairs. The bag she is carrying begins to tear. She knows better than to make her mom angry by asking for help, so she juggles wildly for control. But it is no use. At first it seems as if Lyn will act as an anchor against her over-compensation. Then there is the sound of tearing as the tail of the old shirt rips and both Darcy and the bag tumble to the bottom of the stairs.*

*Confused by topsy-turvy glimpses of familiar things on her way down Darcy is for a moment unable to tell if she is hurt. Gingerly she moves her arms and legs. Shards of glass tinkle. It is only because her head is wet, dripping, that she finally puts a hand to it and removes it, bloodied.*

*But it is not this that sends her running into the rain. It is looking up at her mother and sister on the stairs in almost identical postures of weeping and knowing that none of the tears are for her. They are crying for their own fears and she knows that she will not only have to staunch her wounds herself, but have to comfort the two of them as well. There is no one who will, even for a moment, take care of her. This is what sends her out the door, her hand on the envelope that is always in her pocket.*

Her mother was crying again now. She wasn't hurt, but she was crying, holding up her hands like a little child expecting to be comforted. Darcy reached towards her, thinking that her only intention was to gently remove the keys. She would take them and leave without a word. She thought it up until the moment that she found herself covering Connie's hand with her own. Up until the moment that she began to squeeze it until her mother cried out in pain and dropped the ring on the floor. Even then as she put her hands on her mother's shoulders, she thought that she was just going to explain. She thought that she was going to tell her mother what a terrible, terrible winter it had been and how much difference it would have made to her had she known that her family was still loving her, even though they were somewhere else. She thought she'd tell her mother how her theatrics had made her too late to play in the game, how she had kept her from the one pleasure that she had salvaged.

But as she was lifting her mother six inches off the floor she found that she didn't know what she was doing or planning. She only knew that she was shaking her back and forth as she had never shaken anyone - except her dolls and then only very guiltily in private. It seemed quite unreal, as if she were an observer, rather than a participant and when she started to speak her words made little sense to her. 'I can't do this anymore, Mama. I can't be the good girl and clean up and take care of you. I can't anymore! Nobody takes care of me. Please, Mama, please just care about me. I can't do it all, I can't stay here anymore.'

There was a brief pause during which the shaking did not abate and then she began to repeat the words again, almost mechanically. She didn't think of the game. Time had ceased to exist. It seemed as if the shaking could go on forever.

# THIRTY-THREE

The back tyres spun, and Lyn tensed, ready to leap out of the car and push again. But this time they made contact, and the car moved forward.

'Sorry,' Rick said again, but she tuned out the story of the bald tyres and where the money with which he had meant to replace them had gone. It was her fault as much as his. She had let the time get away from her and now she was probably too late to catch Darcy. Oh, how she wanted to! There wouldn't be time for apologies. But she could go and cheer. She could go and make sure there was one person in the stands calling Darcy by name rather than by her number. She hadn't been to any of the other games. She had known that her voice would choke every time that Darcy made a basket that took her away. But tonight she would yell and try with her whole heart not to begrudge her sister's escape.

She was surprised to see that the truck was still there. True, they had studded snow tyres, but Darcy was cutting it awfully close. Lyn flew in the front door, calling goodbye to Rick over her shoulder. It wasn't good between them yet — she didn't know if it ever would be again. But at least she had taken the big step of telling him a few of her fears.

She could hear Darcy as soon as she was inside the building, but the sound was not comforting. Her voice floated down the staircase, oddly without intonation, like a computer voice. Lyn was frightened. Something was wrong. She ran up the stairs two at a time, almost stumbling on the loose edge of the carpet. Halfway up she dropped her books but she did not stop to pick them up.

The door was ajar. She shoved it, but it opened only an inch or two and then bounced back. Oh, it was on the chain. She could only see the part of the living room that was directly in front of the three inch crack.

'Darcy!' she yelled. 'Darcy. Let me in!' She pounded on the door, but there was no pause or variation in the emotionless voice. She could now hear gasps that sounded as if they were being forced out of someone. Connie? A single limp arm flew into her view, dangling up and down as if it belonged to a marionette. Lyn shouted her sister's name again, then worked her hand into the gap, trying to twist it around upside down so that she could lift the chain. There was a sudden thud against the door, and she cried in pain as it slammed against her wrist. Then it swung back and she pulled her hand free. Now she could see Darcy's face. Her eyes were unfocused as if she were doing a dull, repetitive job.

Lyn threw herself against the door. She was sure she could pull the screws loose. Only a few days ago she had commented to Darcy about how it was only for show. As she pushed, still looking at Darcy's face and the way that the effort with which she was shaking Connie made the tendons stand out in her neck, she wondered how she could have thought that Darcy's peacemaking attempts had meant that she was not upset.

Now Darcy shifted, and Lyn could see her mother. She was confused. When the two of them had fought the night before both of them had been angry and struck out. But now Connie was totally passive, letting Darcy shake her the way a dog does a rat. It was as if they had both accepted their places in some type of awful ritual and Connie's role was to be the victim.

There was a terrible screech as the screws came out of the door frame. The door flew open, jerking Lyn with it. Still holding onto the knob she went down on one knee. Neither her sister nor her mother acknowledged her in anyway.

She had wanted Darcy to do this. She had prayed that somehow she would suddenly become the protectress of old, that she would take Connie in hand and somehow make her act like a mother. She remembered the day that they had run into the landlord in front of their old apartment. Lyn still felt hot remembering how he grasped her by the arm and said,

'Girls, I don't know how to say this. You're both really nice kids. But the other tenants are complaining. Throwing up in the hall, fighting all night long. You're going to have to move.' That was all she remembered though it seemed that they had stood, frozen, listening for hours.

She had panicked. She had resented the rattley windows in the apartment, the way that the heat collected under the sloped roof during the hot days until it seemed thick enough to cut. But, still, she was afraid of moving. After all, it was only the second place she had lived in over a decade.

But Darcy had been mad. Lyn had seen it and she had been

heartened by it. Now maybe she would do something! But when Connie came home later that afternoon it had been about basketball that Darcy had shouted.

'Try-outs are next week! I have to be established in a school district! We're right on the edge of this one and this apartment was hard to find. What if I have to change schools?' She had wanted Darcy to shake Connie then, she had wanted her to pick her up and make her listen as she had shrugged and turned to go back out. But her fantasies had been nothing like this. She hadn't imagined Darcy and Connie would fall into roles that seemed to be operating quite independently of them; she hadn't imagined her sister would radiate despair so raw that it circled her like an aura. She wanted to get out. All she wanted was to crawl backwards out the door and down the stairs, praying that Rick would still be spinning his wheels by the curb. But she couldn't. She couldn't leave them locked together like this. Her throat felt raw and she realized that she was still shouting Darcy's name, though her sister didn't appear to hear. What should she do? Should she try to break them apart physically? To do it she would need a weapon of some sort, a hockey stick or the frying pan to protect her against Darcy's mindless anger.

But she couldn't do that either. Instead she steeled herself and brought both hands down on Darcy's shoulders from behind.

'Darcy, stop,' she said right in her ear. Her lips brushed a strange salty taste.

The effect was immediate and dramatic. Darcy started and turned her head as if she heard someone calling her from far away. She jerked her hands off Connie and Connie dropped soundlessly to the floor without making any effort to catch herself.

'Lyn?' she said, passing her hands over her face as if surfacing from sleep. She began to look around, reorienting herself.

Lyn felt ill. All she wanted to do was get away from the place. She would take Darcy with her if she could, but if she could not she would run alone. She grabbed Darcy's arm, trying to pull her away from the heap of Connie on the floor. She had saved Connie, she couldn't be expected to nurture her too. Besides, she was stirring, she would be fine. Lyn stopped only a moment to stoop and retrieve the car keys.

Darcy tried to turn back on the stairs.

'No, I...'

'She's all right!' Lyn told her sharply. 'You didn't hurt her, it probably did her some good. Come on, we want to get you to the game.'

She pushed her easily before her down the stairs, through the hall, onto the snowy walk. It was not that Darcy's protests were token, but more that she was too, too drained to argue. She pushed Darcy into the passenger's side of the cab and climbed beneath the wheel herself. She wasn't old enough to have a license, but she had been driving for a couple of years on back roads. It was obvious that Darcy could not. She watched out of the corner of her eye as Darcy slumped in the corner against the door, her face ash grey. What was Darcy feeling? Lyn remembered how she had felt the night before, when the accident had pulled the plug on her anger and suddenly she was left with only herself to hate. Was that what Darcy felt like? Was it in fact what she had been feeling all these months? Was that why her routines had become more regimented because she could only be certain she would get out of bed if she trained herself to move autmatically? Lyn saw a visual of Darcy's days as a series of dull grey chores, approachable only if divided into tiny, unwavering steps.

Instinctively she knew that this picture was true. She didn't know how she knew but she was certain of it, just as she knew that Darcy had not been shaking, shouting at her mother now, but the woman of fourteen, fifteen years ago.

The snow was still coming down hard, wet and sticking. The wiper on the passenger's side was beginning to buckle. Lyn knew that soon it would stop altogether. A car honked at them from a cross street, and she hit the brake nervously, realizing too late that she had run a stop sign. The snowy, slick road with the street lights spaced too far apart was nothing at all like the dirt roads she had driven in the daylight.

She glanced at Darcy, checking to see if she had noticed the skid.

Her face was expressionless and her head lolled against the window. Lyn saw what she had tasted now, a dark line of blood caked down Darcy's cheek. She lifted her hand as if to wipe it away, then dropped it without touching her.

'Is this tournament round robin or what?' It sounded so stupid. But maybe instinctively, she had hit on the right thing. Surely she could get Darcy to talk about basketball.

But her sister did not answer. She only stared out the window into the snow.

# THIRTY-FOUR

'Dear Nikona,' Darcy wrote slowly in her head, pushing the thought with an effort. 'Dear Nikona. Dear Nikona.' There she stopped, unable to push any further. What did she say now? 'Dear, Nikona, remember when I said that my mom had totally freaked out? Well, guess what, I did it, too...'

No. There was more to it than that.

'Dear Nikona. When we were kids I envied you so much. I loved Aunt Annie and, even though she loved me too, I knew that she always loved you best, that she wasn't really mine. I was always so astounded when you'd act up. I couldn't believe that you'd risk making her or God, or whoever was in charge of mothers, angry. Because I knew that was why I had my mother. I knew it was because I was so bad I didn't deserve better. I knew that you didn't ever think the same things that I did, that you didn't fantasize about shooting up to be ten feet tall so that you could shake your mother or slap her and tell her "That's enough!" when she cried. I was sure no other kid did, just the way I was sure she would change if I could just stop thinking those things. The mother god wasn't fooled by the way I acted, she knew what I was thinking inside and that I still needed to be punished.

'But I couldn't stop. I couldn't! And tonight it was as if suddenly those fantasies came true. I didn't even remember them till I touched her. But all of a sudden I was bigger than she was, and...'

She stopped. She didn't know how to describe how the gleeful, heady feeling of a five-year-old suddenly in power had combined with the guilt of the teenager who was sure she deserved an alcoholic mother. She felt sick. She wanted to go home. But home didn't mean the apartment where, for all she knew, her mother still lay crumpled on the floor.

Thud! Her head snapped with the jolt as the truck hit a bump.

'Oh, sorry. Didn't see the speed bump.' Lyn spoke without looking at her. She was leaning over the steering wheel trying to find a parking space among the rows of cars. They were at Westminster, then. For a moment Darcy forgot herself, thinking of the big gym, the way that Lee Ann snagged her passes so sweetly. Tonight! Then as she caught her breath she remembered. She had done something awful and the game couldn't make up for it.

'Come on, hurry! The gym's over here, right?' She allowed Lyn to open her door and pull her out and followed her across the parking lot, more because she didn't know what else to do, than for any other reason.

'I won't think about it!' she told herself, but this time it didn't work. The image of her mother crumpling was too stark, too vivid to be blotted out by any picture of scoring.

Lyn was still pulling at her, trying to brush the snow off her jacket as they walked across the lobby. She could hear shouts — the game had started.

'Hey, I need to see your activity card.' Both girls jumped and then stared at the boy sitting by the door.

Lyn started to make her voice sweet and her eyes big, to think of some way to flatter him. No, she wasn't going to do that anymore.

'She's a player. Look at her uniform. She plays for George Washington High. They're already on the court.' She could see that much by twisting her head past him.

'She needs to go in through the locker room. You need to have a card.'

'Where's the locker room?'

'Outside and around the building.' He made a vague hand motion.

Lyn negated it with a wave of her own hand. 'Oh, come on, give us a br...'

'The locker room or not at all,' he said, folding his arms. He was definitely enjoying his power.

Lyn leaned over his table, rattling the muffin tin that held his change. 'Don't give me a hard time. If you want to hassle about it, I can hassle a lot louder. Don't think I can't! I'll have you thrown out!'

'You do that!' Lyn pushed Darcy into the gym while he was struggling to stand up. Two boys came in with their wallets out, and he stood for a moment, torn between Lyn and his table. Finally he turned back to check the cards.

Darcy watched the scene, strangely unmoved. But once they were on the floor she couldn't resist looking at the clock. They were only two minutes into the first quarter. Something must have gone wrong, for some reason they had started very late.

The buzzer went. She looked at the score board. The Westminster team had scored. Their fans, mostly parents, stood up to cheer. Lyn was dragging her in front of the bleachers by one elbow. She pulled back to look at the court.

Something was wrong with her team. She could see it immediately in the way they moved, though for a moment she couldn't tell what the problem was. Lee Ann was playing centre, looking nervous, trying to keep from drifting to her regular position. Where was Sandy? Not on the court, and not on the bench, either. But Joan, sitting two down from Ms Ernst, had spotted her and was waving wildly. Darcy shook her arm loose and walked by herself, trying to ignore the voice screaming inside her head.

Joan grabbed her arm and began talking before she could sit down. 'Sandy made herself so sick on that food, her folks just took her home. She decided not to tell Ms Ernst because you weren't here, and she went out on the floor and threw up all over! It was so gross! We had to stop the clock so they could clean the floor, plus one of the Westminster girls fell in it and she had to go shower...'

'It wasn't the food,' corrected the girl beside her. 'It's the flu. Everybody at school has the flu. I had it last week. If it was the food we'd all be sick.'

'Well, to tell the truth I don't feel that hot.' Joan rubbed her stomach.

'Don't say that. You're only sick because Sandy threw up. That was enough to make anybody sick.'

'Anyway, it's great that you're here.' Joan was peeling Darcy's jacket off. 'Lee Ann just about shit herself when she had to go in as centre and Ms Ernst says I have to do it next...'

Darcy looked down at the coach. Would she even let her play? She had been willing to tell her the story, her whole life even, to get cab fare. But she knew she could no longer choke it out.

Ms Ernst caught her eye. She gave her a long, unreadable look, then said so softly that Darcy barely heard her, 'You went home, didn't you?'

Then, before Darcy could answer or even think of any answer, she became brusque and businesslike.

'Dress down. I hate to put you in cold, but all those ninnies out on the floor are panicking. I just want to put you in long enough to calm them down so they know they can pull it together. Go tell them you're in.'

Crouching by the scoretable Darcy found that her hands were

sweating. She wiped them on her uniform, trying to tell herself that it was only the game. There was nothing else upsetting her. The buzzer blared and she ran onto the court. To her relief Lee Ann gave her a thump on the back that bent her over. Then they were playing.

The guards were bringing the ball down the court and she ran with the rest of the team, setting herself up for a play. The ball went to the right of the key and then up for a shot. It bounced off the backboard and was snatched by one of the forwards. She found herself blocked and passed back to Darcy.

She didn't know what made her look over at the bleachers. She liked to have her family at games, but usually she never noticed them while she was playing. But as the ball went up again she glanced over behind the player's bench. Lyn had wormed her way into the very front row, ignoring the glares from other fans. Her face as she watched, looked strangely peaked and anxious and Darcy was reminded of those few weeks she had gone to kindergarten, that first time. That was the way Lyn had looked when she had stood at the window to watch her go. She also remembered something from that time she had forgotten. Her mother hadn't let her stay home with Lyn until she had complained of a stomach-ache. Eventually, she had complained so long that she actually did start getting an upset stomach in the morning.

It all flashed through her mind in a moment. Then the ball rebounded again and she was up fighting for it. She pulled it loose fiercely and jumped up to shoot, jumping higher than anyone else on the court could jump or block. She knew without watching it clear the hoop that it was good. That one shot that was on the video was perfect.

But as she came back down she looked back over her shoulder at Lyn and she allowed her bad ankle, which wasn't wrapped, to twist beneath her so that she landed on the side of her foot. Half way down she thought she heard Lyn from the crowd calling, 'No!', but it was too late to stop then.

A sharp rush of pain shot through her ankle so intense she could not keep from crying out loud. She crumpled onto the floor and another player stumbled and fell over her. She was panting from the pain, but she also felt strangely calm and relieved. There were no more choices to make now.

The ref had not yet blown her whistle, but there were extra people on the court. Darcy's eyes were closed. She heard Ms Ernst near her head calling, 'Ice! Ice!' Then, 'Oh, no, it's swelling already. She's going to have to get it x-rayed.'

'I'll take her,' she heard Lee Ann say. 'We're screwed anyway.'

'You have an attitude problem, young lady, and that's what's going to lose this game. Hilary can take her.' She did not bother to add the obvious, that Hilary would no longer be needed to run the video camera.

# THIRTY-FIVE

The emergency room was chilly. The girls kept their coats on. Hilary was usually talkative, but after filling out the paperwork she sat in the orange plastic chair across from Darcy at a loss for words, obviously wishing that she were back at the game. Darcy didn't care. She hunched down into her jacket, waiting for car casualties and gunshot wounds to be taken care of ahead of her.

She had just closed her eyes and let herself be taken care of on the court. It was not much in the way of taking care. She was treated more like a problem than a person. Still, it was better than nothing. Lyn had never come over to her on the floor. She had not seen her in the gym as the ref and Lee Ann carried her out to Hilary's car. She must have decided that it was too much to deal with and left alone. Darcy felt a pang but put it off sternly. She was not to think of herself anymore. That was her penance.

The double doors from the lobby swung open and Hilary glanced over at them. Darcy did not. She was allowing the pain to throb in the front of her mind, blocking out everything else.

'Darcy! Haven't they even looked at you yet? How does it feel?'

She reacted slowly, pushing the throbbing back with an effort.

'Lyn? How... but why...'

'That jerk at the door actually had me thrown out! Can you believe that? He got some other jerk, the football coach maybe, and they dumped me right out in the snow like I was a drug dealer or something. It was right when you were hurt. One of your friend's dads offered to pay for me, but they wouldn't even listen. I ran around and waited and waited at the door of the girls' locker room, they never brought you out.'

'Oh...' Darcy was unable to think of an answer.

'We came through the boys' locker room,' Hilary volunteered. 'That's where they always put the visiting team and I was parked right by the door.'

Lyn spared her no more than a glance. She dropped down by Darcy's chair. 'Your ankle,' she said. 'I tried to call to you... it's no good! I don't want you to do this anymore!'

'What are you talking about?'

'Don't pretend you don't know! You didn't have to get hurt! You let that happen. That way you don't have any choice except to stay home. But I don't need you like this!'

Darcy's head was reeling. 'You said...'

'I know what I said. I know what I did. But I was wrong. That's what I was trying to come home and tell you. Don't you see, I don't need you like this. I need you... I need you to be strong and happy for yourself. I need to see that you can do that. Then maybe I'll believe I can do it, too.' For a split second Lyn saw Robin leaning against the sink with her hair down, talking about the other girls who would find the programme easier because of her.

Darcy shook her head, not believing her ears. The pain was almost forgotten in the welter of other emotions. She turned and slammed her fist into the chair, hardly aware of what she was doing.

'Damn!' she said, but she didn't know who or what she was cursing. It didn't matter how hard she tried. Without warning she began to cry, harsh sobs that became louder as she tried to control them.

Lyn found herself in a comforting role that she had not experienced before, and gracelessly she groped about for something to say. 'Don't cry, Darce. Maybe they'll take you anyway, maybe...'

'It's not that!' It was all she was able to gasp out which was fine, because she didn't know what it was. Maybe everything.

'Umm...'

Lyn had forgotten that there was anyone else in the room until Hilary cleared her throat.

'Are you going to wait here? Could I maybe leave?'

'Yeah, go ahead, I'll take her home. Thanks.'

'Bye, Darcy. Bad luck. I'll talk to you tomorrow at school.' Hilary leaned forward to put her hand on Darcy's shoulder. She had stopped sobbing and nodded acknowledgement.

Lyn stood up and put her hands awkwardly in her pockets.

'Darcy, I want to talk to you. I want us to help each other. I...'

The opposite door flew open, this time to admit a nurse with a gurney.

'Well, it's finally your turn,' she said briskly. 'Oh, surely it doesn't hurt that bad, does it? A big girl like you? Well, never mind, we'll get it all fixed up. Up you go.'

Suddenly Lyn was alone. She sat down in one of the chairs and glanced at the religious tracts on the table. After a moment she jumped up to pace.

'Umm...'

Lyn jumped.

'I thought you had gone back to the tournament!'

'I started to,' Hilary said apologetically. 'But I thought of something that I wanted to tell Darcy.'

'They've taken her.'

'Well, maybe you could tell her then. The thing is, we couldn't tape her tonight. But maybe it doesn't have to be her last chance. How long will it be before she's back on her feet?'

'I don't know, a couple of months if she's really good. But isn't this the last game of the season?'

'Yeah, but Ms Ernst really likes Darcy. She wants to see her do good. I'll bet she could call one of the other coaches and arrange an out-of-season scrimmage. It's a thought anyway.'

'No!' Lyn thought. 'It's settled now!' Suddenly she wondered if she had been able to say those things so easily because Darcy couldn't leave her now. But aloud she simply said, 'Thanks.'

Then, as Hilary left for the second time she sank back into the chair and looked at the wall.

# THIRTY-SIX

Thump. Thump. Thump.

As they went up the stairs to the apartment Darcy's cast hit each step resoundingly. Lyn knew that it must hurt, but Darcy was too drugged to feel it. She neither winced nor slowed, but continued up. Thump, thump, thump. Lyn couldn't make her tired mind think of any way to help her, so she just stared at the hood of her sweatshirt, letting it lead her up in the dark. She wished they hadn't given Darcy so many pain-killers. Except maybe they hadn't. Maybe they had just given her a few and it had just combined with everything else. Whatever it was, she was really out of it. They hadn't been able to talk at all in the car.

She passed Darcy at the landing, pulling out her keys, but the door was already open a few inches. Connie must have gone out without pulling it behind her. Lyn didn't even allow herself to consider that there might have been a break-in. She just didn't have the energy to worry about anything new.

She shoved the door but it stopped after opening only a foot. Impatiently she kicked it hard, not even thinking about what might be on the other side until she heard a muffled groan.

Shit. Shit. Shit. She thought each word slowly and carefully, banging her forehead against the door-frame at the same time. More than anything she just wanted the day to be over. But it wasn't. Why, of all evenings, had Connie chosen this one to stay home? Why couldn't she have gone out partying? Lyn hit the door again, not with malice, but just hoping that she could get Connie to roll over.

It didn't work. Darcy had clunked up to the landing and was standing beside her, leaning on her crutches, without urgency or even interest, as if she would be willing to stay there all night. Lyn sighed, then forced the door a few more inches so that she could slip sideways into the dark room.

She hit the overhead light. Connie was lying on her back. Her mouth was open, but she was not snoring. Lyn moved her by one arm, again not to hurt her, but as if dealing with a piece of furniture. Be a lamp, Connie, be a chair. Be something I can move around and deal with without pain.

It did occur to her, in a very uninvolved part of her mind, that tonight Connie had really tried one on. Lyn had never seen her passed out before. There went the old 'I never fell asleep with my shoes on' brag. She wondered if Connie would be embarrassed to find herself on the floor in the morning. But then, what did that matter? Even if she was, even if she couldn't find some way to make it someone else's fault it wouldn't change anything.

Darcy swung in beside her, still dragging rather than lifting her foot. She caught the tip of one crutch on Connie's blouse, almost stepped right on her, but she didn't look down or comment. Only when she had crossed the room did she stop.

'Did I do that?' she asked Lyn tonelessly, pointing in Connie's general direction with her chin. She might have been asking about a spill on the floor.

Lyn had had the same thought. But there were a number of things that showed that Connie had been up and around since Darcy had dropped her. She was in a different position for one thing, and for another, she had changed her shirt.

'No,' she answered, not wanting to say more. She wondered why. The time was long past when either of them could deny what was happening, yet there was still that stupid superstitious feeling. As if each time they said the words the problem became more real, as if it would go away if they only refused to acknowledge it out loud. It made little sense with Connie lying there on the floor between the two of them, but still Lyn couldn't bring herself to say, 'No, she's just drunk again.'

'Oh,' was all Darcy said in reply. She continued into the bedroom without looking back. A moment later Lyn heard a great thud as if she had simply let herself fall into the bed on the floor. Then there was silence.

Lyn walked aimlessly around the small living-room. She picked up a shoe and set it back down and then did the same thing with an ashtray. Darcy was lucky if she could go to sleep. She wished she could. But she was too wired, even though she was exhausted. Tapes of her day still played through her mind at fast speed, bigger than life and garish with colour: Robin's look when she said, 'There's a lot you don't know about me, Lyn.'; Connie, set in the role of the victim; Darcy's one jump, high above everyone's heads and then down with a crash. She could not shut her mind down.

But there was another reason that she had known that Connie hadn't just lain on the floor the whole time they were gone. Under the couch, where Darcy hadn't seen it, was a bottle half full of wine. Lyn pulled it out and flipped on the TV. She didn't bother to try and choose between the late night shows already in progress, but settled down in front of the first thing that came on, hoping she could distract herself into sleep.

# THIRTY-SEVEN

Darcy's head was much clearer when she woke. But as she got up she was still muzzy enough for part of her to pretend she was once again on the farm. She knew it wasn't true but she kept pretending anyway. She pretended she was climbing down the bunk ladder instead of getting up off the floor, pretended that she would hear Nikona's sleepy voice mumbling at her in the darkness. It didn't hurt anyone. She just didn't want to think anymore tonight, wanted to pretend long enough for a trip to the bathroom and back.

She only opened her eyes half way, the better to sustain the illusion. She had not meant to look into the living room at all, but she found herself standing in the doorway.

Her mother was sitting curled on the couch, bathed in the weird, flickering light of the TV. The flower garden quilt that belonged on Sadie's bed was wrapped around her, one corner of it pulled up over her head like a hood. She looked tired.

Darcy stood without moving, remembering other times that she had crawled out of her bed late at night to watch her mother. It had been something she had done often at one time, long ago. At night, weariness would chase away her mother's look of fear and need and she would look just like any other young woman. Standing in the darkness, out of sight, Darcy had wrapped her arms around herself and rocked from side to side, pretending that her mother was holding her.

She realized that she was holding herself again in the same way and angrily she threw her hands down. It had not been enough then, and it was not enough now.

She wondered how late it was, if perhaps her team was still out celebrating. A wave of self-pity rolled over her. For a moment she wondered if this was the way her mother felt — unwanted, unloved. But she quashed the thought. She couldn't bring herself to feel sorry for Connie anymore, no matter how pitiful she might seem, no matter how much she hurt herself.

But even as she resolved it the light from the TV smoothed the harsh lines in Connie's face and she looked young, and somehow innocent. The illusion was not dispelled even when she raised an almost empty wine bottle to her lips. It was only when she half turned her head in

Darcy's direction and the blanket fell down around her shoulders that
Darcy blinked. Her throat went suddenly dry; her vision seemed to
blur and then refocus sharply. She saw a series of pictures super-
imposed one upon the other. Her mother, her sister. Connie, Lyn.

No. No. But a quick glance at the floor told her that she wasn't
imagining things. It was true. Connie was still lying by the door. She
watched in horror as Lyn took a long swallow of the wine, throwing
it to the back of her throat with a jerk, then allowing it to trickle down
slowly. Her eyes were closed. The gesture was so like Connie that
for a second Darcy thought again that she was mistaken. But it was
only for a second. Then Lyn drew her fingers back through her spiked
hair and the illusion was gone for good.

She didn't know she had cried out until she heard her own voice.
She was remembering. Remembering the night her mother had come
home with Aunt Annie covered with beer and how she had smelled
it as she ran to greet them in her nightgown. She was remembering
how she had screamed and screamed and screamed. That horrified
breathlessness. That feeling that she would slip under and not be able
to surface again, that a sanctuary had been breached. She was not
just remembering, she was feeling it again.

Lyn turned slowly towards her. Darcy saw it as a progression of
stills, each in a slightly different position. She turned. She turned.
She turned. Her eyes opened wide. She began to stand. It was an eternity
before she crossed the floor, and the whole while Darcy could not
stop the moaning sounds that were coming out of her mouth.

'No, no, no!' She shook her head back and forth, only realizing that
Lyn was by her as she reached out and grasped her shoulders. For
a moment it seemed as if she would relax and allow herself to be
embraced. Then she jerked away ungently.

'Jesusfuck, Lyn!' A swear word from school, one that only the really
rough kids, the rebels and druggies used, one that she had never before
even considered saying.

'Jesusfuck, why? Why?'

She could see that Lyn was trying to answer, but just as she had
been unable to stop the moaning she now could not stop the angry
questions.

'Why? Why are you doing this to me?' She had not meant to
mention her leg or fairness, but in fury she thrust her cast forward.
'Look at this! That's my scholarship shot right down the drain! That
was for you, Lyn! Is this how you say thank you?'

'I didn't ask you to do that! You did it yourself! How could I know that you'd think up something stupid like that?'

But Darcy didn't seem to be listening, for she only shouted, 'God dammit, you're not only drinking. You're drunk!'

*They are once again at the trail's head. The dust rises around them as they run to meet the truck, Darcy as usual holding back a little. Lyn is almost in her mother's arms when she hears Darcy say, as if from far, far away, 'You've been drinking, Mom. You've been drinking again.'*

*Only then does Lyn smell the liquor and only when Connie pushes her aside and she sees her face, twisted with anger, her hand upraised as if to strike, does Lyn believe the words are true.*

Lyn looked at her own right hand, clenched into a fist, as if it belonged to someone else. Darcy was still shouting, but it was Robin Lyn was thinking of: of when the two of them were together in the bathroom and Robin said she'd had a blackout. She wondered if her fury had shown ugly on her face then the way her mother's had.

'Oh, no,' she said, as if to herself. 'Oh, no please.'

She felt suddenly weak and her hand dropped, limp, down by her side. She took several steps backwards as if she were trying to get away from herself. On the third step her bare foot struck something that felt unpleasant; soft but unyielding, and unnaturally cold.

It was Connie's arm. She kicked at it impatiently with her toe. Then something made her kneel for a closer look. Maybe it was the clammy feeling, maybe the total lack of response. She felt Connie's wrist, then her neck for a pulse. She slapped her on her face, gently at first, then harder.

'What now?' Darcy demanded, her voice still raw with anger. 'I'm not enough by myself? You can't create a really high quality scene unless she's in on it, too?'

'No, something's really wrong.' Lyn's answer was so quiet, so absorbed, that Darcy stopped short. She turned on the overhead light and knelt beside them.

'Look.' Lyn pressed on a fingernail and silently they watched the blood slowly return.

'She's just passed out, isn't she?' asked Darcy uncertainly.

'No. I've seen people who're passed out before. They move if you poke them. They mumble.' They look alive, she thought but did not say, while Connie looked dead. 'This is like a coma or something.'

Even as she said it she remembered the drug prevention assembly they had been forced to attend at school. She had sat in the back with Rick, messing around mostly, but she remembered a couple of the things that the earnest little woman in the pants suit had said between her film clips. Like the part about alchohol-induced comas. And she also remembered, as she looked at her mother limp beneath her hands, that they were something from which you could die.

'We have to get her to the hospital.' Darcy laced her hands together and made her forefingers into a steeple against her lips, visibly composing herself. For a moment Lyn waited for her to take over. Then, once again she heard Robin's voice urging, 'Let her go.' She remembered what Hilary had come back into the waiting room to tell her. She had to tell Darcy. She had to let her go, even if it came to pushing her out. The first step was trying to deal with this herself.

'Okay,' she began to think aloud, 'the school insurance paid for your ankle, but Connie's got a Blue Shield card in her wallet. If it's not good they have to take indigents; there was a sign up in the waiting room that said that. We need...'

But Darcy was talking over the top of her, not listening at all.

'I can carry her easy. You start the car. I'll drive...'

'Wait a minute. Listen to me! We'll be lucky if you get down those stairs yourself without falling. I can carry her. You just get your coat and the car keys.'

'You can't either. You're not any bigger than she is.'

'You don't always have to be the biggest and the strongest and the best to do something! I can carry Nikona piggyback — you know that! And she,' she nodded towards the floor, reluctant to validate the relationship with the word, 'must weigh twenty pounds less, now.'

'No, I...' Suddenly Lyn was angry.

'You have to be in charge, don't you? You tell me to take care of myself but, boy, you're not going to let me if you can help it, are you? Dammit, Darcy, let me zip up my own coat for once.'

Darcy was silent, looking from one to the other. Then she said, 'I'll get you a blanket to wrap her in. Then I'll go start the car.'

In spite of the seriousness Lyn's heart was pounding over her victory. Then she thought of the narrow staircase and all the things she had not said about carrying Nikona — that she held on and balanced herself and jumped off when Lyn stumbled.

'If I can't carry her,' she said hesitantly, 'you could help me.'

# THIRTY-EIGHT

In the end it took both of them to get Connie down the stairs and out into the truck. Connie, over a hundred pounds of passive weight without a handle, was nothing at all like a cooperating partner. They were not able to be gentle. Connie didn't respond to any of it; not the jostling and bumping, or the near drops and recoveries. It frightened Lyn. The night before in her rage she would have shouted that Connie deserved whatever she brought on herself. But now she was frightened. Like a child she remembered all the recent times that she had wished her mother harm and like a child she wondered wildly if somehow her angry thoughts had come home to roost on Connie's deathlike head.

The snow was still falling heavily. The huge flakes caught in the light of the street lamp on the corner added to the nightmarish quality of wrestling Connie across the lawn. In fact several times Lyn caught herself watching the three of them with her mind's eye, the same way that she sometimes watched her dreams when she knew that she was dreaming. Then she had the same appreciation for detail, the same amazement at what her mind could create. But the snow drifting down the folds of the blanket was no dream and it wasn't a dream when Darcy slipped and fell flat, jerking them into the snow with her. Her cast hit the sidewalk with a muffled clunk and Lyn could see tears of pain already freezing to her eyelashes, but neither of them said a word as they hauled themselves to their feet.

There was a whole new set of problems when they reached the truck and for a moment Lyn was tempted to withdraw again, to let Darcy handle it. Instead she steeled herself and began again to think aloud.

'We'll never get her into the cab. We can hardly fit when we're sitting up and you'll have to drive.'

'I was counting on it,' Darcy put in. 'I do remember a little of that ride to the game.' She flashed a quick smile that heartened Lyn, made her think that perhaps her mother was not dying after all.

'The back, then?'

They both looked at the homemade camper doubtfully. It had been a dubious shelter even at its peak. They could see the snow sifting down between the boards.

'It's so cold,' Darcy said.

'But it's not far. And we'll kill her for sure if we keep wrestling with her in the snow.'

They both looked at the bundle for a moment, and Lyn could see quick panic crossing Darcy's mind as it had her own. What if she was already dead under the blanket?

'Let's give it a go.'

Lyn pulled the tailgate down and scrambled over the two bags of sand that they were carrying in the back for weight during the snowy weather. It was only at the last moment as Darcy was pushing Connie up to her, that Lyn realized she meant for her to ride in back with Connie, and not only to ride but to hold her up off the wet bed of the truck in her arms. She was too startled to protest. She sat dumbly, legs crossed, arms outstretched, without speaking as Darcy placed Connie in her lap and then climbed out and slammed the tailgate. Her mother was like a child, no, like a big lifeless doll lolling against her. Again she noticed how thin she had become. She seemed lost in the bundle of bedding. But still Lyn could not bring herself to cradle her. It didn't make sense, but it was as if it were a sign of approval and love that she simply could not bear to give.

The truck lurched forward, and Connie had slipped away from her. Lyn hauled her back and held her with handfuls of the blanket. As they began to move the wind whistled in through the boards, and she crouched over Connie, trying to shield her with her body.

As she sat in the dark she suddenly remembered a time some years before when she had been sitting at the kitchen table with Louise. She could see the woman clearly, down to the blue t-shirt, covered with sawdust and paint, but she had no picture of herself, except to think that perhaps her hair was at a straggly stage. She knew, owever, that she had been angry, that she had been fighting with Nikona. She could still hear the sound of Louise's voice, always rich with the tones of singing, even when she spoke.

'Sure,' she'd said, 'Nikona is a bad sport. She's a terrible sport. She even embarrasses me sometimes and I'm just standing on the sidelines. But you think people are like apples, Lyn, and want to cut out the bad spots and throw them away and be done with it. Or, if you can't do that you want to destroy what you don't like with your anger, like it was a laser. But people aren't like that, darling. It's hard to hate one part and not have all the parts that you love not feel it.

You can tell Nikona you don't like that part of her, but when it comes right down to it you can't change her. She has to change herself — if she wants to — and all you can do is decide if the good outweighs the bad enough for you to want to stick around.'

Then, right on the tail of the memory, she thought of how strong and gentle her mother's hands had been that morning, of how she had killed the kitten because it was the right thing to do even though it was hard, and how beyond that she had stayed to talk to the children about its death.

Lyn sat motionless for a moment. Then she sighed heavily and slowly she brought Connie's limp body in toward her so that her head rested against her shoulder.


# THIRTY-NINE


Darcy was awakened by a sharp pain in her neck that outweighed all the other little aches that came from sleeping upright in a plastic chair. She stood carefully, bending her head away from the bright fluorescent light. She shook out her arms and legs, silently apologizing to each for the abuse it had been put through. She was the only one in the waiting room. Lyn was nowhere in sight. Darcy ran her hands back and forth through her hair before turning towards her mother's room down the hall.

But before she could take more than a few awkward steps in that direction a woman popped out of the nursing station.

'Hi. Awake?'

'Kind of.' Darcy remembered her only vaguely, in the same dreamlike way that she remembered the floor and the waiting station. The only clear memory she had was the relief it had been to get out of the emergency room, away from the curious eyes that had seen them twice in one evening.

'Do you remember the doctor talking to you last night?'

'Sorta.' Actually she hardly remembered it at all. It had been just too hard to hear. Neither she nor Lyn had asked any questions when the doctor had paused. They hadn't looked at one another when she left. The last thing that Darcy remembered was settling into the chair, thinking that in just a moment she would have enough energy to get up and go home.

She rubbed her eyes now, trying to focus on the voice of the woman speaking to her.

'My mom...'

'She's going to be okay. The doctor says that she's out of danger for now. I didn't want to wake you — you looked like you were really beat — and since it was so close to morning I thought you'd probably want to stay and see her.'

Darcy tried to smile her thanks while still rubbing her face. She took a step in the direction of Connie's room, but the nurse put out a hand to stop her.

'She's sleeping now. Why don't you wait just a little while, have a cup of coffee? We'll be waking her up soon for breakfast.'

She sat back down without arguing. Giving in was easy. It wasn't because she agreed, but because as she had started waking, she had realized that she had no idea at all what she was going to say. What if she just walked out? The idea seemed wonderfully free. No more refereeing, no more comforting and taking care of. She could let her mother find her own way home. She stood. She would do it!

Then she sat back down. Who did she think she was kidding? She was bound too heavily with her own chains of caretaking. She'd never get away. With a sigh she reached out and picked up one of the women's magazines on the table.

'Hi.'

She glanced up and then did a double take. Lyn, with a bandanna over her hair and no make up, looked as if she had slid back six months. Her hands were covered with a network of fresh cat scratches.

'What happened to you?' Darcy asked, eyeing the jeans that she barely even wore at home anymore. The knees were dirty and wet, as if she had been kneeling in the mud. 'Did you drive through that blizzard?'

Lyn answered the second question first. 'What blizzard? You know how crazy the weather is around here. It's in the sixties, the streets are flooded and people are walking around in shorts. You can dig in the ground now.'

She sat down beside Darcy and did not say more.

'Mom's okay,' Darcy told her after a moments silence. 'We can go in in a minute.'

'Oh.' Lyn said in a preoccupied tone. 'No, you go ahead. I don't want to.'

'Oh, for...' Darcy started to burst out. Then she stopped. She just didn't have the energy.

Lyn didn't seem to notice. Instead she hopscotched back to Darcy's first question. 'I figured that if I didn't tone it down a little Nikona might die laughing, and I'd hear about it for months.'

'What?' Darcy passed her hand over her face, confused. Surely she wasn't hearing right.

Lyn spoke slowly and carefully, as if to a child. 'I was afraid that if I looked too chic that Nikona wouldn't stop making fun of me for weeks after I got home.'

'What?'

Lyn was nodding her head up and down, looking seriously straight ahead of her, rather than into Darcy's face.

'What do you mean? I mean, even if you had a way back you know what Mom told us they said...' She trailed off.

Her mother had said something totally different the day before. But Lyn didn't know that. She kept on talking.

'If they don't want me they are going to have to say that to my face. I can't stay here anymore. This is killing me.' She spoke in a monotone, the speech obviously prepared. Only at the end did she turn her head towards Darcy, and as she did Darcy caught a very faint smell of beer on her breath.

Suddenly her control broke. 'Darce, she's lying. Don't you see that? She's been lying to us all along. Nobody threw us out, nobody threw her out. She's just like a kid. They said, "Hey, you agreed not to drink here. Hold up your end of the bargain," and she said, "Fine, if I can't have my own way I'll run away and, boy, then you'll be sorry. And not only that, I'll take my toys with me." That's all we've been to her, Darcy. Just a couple of things that she took with her to hurt them. There wasn't anymore thought to taking us than there was to taking Louise's sewing machine. She just packed drunk.' Her voice was not bitter. It was resigned.

'Lyn, that's not true.' Vaguely Darcy wondered why it was she, who had always been the outsider, who was explaining this to Lyn. 'She took us because she loved us, because she needed us.'

'No. No!' Lyn was shaking her head vehemently. She held up her hands to stay the protest. 'Maybe because she needed us. Not because she loved us.'

'Yes! It doesn't turn...'

'No! Or even if she does, it's not the kind of love that I need now.

I need to be loved by someone who cares about what's happening in my life and can show it. It doesn't matter how much she feels or how much you think she feels. She just can't do that. She can't love me the way that I need to be loved now. She can't be a mother to me. And Darcy, I still need a mother.'

'Lyn, she can't help it...'

'That doesn't matter now, either. All that matters is that she can't be what I need. She doesn't love you either, Darcy, not in a good way. She's just using you. She uses you to pick up after her, to take care of her. She's using you to help her go on drinking, and the two of you are calling it love.'

'That's not true!'

'It is.' Lyn was calm, earnest now. 'You can't give her what she needs now anymore than she can give it to you. She's needs to be told if she wants to do this that she's going to have to do it alone, that we're not going to hang around to watch. That's what Aunt Annie told her the first time. But whenever you clean her up, or wash her clothes, or put her to bed, or pay the rent you're really telling her it's okay for her to drink, you'll take care of her. You're being the mother again. And she doesn't need a mother now, Darcy. She needs to be a mother.'

Darcy bowed her head. It wasn't fair. It wasn't. Not when she had tried so hard to hold them all together. Yet, it wasn't unexpected, either. Weren't they thoughts she had been having herself in the back of her mind?

As if reading her mind Lyn said, more gently, 'You did the best you could. But, don't you see, it's not what she needs to get better. And if we're not here there won't be anybody to take care of her.'

'We?'

'Of course "we", dumb-ass. Do you think I just came back because I like to read *Good Housekeeping*? Your stuff is in the truck, we're ready to go. We can get there by tomorrow.'

'How could we even get out of town?' It was not the most important thing that was bothering her, but it was the first that popped out of her mouth.

Lyn spoke slowly. 'I have a thing called a map. I hear anyone can read it. Come on, she got us here drunk.'

'Yeah, but who knows where she was really aiming?' Their laughter was too long and loud, but it felt good to break the tension.

'I can't.' Darcy broke off suddenly. 'I just can't leave her like this.'

'Then I'm sorry. I'm really sorry. But I'm going anyway.' Lyn pulled her wallet from her jacket pocket and took from it a sheaf of bills.

'That's my rent money!' Darcy protested, spotting the two that were dotted with paint.

'Yeah, it is. I'll leave you as much as I can, but I'm taking the rest for gas and in case I have any problems. That rear tyre is ready to blow and I think she sold the spare.'

'What good will it do if you only leave me part? You might as well leave me nothing!'

'If you want it that way. Darcy, I'm making a choice. I can't choose for you, but you can't choose for me, either. If I can't force you to come, and you can't force me to stay, what can I do?'

Then, as Darcy said nothing, rubbing her head in bewilderment, she added softly, 'I don't want to be like her, Darcy. Not the way she is now. I don't want to.'

Startled, Darcy looked up as if to question her but she had moved to the window. Her turned back, crossed arms, told Darcy that she had said all she was going to say. For a moment as she bent her neck away, Darcy saw her as she had the night before, the image of their mother fifteen years earlier, sucking love out of a bottle.

The choice was sudden.

'Okay. Yes. I'll go with you.' She sprang to her feet, forgetting her cast and came close to toppling over. 'Where are my crutches, anyway?'

'I could point out that you didn't use them last night. But they're behind your chair.' She smiled for the first time, a smile so bright that it seemed inappropriate in the hospital, though it lasted only a moment. 'I have a surprise for you in the car,' she said.

Darcy picked up her crutches and adjusted them carefully, taking the time to gather her words convincingly. Only when the weight was off her foot did she realize that it still throbbed.

'But we have to go tell her,' she said without looking up, in a voice that was less confident than she had tried for.

'No.'

'But we...'

'No. You go if you like. I'll wait fifteen minutes before I leave.'

Again Lyn turned to face the window, totally absorbed in the picture that was playing inside her head. Her mother sitting on the roof on a hot day, sweat darkening the back of her tank top. A mouthful of nails, all her concentration on prying up a shingle. And braced against one outstretched leg, so she couldn't possibly fall, Lyn at nine, a perfect imitation down to the scowl on her face as she levered her small hammer, the sweaty hair pushed back beneath her ball cap.

'Goodbye, Mama,' she whispered to no one, 'Thank you for not letting me fall.'

# FORTY

Darcy entered on the wake of the breakfast tray. The nurse was still in the room, opening the drapes so that the sun shone in on the woman in the far bed. She was very small, with grey hair in a coronet and she seemed lifeless. Darcy looked at the other bed, but there was no one in it. The grey bedspread that matched the sheets was pulled tight.

On her way out the nurse said, 'Not too long now,' and inclined her head towards the bed by the window.

Hesitantly Darcy approached. She could see now that most of the grey was a trick of the morning sunlight. Most, but not all. There really were some grey strands among the blonde. She wondered how long they had been there. Her mother's eyes were closed and she considered for a moment just leaving, as Lyn suggested. She even backed up a couple of steps. But then she bumped into the bedside table and the purple lids fluttered open.

'Hi,' her mother said weakly. She attempted what Darcy surmised was a smile.

'Hi.' Darcy could think of nothing else to say. She glanced at the visitors' chair, then decided to stay standing.

'I hear we had a lot of fun last night.'

It was an invitation to joke the situation away, but Darcy could not bring herself to respond.

'No,' she said bluntly, 'we really didn't.' She winced in advance, anticipating the flood of tears this might loosen. At least she could not capture her physically. But her mother just turned her head towards the window for a moment and sighed heavily, and when she turned back her eyes were clear.

'What happened to you?' she asked, eyeing the cast and crutches.

'Basketball.' It was not what she wanted to talk about, but at the same time she was furious when her mother's only reply was,

'Oh.'

Dammit, she knew she was sick and hurting, but to dismiss the death of four years of dreams in one syllable! It made the next sentence easier to say.

'Lyn and I are going home.'

There it was between them now, blunt and hard.

'Of course you are. You should go to school, too, unless you're too tired.'

Darcy did not correct her. She knew that she was misunderstanding deliberately. Connie knew that she had never called the third floor apartment home. Sure enough, after a moment she sighed again. Now her eyes were brimming with tears, flowing from the corners down both sides of her face.

'I could have them arrested, you know. I could have you arrested for that matter. For your own protection.' The threat was weak, the threat of a child resorting to one last pitiful try.

Darcy said nothing. After a moment her mother sighed again.

'It's always been you, my beautiful girls.' The tears, all the more horrible, somehow, for the fact that she seemed unaware of them, continued to darken her pillow. 'I'm sorry. I'm so sorry...'

'I know.' For the first time Darcy cut her off. Lyn was in the hall with the truck keys, watching the clock. 'I know you really are. But it doesn't matter how sorry you are.' She found herself echoing Lyn. 'Your sorries can't do me any good now. My sorries can't do you any good.'

She held her breath hoping for a moment that her mother would disagree with Lyn, protest that Darcy's love had been the best thing for her. Instead she closed her eyes and nodded painfully, as if in agreement. It was true then. Even Connie was able to see it. She sucked her breath in painfully and missed the first part of her mother's next sentence.

'What?'

Her eyes were heavy now, Darcy could see the pain it cost her to talk. 'You going to graduate this year?'

Had she missed something? Warily she said, 'Yes.'

'Get me a ticket, okay? Save a seat for me.'

'All right.' She turned then, again jostling the table, knowing now was the time to leave. She did not know what made her pause at the door and say over her shoulder, 'I'll count on it.'

It wasn't true. But perhaps it would help her mother to think that it was.

The halls were bustling now. Nurses, orderlies, even a few visitors who had come early or, like her, spent the night. The nurse with the honey voice nodded at her from the glassed station. But she did not see it. She was headed towards the door, on the other side of which her sister waited.

# RESOURCES AND SUGGESTED FURTHER READING

If you would like to contact someone regarding a drink problem or its effects on you, here is a list of some organizations to contact. This list is by no means comprehensive. All information correct at time of printing.

## ACCEPT
724 Fulham Road
LONDON SW6 5SE
071-371 7477
Organization for alcoholics and their families and friends. Run a range of services.

## ALATEEN
Al-Anon Family Groups UK & Eire
61 Great Dover Street
LONDON SE1 4YF
Self-help groups for young people aged between 12-20 who are affected by someone else's drinking.

## ALCOHOL CONCERN
275 Gray's Inn Road
LONDON WC1X 8QF
Please write.

## THE ALCOHOL COUNSELLING SERVICE (ACS)
34 Electric Lane
LONDON SW9 8JT
071-737 3579
Offer free and confidential counselling service on a one-to-one basis. Counsel both problem drinkers and friends and family of problem drinkers. Policy to meet clients needs as far as possible. Offer male and female counsellors. Counsellors for ethnic groups as well as lesbian and gay counsellors.

## ALCOHOL PROBLEM ADVISORY SERVICE
4 Greenland Road
LONDON NW1 0AS
071-482 0837

## ALCOHOL RECOVERY PROJECT (ARP)
68 Newington Causeway
LONDON SE1 6DF
071-403 3369
A social work agency and housing association for people with drinking problems. It has specialist services for women.

## ALCOHOLICS ANONYMOUS
11 Redcliffe Gardens
LONDON SW10
071-352 3001 (This is a 24-hour helpline or check your local directory for local helplines.)
Support Group for alcoholics .

## BLACK WOMEN AND ALCOHOL GROUP
Part of ACS above.

## CHILDLINE
0800 1111
The free national helpline for any child or young person with any problem.

## NATIONAL ASSOCIATION FOR THE CHILDREN OF ALCOHOLICS (NACOA)
PO Box 64
Fishponds
BRISTOL BS16 2UH
0800 289061

## SCOTTISH COUNCIL ON ALCOHOL
5th Floor, 137 - 145 Sauchiehall Street
GLASGOW G2 3EW
041-333 9677

## WOMEN'S ALCOHOL CENTRE

Contact through ARP above. A service for lesbians is available.

## SUPPORT FOR THE CHILDREN OF ADULT DRINKERS (SCAD)

10 Sansome Place
WORCESTOR WR11UA
0905-23060

Aimed at directly helping young people living with drink. Steering group consists solely of people who have parents who are problem drinkers.


## SUGGESTED READING LIST

*Coming Off Drink*, J and J Ditzler (Papermac £5.95)

*Problem Drinking*, N Heather and I Robertson (Oxford University Press, £5.95)

*Alateen - Hope for Children of Alcoholics* (available from Al-anon Family Groups UK & Eire, see ALATEEN above, £5.50)

*Alcohol: Our Favorite Drug*, The Royal Society of Psychiatrists (Tavistock Publications)

*The Courage to Change*, D Wholey (Fontana)

# FORTHCOMING AND RECENT TITLES FROM SHEBA

These books are available from most good bookshops or by mail order from SHEBA, 10A BRADBURY STREET, LONDON N16 8JN. Please send cheque or postal order and add 85p p&p per book.

*POSITIVELY WOMEN: LIVING WITH AIDS*, Eds. O'Sullivan and Thomson
ISBN 0 907179 47 9   £9.99   May 1992

For the first time in the UK, in their own words, a variety of women tell how they coped with the devastating news that they were HIV positive. As well as moving personal testimony and experience the book also includes factual advice on housing, treatment and other issues as well as a comprehensive resource list.

*THE GILDA STORIES*, Jewelle Gomez
ISBN 0 907179 61 4   £7.99   June 1992

An American odyssey, a romantic adventure, a magical tale that sweeps you along as the immortal Gilda strides across time. A unique vampire, Gilda listens to the world and tries to add her own voice. History offers cataclysms and everyday horrors but it also offers community and kindred spirits.

*WILD HEARTS*, The Wild Hearts Group
ISBN 0 907179 59 2   6.99   October 1991

The first collection of original melodrama of its kind: passionate, intriguing, witty, bitter-sweet stories to capture the imagination. These wildly imaginative writers have produced a thoroughly engaging volume which speaks to the inexorable rise and fall of the lesbian heartbeat.

*GIRLS, VISIONS AND EVERYTHING*, Sarah Schulman
ISBN 0 907179 58 4   £6.99   November 1991

This is a sexy and spirited novel from the author of AFTER DELORES, PEOPLE IN TROUBLE and THE SOPHIE HOROWITZ STORY (also published by SHEBA). With her keys in her pocket and a copy of On The Road in her hand, Lila Futuransky is looking for adventure....